WAR BONDS

Book One of
God Bonded America
a Trilogy

MICHAEL W. WEAVER AND WILL SCOTT

BALBOA.
PRESS

A DIVISION OF HAY HOUSE

Balboa Press books may be ordered through booksellers or by contacting:

Balboa Press
A Division of Hay House
1663 Liberty Drive
Bloomington, IN 47403
www.balboapress.com
1-(877) 407-4847

Because of the dynamic nature of the Internet, any web addresses or links contained in this book may have changed since publication and may no longer be valid. The views expressed in this work are solely those of the authors and do not necessarily reflect the views of the publisher, and the publisher hereby disclaims any responsibility for them.

The authors of this book do not dispense medical advice or prescribe the use of any technique as a form of treatment for physical, emotional, or medical problems without the advice of a physician, either directly or indirectly. The intent of the authors is only to offer information of a general nature to help you in your quest for emotional and spiritual well-being. In the event you use any of the information in this book for yourself, which is your constitutional right, the authors and the publisher assume no responsibility for your actions.

Any people depicted in stock imagery provided by Thinkstock are models, and such images are being used for illustrative purposes only. Certain stock imagery © Thinkstock.

Front Cover: current picture of Chateau de Beynac in Dordogne, France

Printed in the United States of America.

ISBN: 978-1-4525-7974-0 (sc)
ISBN: 978-1-4525-7976-4 (hc)
ISBN: 978-1-4525-7975-7 (e)

Library of Congress Control Number: 2013914412

Balboa Press rev. date: 09/05/2013

Dedication by Michael W. Weaver

As a disabled veteran of the Vietnam era, I would like to dedicate this book to all my brothers and sisters who ever wore a uniform and served in any military branch of this great country. I also wish to recognize those families of fallen soldiers for all they have sacrificed.

The book title implies a reference to war bonds, the debt securities issued by a government for financing military operations during times of war. However, the title is a play on words, as the book is actually about the bonds forged between and among soldiers while in the service and beyond because of the experiences they shared or had in common. On a personal level, this book is dedicated in part to Jackie Arnold, Frank Cashwell, Jim Cooper, Harry Frey, Gary Gardner, Jerry Garvick, Randy Henderson, Paul Kreiner, Donnie Lagana, Terry Schlicker, Rick Sherman, and the late Jim Newberry. They are friends I made in the service and since then. I think about every one of you often. Most important to me is my older brother, Hank. This book may remind you of people we know, with different names, of course.

I also dedicate this book to the memory of my late father, Russell Kenneth Weaver, whom we lost to cancer in 2009. Russ was a disabled veteran from World War II. Some of the stories in this book are based on actual events in his life. He is one of the main characters, although the story puts him in the service during WWI, and by book three, I (his son, Mikey) will be in World War II instead of the Vietnam era.

Dedication by Will Scott

I would like to dedicate this book to God, the father of Abraham, Isaac, and Jacob, and to God's son and my brother, Jesus Christ. Please don't misunderstand me. I spend as much time looking out over our world as I do looking up into God's world. Therefore, I would also like to dedicate this book to Mike Weaver and Mary Henderson, who have devoted a significant portion of their lives to writing and editing two of the three books (so far) of this trilogy.

Mike and I interweaved parts of my father's life into this book. Jack, my father, is the other main character in the trilogy, and I dedicate this book to him for being the rock that I built my faith and life on. I also dedicate this book to my wife, Megan, who has tolerated and supported me in all of the unusual things I have done. This would include being a carpenter, running a Christian newspaper, and now coauthoring books.

CONTENTS

FOREWORD

By William G. Williams

A this point in history, no one can truly comprehend the horrors of World War I or any other war that blasted upon the earth prior to the twenty-first century. Because people are different and technology has evolved, wars are not the same now.

The training, the attitude, and the fears build up in a person facing the ugliness of warfare with other humans. Combat is not a learned social skill and often creates ongoing problems for the person long after the war he or she fights in is over. Killing is not a natural objective for citizen soldiers or even for the military professional. I have been told that killing another human being is not necessary to complete a man's life cycle.

Authors Michael Weaver and Will Scott get the ball rolling in this book, which they have titled *War Bonds*, the first in a trilogy gathered under the umbrella title of *God Bonded America.*

They have followed the rightful path of placing their story within the bounds of where they grew up. They know the important sites, the histories of their hometowns. Fictional characters have to live somewhere; it always seems right to put them in locations where history has been made. The combination of the real and the imagined characters and locations lends body to the work that Weaver and Scott have developed.

These two writers have had varied careers, but they use the words that connect author with reader. Weaver, with *War Bonds*, is marching through his sixth book, holding close to heart the average student reader, as he is one. Scott, who ran a Christian newspaper, dedicated a good bit of his time to the missions of God. Those endeavors gave both a watchful eye on the human problem in Christianity today, the essence of their trilogy.

As an author, I understand the careful selection of subject and the actors in any work of fiction. Such characters have to appear real, not fictional. The readers of *War Bonds* are able to visualize all the characters whenever they read their names. After all, readers must see the story as a possible reflection of their own lives or those of people they know. Scott and Weaver have carved out the language and the events to reach the souls of their readers. They enable them to enjoy the adventure and guess about the final chapter.

One key character sets the stage for a wild ride through childhood and beyond. Who is this kid, this Russell Kaye? Why does he seem so much like me (or someone I know)? What will become of him? Another main character, Jack Earl, is a boy of intellect and Christian values. Why would he befriend such a fellow? What does he see in Russell? You find yourself wondering about the lives of these and other characters whenever you lay the book down. These are among the questions everyone wants answered. This book has the theme of great fiction, and the process that these authors have faithfully followed as they draw the reader deeper and deeper into their story is wonderful. It is a must-read.

I am anxious to follow their trail, to the end of this book and the two books that will follow.

—William G. Williams, author of the nonfiction *Rescue from Ploesti* and four historical novels dating back to 1990, including *Days of Darkness: the Gettysburg Civilians*

PREFACE

By Will Scott

This book and the rest of the trilogy have been a long time in the making. God has instilled in me the importance of the United States of America—not just its importance now but from its conception. This nation's people are free of a dominant ruler, free from a government that dictates their religious rights, free from a government that tells them they belong to a certain social class and have no hope of change, free to be the best they can be, and free to think outside the box. There have been obstacles in our freedom, such as slavery, confinement of Native Americans to reservations, wars, and many others things, but as my father says, "Despite this country's problems, it is still the best one."

The purpose of writing this trilogy is to help people see beyond everyday troubles, to see the big picture, to see that God built this nation for a purpose. This nation exists out of necessity, not out of random chance. Without this nation, the world would be completely full of kings and dictators. An overwhelming number of the people of this earth would live under oppression, and we would still be in the horse and buggy days.

The freedoms I spoke of created the opportunity for the industrial age. With its primarily Christian values, this nation helped lead the Industrial Revolution with mass production capabilities. The United States was in a position to defend itself and other countries from the old ways of aggressive leaders wanting to dominate the world.

Mike and I continually look to God for guidance as we write. We often find ourselves, as I call it, "backing into a new direction." We started out with a short outline of what was going to be one book, not three. However, as we began to develop characters and events, it was evident that one book would not be enough. We knew where we wanted to end up but not how to get there. Mike and I would sit down and outline a little more of the book. Then Mike would ask me, "Where do we go from here?" I would say, "I don't know, but God will let us know when the time is right."

Frequently, something would pop up when we were not even working on the book, giving us direction about the next step we needed to take. For instance, while researching the second book, we read about a man who lived during the same era we were researching. Multiple significant things happened during his life that made him a perfect character for an important role in book two, so he was included.

God also gives us confirmations that we are heading in the right direction. Mike, Mary, and I are Philadelphia Phillies fans. In this book, Jack Earl and Russ Kaye go to a Phillies baseball game and have what we call a "God moment." That story in the book was completely written when Mike, Mary, Megan, and I decided it would be good to go to see the Phillies in person, not just on TV. We purchased our tickets about two months in advance. The Phillies were doing well that year, and we were excited about going to see them play.

About a week before the big event, a storm formed in the Atlantic Ocean. We didn't think much of it at the time. It was hurricane season, and such storms happen regularly. Then it got stronger and had a projected path that included Philadelphia. This got our attention. When it became a hurricane, it was named Earl. So there was a hurricane named Earl, my father's middle name is Earl, and Jack Earl is a main character in the book. That had been the character's last name for several years prior to the hurricane, but it seemed like a confirmation to us.

Fortunately, the hurricane just missed canceling the game and we had a perfect day at the ballpark. However, we definitely had a God moment. What are the odds of a hurricane with the name of one of our main characters almost stopping us from going to the ball game? This kind of thing happened again with a Washington, DC, storm at the end of this book, in addition to many other times. We are trying to create the books that God wants us to write, and He is definitely telling us that we are heading in the right direction.

ACKNOWLEDGMENTS

By Michael W. Weaver

First, we thank God the Father, Jesus the son, and the Holy Ghost for their guidance. Second, we must make a disclaimer. Some of the anecdotes that we share throughout this book are real-life stories from our family memories. We took a bit of poetic license, so in many cases, what you read could be totally factual, while others are created for entertainment purposes only. You will have to figure out what is real and what is slightly embellished. Characters might be slightly exaggerated to create at least partial anonymity.

Perhaps Will's and my children and grandchildren do not need to know all the family warts, foibles and wrinkles. We may keep them guessing, or maybe not, as we go to our graves (or urns to become doorstops, allowing the future generations to enter the room). Many of our friends and family members' names have been changed in an attempt to protect them.

For many years, I complained and whined bitterly at my parents because they never took the time to tell us much of anything about their lives or families. Now they have both passed away. In this book, Dani is no more like my mother than my having a shot at being the next pope. My mom was a coal cracker from Shamokin, Pennsylvania. To me, she was also the most wonderful person in the world. My siblings say I was her favorite.

When Dad was dying of cancer, he lived with Mary and me. That was when the stories started coming. Oh, the things we were told!

Many times, they were morphine-induced stories that produced more information than you really wanted. His stories became so extremely exaggerated that they bordered on pure imagination. I guess with my taking poetic license, you could say that the nut doesn't fall far from the tree. Could it be that I am like my father?

Will and I thank my wife, Mary, for her tireless hours of editing, and Carolyn Kimmel for her run-through and editorial comments. In addition, thanks to Will's dad, Jack (Jack Earl), who gave the book a critical look insofar as fact and content checking on the historical points.

We also want to thank Barb Ivy for her research work at Thomas T. Tuber Museum of the Lycoming County Historical Society. Thanks also to the people who so willing assisted me in my research at Muncy Historical Society, Northumberland Historical Society, Snyder County Historical Society, and Dauphin County Historical Society. Big thanks to Dave Housell, the historian at The Pennsylvania National Fire Museum.

References to Bible verses are based on the New King James Version (extreme word), Thomas Nelson Publishers, Nashville. We wish to acknowledge Ken Frew, who wrote *Building Harrisburg: the Architecture and Builders 1719-1941.* This book was invaluable to our research, as was the twelfth edition of *Handbook of Denominations in the United States*, and we acknowledge its authors, Frank Mead, Samuel Hill, and Craig Atwood. The book *Weird Pennsylvania*, by Matt Lake, and articles from the *Patriot-News,* a Harrisburg, Pennsylvania newspaper were also referenced.

We researched numerous Internet articles on the burning of Pennsylvania's capitol; WWI; Hitler's rise to power; the Great Depression; German spies and gangsters in American history; the history of *Stars and Stripes* magazine; vintage automobile and planes; and Washington, DC, and surrounding communities. We also referred to the Philadelphia Phillies web page as well as several sources on the Internet about the history of the Philadelphia Phillies.

The self-guided tourist program for the Château de Beynac castle in France was the basis for the prisoner of war camp where Jack was held. The catchy one-liners that Colonel Sergeant Major Garfield shared in the book were treasures spoken by Arthur Garfield Bigelow, my wife's father. Most of them used in the book were read at his funeral by his son, Timothy Allen Bigelow, to express that down-home Vermont humor that endeared him to many.

INTRODUCTION

It is true that God sometimes seeks out less-than-perfect people, even heathens, to spread His gospel. As we wend our way through this book of friendship, faith, and fellowship, you will experience both religiously blessed God-fearing people as well as colorful, not-so-perfect folks. You will probably recognize a few racists, grumpy souls, antagonists, nonbelievers, and the so-called regular people. You will read about how, strange as it may seem, all sorts of people can work together on a common project and achieve personal and group goals.

This book is a gift to readers who believe that those deemed unworthy of walking with the righteous can end up being accepted into the arms of God, as can those who are His strong followers. This book interweaves the life stories of two very close if dissimilar friends with stories of their fathers' lives. This first book of an adventure trilogy that takes place from the late 1800s through World War II is filled with interesting historic information and facts.

There is no such thing as a perfect human being. This story validates that those who are truly righteous should put aside the flaws of their brothers and accept them as God does. We are all His children and can walk with Him, just like the two friends in this book.

Scripture says, "I will take you as my people, and I will be your God. Then you shall know that I am the Lord your God who will bring you out from under [the burdens of the Egyptians] your burdens." (Exodus 6:7) When God spoke these words thousands of years ago, He did not mean just the people of Israel. He meant followers of all sorts, through all times and situations. He knew that through time, people would endure, and He wanted to be sure that they knew He was always with them. Simply by being in God's kingdom, you are worth something, no matter what your flaws. Nobody is perfect. We all have faults. Just remember that Jesus' disciples were far-from-perfect men, yet Jesus chose them to spread His word.

This being said, Jack Earl's life was what one would probably think of as religious and righteous. He was close to God in all aspects of his life, from church to evening prayer. His grandfather was a minister, and his father helped as a lay minister. Jack was involved in the choir and other functions at the church his family attended every Sunday. He was baptized and confirmed there, and he attended church camp during the summer months. As an adult, Jack was everything you would associate with a good, kind, God-fearing man who had grown up in a religious family.

On the other hand, Russell Kaye had his difficulties on bumpy roads. His family would be considered dysfunctional, mainly due to his father's drinking problem. Saying that Russ lost his temper with little or no provocation when he was young was an understatement. Nobody ever thought of him as a choirboy, and certainly nobody ever pinched his cheek and called him an angel.

Russell was what many think of as a "CE Christian"—a Christian who practices religion only during Christmas and Easter. Russell was surely not in church every Sunday, but when things were tough in his life, he did turn to prayer. To his credit, instead of turning to booze or drugs, he would turn to church until all was well again. Then he was back to "CE Christianity." He was called "the foul one" for several years by many friends, and for good reason. This nickname had nothing to do with baked beans, green peppers, onions, or other foods he ate, although it easily could have. The words that spewed from his mouth with some frequency were what earned Russell that handle.

CHAPTER

RUSSELL KAYE

In the early 1880s, a young Mae Rodgers, the third oldest of fourteen children, lived with her family in a small Harrisburg, Pennsylvania, home. Nine of the fourteen children were boys, so two of the boys had to sleep with the girls in the three-bedroom house.

Mae, with her brown curls and steel-gray eyes, turned many heads as a young woman. She could likely have done better, but she began a long, difficult courtship with Calvin Kaye. Calvin, or "Pop," as he came to be known, had a bad temper, was a hard-core racist, and had a severe drinking problem. Even so, he was no better or worse than Mae's father, Bill Rodgers. Mae really wanted to make the relationship with Calvin work, as she longed to get out of the overly crowded home. Mae and Calvin finally married around 1895 and set up housekeeping in Harrisburg.

The thriving metropolis of Harrisburg became the capital of Pennsylvania in 1812. From the grounds of the capitol building, one could look down onto the Susquehanna River, the city's western border. The Native American Indians who first inhabited the general vicinity knew the area as Peixtin.

When Harrisburg was first established, it was a major crossroad of trade between the white men and the Native American Indians.

John Harris, an English trader, was the first white man to settle in the area. By 1785, John Harris Jr. and William Maclay had mapped out the original city, from Pine Street to the north, Tuscarora to the south, the Susquehanna River to the west, and Cameron Street to the east. In 1791, John Harris Jr. named the city Harrisburg in honor of his father.

However, none of that mattered on the morning of February 3, 1897. A typical winter morning, the wind gusts howled straight up State Street, and the choppy whitecaps on the river separated the city from the river's west shore. The freezing rain stung when it slapped against bare flesh, and it was starting to change to a heavy, wet snowfall.

Calvin Kaye and several of his scrawny Rodgers brothers-in-law—Bill, Frank, Charlie, Walter, and Paul—were among the many volunteers of the City of Harrisburg Fire Department responding to the fire at the state capitol building. Flames quickly ate up $1.5 million worth of property. The state capitol building was destroyed, and the legislative halls fell in ruins.

It started on a day when the House of Representatives was in session. The Senate was about to come back into session after a short recess when someone noticed smoke pouring out of the windows of the House. Instantly there was a motion to adjourn. Meanwhile, in the Senate, the smell of fire pierced the senators' noses, and then smoke clouds surrounded them. Senator John Grady of Philadelphia quickly warned the senators, and they began ripping their desks loose from the wooden floors and carrying them out. The representatives did the same in the House chamber. Once outside, the desks were placed on the capitol grounds under trees and then covered.

Crowds of people gathered from all over the city to watch, as if the fire were a Wednesday afternoon show. Flames shot from the roof over the lieutenant governor's chamber, where the fire had originated. The people began shouting when they realized that they were able to get there from their homes but the fire department still had not yet arrived. When the firefighters did finally get there, the first thing the hose crews did was walk around the capitol, assessing the blaze. To the crowd, that was another waste of time.

The fire licked through the roof of the capitol. In numerous places, flames skipped about like burlesque dancers. At last, the fire companies started spraying water on the roof of the Senate wing, which seemed fruitless, as the fire had grown into a wall of flames, with embers of hot ash floating to the ground close to the spectators. To add to the mayhem, the water hardly had enough force to reach the roof's edge, let alone get to the blaze that was breaking through the roof.

Much of the water was evaporating from the flames and heat, but what was falling back to the earth was turning into ice on that cold February morning. Although the morning was stormy and a lot of wet snow was falling, the dry wood was defenseless against the fire. The capitol burned as if it were made of matchsticks.

The roof quickly collapsed into the building, and the fire rapidly ate its way down into the Senate chambers. Those who were trying to get furniture and documents out of the building were suddenly driven out and reduced to spectators like the hundreds of others. Within an hour or so, every part of the capitol was on fire. There was no hope. Nearby apartments were in danger of catching fire but were saved by an act of God—the wind had shifted in the opposite direction.

Numerous firefighters were injured by falling burning timbers. The flames finally burned themselves out when there was nothing left to burn.

The finger-pointing started while the fire was still smoldering. The locals and the news media all blamed the inefficiency of the City of Harrisburg Fire Department, staffed only by volunteers.

Pop, the Rodgers boys, and many other firefighters were on the hill at the capitol, putting out hot spots well into the next day, February 4. Once they were given the okay to return to the station, they cleaned up the gear and stowed it away. They then left the station and, realizing that their wives had no clue whether they were back from or still at the fire, went to their favorite watering hole for a few pints of ale before going home. They just had to unwind after a tough day and a half of fighting the fire and, frankly, to bitch a bit about the finger-pointing and nasty comments and accusations being hurled at them. After all, they were the ones putting their lives in jeopardy. What if those cruel comments about the fire department made the newspaper?

*   *   *

Pop and Mae's home was a third-floor flat at 13th and Vernon streets, off Derry Street, by the Mulberry Street Bridge. While the fire burned, Mae was having her own adventure. Dixie, the colored indentured girl for the other family in the main house, lived in a room on the second floor. At Mae's request, Dixie ran the entire way to the Rodgers house, which was right up against the canal, just south of Paxtang Street and next to the Harrisburg Barrel company. She was to bring Mae's sisters to Mae.

Two of Mae's sisters, Stella and Zena, readied their father's barrel wagon, declaring that the only part of them that was running that day was their noses. Stella was built like her father, short and round, and she could not get around as fast as Zena, who could have passed for Mae's twin. Riding the wagon was also good for little Dixie. Sitting between Stella and Zena, Dixie warmed up from her almost two-mile run in the awful weather.

Once they got to the flat, they stopped at the top of Derry and Mulberry streets to water the horse at the water fountain. They could see the fire out in the distance and wondered what it was. They guessed that it was one of the churches over on Third Street.

They knew that Pop and their brothers were certainly over there. However, they had no time to dillydally around, as Mae needed their help. Stella waddled up the steps, having to take a breather a few times when she became winded. Zena ran up the stairs, opened the door, and yelled out, "Mae!"

From her bedroom, Mae responded, *"Ahhhhhhhhh, daaammmmmnnnn!"*

They rushed into the room to see her legs spread, a puddle of wetness between her legs, and sweat rolling off her face in the relatively cool room. She again yelled, *"Ahhhhh!"*

Zena turned and went to the kitchen to warm water on the stove. She told Dixie where Mae kept her towels and told her to fetch a few.

Stella, moving about as quickly as cold molasses running uphill in winter, lowered herself to her knees like an elephant taking a graceful bow in the center ring of the circus. She stationed herself to receive the newborn child Mae was laboring to deliver.

Stella said, "Sis, stand over the top of me and push like you are trying to poop." She continued, "Dixie, honey child, get one of those towels wet with the warm water and stand behind Mae's tush. Wrap the towel around her belly and pull it tight like it's a girdle."

Mae said, "Oh my God, I'm going to kill Pop."

Stella said, "Sis, lean forward a bit. It will take the pressure off."

Mae groaned and said, "I wish I was still a virgin."

Zena laughed and said, "It's a bit late for that now."

Mae only labored for about an hour, during which she twice threatened to destroy Pop's manhood and three times threatened to kill him. Dixie and Mae's sisters also heard numerous cuss words. Nevertheless, it was soon over, while several miles away, Pop and his brothers-in-law were in the worst throes of their personal hell while fighting the fire.

Russell Kenneth Kaye came into this world that day. Dixie started cleaning up the mess made on the floors in the flat while the Rodgers girls took care of little Russ.

Pop and Mae ended up having two children, and both were boys, Russell and little Cal. "Barrel" was Cal's nickname, as his physique, even as a small child, resembled one of the barrels coming out of the factory by Mae's childhood home.

Calvin Jr. was born November 2, 1902, which, ironically, was the day of the groundbreaking for the new capitol building in Harrisburg. Joseph Miller Huston designed the new building.

Pop found work at a doughnut shop. As soon as he got off work there, he went to Bethlehem Steel to put in another five or so hours during the day. He got off work at about one or two o'clock in the afternoon and did his drinking until early evening. Then he passed out until about eleven thirty at night, when he woke up to start the routine all over again.

Pop thought that if he got five hours of sleep, all would be well, giving him the weekends to spend with his family. However, most weekends he spent more time nursing a bottle and running his vulgar mouth than he spent with his wife and two sons. Pop essentially forced Mae to find things to do with their boys outside of the apartment to protect them from his mouth and behavior. Unfortunately, the boys were destined to be a product of their environment.

Mae walked to work in all weather conditions. She sold fresh and canned produce at a fruit stand in the fifty-year-old Broad Street Market. She took the boys with her, and they had to sit under the apple bin and play quietly so she could keep her job. She usually earned just enough money to buy some needed food items before she went home.

There were weeks when Mae didn't need things like Pop's three-pound crock of apple butter at fifteen cents, five cakes of homemade soap for twenty-five cents, and fresh coffee beans at thirty-five cents a pound. In the spring of the year, if you were willing to pay extra for the transportation needed to get it down here all the way from Vermont, there was Vermont's delicious maple syrup, which was a yearly purchase at ninety cents a gallon. Mae tried her best to have such extras around the house. She called them frills, and she tried to spend no more than fifty cents of her three-dollar pay on them.

She needed other things almost on a weekly basis. Kidney beans were ten cents per quart, peas were seven cents per quart, and tomatoes were eight cents per quart. As for meat, she would walk around just at the close of business on Saturday and in many cases get deep discounts on meats from the regular price of beef roast at ten cents a pound, cured ham at twelve cents a pound, and sausage at twelve cents a pound. If she played her cards well and took the boys in tow wearing their mismatched, patched, and hemmed clothing, she could get ten or twelve pounds of meat to get them through the next week for fifty to sixty cents and take home about eighty cents of her pay to get things during the week. For the most part, she could not depend on Pop's check. Some of it would have gone to drink before he even got home. Mae usually forced herself to stay away from her weakness, peanut brittle. Even though Pop drank at least half of his pay, Mae felt guilty if she took even five cents out of her earnings for a half pound of peanut brittle.

The Broad Street Market was founded pre-Civil War and helped feed over five hundred troops coming through Camp Curtin. Mae took pride in her job, as the market had helped feed her father and several of her uncles when they fought in the Civil War. The original building that ran from Third to Sixth streets was still part of the market. The stone end of the building was built in 1863, and the brick end of the structure was built about ten years earlier. The market remained a community gathering place even thirty-five years after it opened. Moreover, it was still growing.

As little Russ and Barrel got too old to hang out at the market under the apple table, they started to resist going to the market and wanted to stay home. However, Pop made it clear that he wasn't a damn babysitter and they needed to be out of the house.

Russ and the bigger boys in the neighborhood played "conkers." When the pods, called conkers, fell off the horse chestnut trees, the boys would select the firm ones and bore a hole in each one. Then they would run several feet of twine through them. Conkers was played in pairs, and the idea was to swing your conker to hit the opponent's conker. The game ended when one conker got broken. Then the unbroken conker was declared the winner. Barrel would never play with Russ after Russ's conker accidentally hit him in the face when the twine slipped out of Russ's hand.

When they got bored, they played "knocking down Ginger," a game in which the boys ran up to somebody's house, knocked on the front door, and then scooted away. Lord only knows why the game amused them so much, but it passed the time.

Then there were the things that really made Pop raise the roof when he found out about them. The boys would steal some of his booze, gather some corn silk and a few pipes, and head down the alley to act like little men. Then there was lifting a few of Pop's private collection of early nudie magazines that the Rodgers boys got shipped in mass quantities all the way from France to resell. Pop had at least twenty-five of them hidden away in a metal box in the closet, and the boys snuck a few out at a time. They were early titles, and Pop had at least two of most, including *H&E Naturist*, *Photo Bit*, *Body in Art*, *Figure Photography*, *Nude Living*, and *Modern Art for Men*. Once they and the neighborhood boys saw these, there was no going back to the lingerie section of the Sears catalog.

As the boys grew older, the little flat on the third floor was no longer working for them. The family moved to 230 S. 15th Street to give them a little more space. The boys knew all too well from living in the flat that if they made the least bit of noise in the evening, Pop would get up and wear out their butts with a hickory switch or his leather razor strap. The names and curse words he would call the boys were not fit to call an animal, let alone one's child. He also was known to hit Mae if he felt the boys were not "under control," for he held Mae responsible for the effective discipline of their sons. The hope was that the bigger house would lessen that feeling of imprisonment and keep them off the streets a bit more, for their parents had starting hearing stories about their behavior.

The new neighborhood was nosier than the old one, and this became a problem for Pop and, in reality, for the entire family. It defeated the purpose of the move, and the noise drove the boys to the streets early in the day to escape Pop's carryings-on. Russ and

Barrel were running the streets of Harrisburg at the ages of thirteen and nine years old. Because of the foul language and other crap Pop spewed around the house, Russ and Barrel stayed away from home more and more to stay out of trouble with their parents.

Mae tried her best to expose the boys to religious values and community at the Salem United Church of Christ as a replacement to running the streets. At best however, the church only saved the boys from being worse than they were. They grew up with troubled lives, and because of that, they found their way to the bottle, loose women, and fist fighting. Their father was their role model, and by the time they were in their mid and early teens, they were nothing but trouble. Mae was deeply despondent.

Maxamillion Kline, Max for short, was a Jewish friend of Russ's, and he called him "my favorite kike." He lived just off Forster, on South 17th Street. Max was quite tall and had sandy brown hair, blue eyes, and more freckles on his face than there are stars in the sky. The two of them would regularly skip school and take their fishing poles, a pouch of corn, and some potato mash to the lower side of the Dock Street Dam. They would fish, catch carp, and measure them across the tracks of the railroad bridge. If they were not longer than the width of the track, they would throw them from the bridge, through the air, and try to get them to the top side of the dam so they could watch them go flying back over the falls.

Now for those who know where the dam is in reference to the railroad bridge, or if you know that the width of standard railroad tracks is fifty-six inches, you know this is one of the greatest fish stories ever told. Or was it simply Russ trying to bamboozle the crowd?

Even though Max was Jewish, he often went to church with Russell at the Salem United Church of Christ. One of their favorite pastimes at church was a game to see who could get the most money out of the collection plate as it passed by without being caught. Sometimes it gave them spending money they otherwise wouldn't have for Adam Reel's Grocery Store at the corner of 4th and Market streets.

Both Russ and Barrel went to Technical High School in the old DeWitt building at the corner of Walnut Street and Aberdeen Alley to learn a trade. Barrel was working toward becoming a glass master, but Russ decided to take up Pop's trade, baking and a little drinking. Who are we kidding? There would be a lot of drinking.

Russ had another problem at school that went beyond not attending class regularly, not doing his studying, not paying attention when he was in class, and smoking in the bathroom with James Minnick, known as "Red." Red was the well-liked football star, admired by all the popular girls, who flirted and hung all over him. Red didn't have any humility. In fact, he was once heard saying about himself, "I'm a man of great renown."

Red was a damn good cartoon artist, and every classmate was made the butt of his jokes through the humor of his cartoons. He did two drawings of Russ, one entitled "He's a dough boy. He has a woman's job." The other was "Dough Boy the Slow Boy." Comments like this about a kid with an attitude bigger than life itself were an invitation for a royal ass kicking of a boy in love with himself. That is just what happened to Red. That encounter resulted in Russ's expulsion from school when he was just a sixteen-year-old kid, and the end of his friendship with Red.

Russell was spiraling out of control. Without the structure of school, it seemed that he found more trouble to get into every day. For instance, several times Russ snuck down into the dirt cellar and stole some of Pop's potato mash from his stash. He and Max took it and a couple of naughty girls to Reservoir Park after dark. Those two girls were only fifteen, but they already knew more about what it takes to please a man than women half again their age. They told certain friends the stories from these little trips up to the top of the reservoir on moonlit nights, and the word spread. That was just what Russ and Max had in mind to build their reputations.

One night while doing things that kids their ages should not do, one of them noticed a colored boy watching them from behind a tree. Half-dressed, Max and Russ took off after him and tackled him on the Market Street side of the park. They stripped him down naked as a jaybird. Then they ran away with his clothes, leaving him naked at the top of Reservoir Park late at night.

The boy stole some clothes from someone's clothesline on his way home. When the boy walked into his home dressed in a woman's muumuu, his parents had more than a few questions. In the morning, after answering his parents' questions for half the night, he was still furious.

What Russ did not know was that the colored boy knew him through church. Since the boy was black, Russ wouldn't have ever spoken to him, which was the way he was raised. You just did not speak to blacks or Catholics. They were virtually the same breed, which is just the way it was. The colored boy and his parents went to the Kayes' house to speak with Russ's parents. When the boy's parents confronted Russ, Pop Kaye was angry with his son because he would not identify the other boy who was with him. However, Pop did not give much sympathy to the boy's parents either. He told the boy's parents only that he was disappointed in his own son and that he would handle it with him. They needed to deal with their son.

When the boys' parents left, he called Russell out to the kitchen, and with a mug of coffee in hand, Pop made Russell tell him the whole story. Russell, of course, left out some of the details such as stealing the potato mash, and he gave limited detail about his activities with the girls. By the end of the conversation, for one of the few times he could remember in his life, Russ was laughing with Pop.

It was also the first time in his life that he remembered his dad embracing him. Pop said, "Son, soon you might be dragged into this war, and I need to tell you, in case anything happens, that I love you." As he hugged his son in his arms for the first time since he was a baby, Pop was thinking that if his son went to war, he might never come home alive. He could also see that his son was growing up to be a chip off the old block. Unfortunately, there was not much of a chance to change the fact that the boy lacked a strong role model, and if he were to die at war, Pop would know that he had failed as a father.

It took a matter of only four days from the time President Wilson outlined his case to go to war in defense of France and Britain for Congress to give the thumbs-up. Cities, towns, and villages all over the United States were in shock on Monday evening of April 6, 1917, when people all over the country woke to hear newspaper boys screaming on street corners. They could be seen swinging newspapers over their heads and yelling, "Hear ye, Hear ye! United States declares war on Germany."

By May 18, the Selective Service Act passed, creating the draft for men ages twenty-one to thirty (and subsequently eighteen to forty-five). The goal was to raise a national army to enter the war and fight the Germans. Both President Wilson and Congress were criticized for destroying democracy at home and sending our boys off to war.

Max pondered whether he should enlist just to keep from getting in big trouble with Russell. An angry Russell held out on enlisting in the war effort and looked for the support of his family in that decision. Boys like Barrel thanked God they were too young. From Harrisburg, young men were flocking to the New Cumberland Army Post to join and go fight the "Krauts."

Max decided that a life as a follower of Russell Kaye was going to get him nowhere except maybe in a jail cell. He made a grown-up decision and enlisted in the army in early May. Russell could not bring himself to enlist, and he was too young for the draft. Max left for Camp Meade, Maryland, for training. Leaving home was a big deal for Max, but he did not realize how much so until he got to Camp Meade and became a part of a larger (military) family. The sight of thousands of young men from all parts of Pennsylvania, Maryland, and Delaware who were in training under the guidance of older men wearing work utilities was almost overwhelming. The reality was that by the end of training, those young men would become United States soldiers ready to fight the Germans in France in World War I.

On the other hand, Russell said, "Ain't any sweat off my back. I didn't lose anything over there, and I have no desire to be involved." He heard about what others were doing so they wouldn't qualify to be drafted. Guys chewed wads of tobacco and swallowed its juice. Others sucked the juice out of a beetroot and chased it with a bit of sour mash. Some drank large quantities of saltwater. All of these were considered to be methods to raise their blood pressure so they would not be eligible to be drafted. He told Max that he was pissed off at him for going, but in the privacy of his own room, Russ punched the wall a few times, saying he was afraid to die over there and admitting his admiration of Max. Russ felt that his family wouldn't care if he lived or died, but he did, so why should he go and take the risk?

CHAPTER

ARMY TRAINING
AND DEPLOYMENT

R ussell was getting a haircut at L. M. Cassel's barbershop
at 1444 Regina Street when he ran into Max's papa. Their
relationship had always been strained because Mr. Kline had
always seen Russ for what he was, a troublemaker with insufficient
parental guidance. To say the least, Mr. Kline, a short Jewish man
with dark curly hair and a big nose, was glad that Max and Russ were
separated. He did not really want Max to go off to war, but at least
he was away from Russ's influence. More than likely, he would have
rather had Russ, a scalawag, standing in front of Max to protect him
and let Russ be the one who was shot at overseas.

Mr. Kline told Russ that Max was very happy that he made the
decision to go. He felt manhood was forming within himself, and it
was better than the life of delinquency he had been living around
Russ. Mr. Kline went on to say that Russ would probably find the
family that he had longed and searched for within the military. He
told Russ that Max said he would like to talk to him about it but
figured Russ would just tell him to take a hike.

Russ walked away from that encounter with two things that made
him unhappy: that military crew cut that he hated and wanted nothing
to do with and the fact that a big-nosed kike like old man Kline knew

his innermost personal and emotional struggles as he searched for stability. Why would Max tell his old man about his private, personal challenges?

That night, Russ lay in his bed sulking about Max, who was his one and only trusted friend. Russ was madder than hell about Max talking about him behind his back and wished he had his hands on Max's scrawny pencil neck. In reality, Russ had been alternating between being in favor of and then against enlisting. He searched his heart about Mr. Kline's comments that the military could possibly be the family he was longing for. Why would he or should he join the military? Russ actually knew little about the military and didn't have a good enough relationship with his own father to ask for his input. Then he would wonder if he was pushing himself to join just to stay out of jail or maybe to be with Max again.

After about two weeks of pondering the question, Russ turned to Mr. Kline because going to Pop would just bring insults and ridicule. He met with Kline twice, and after the second meeting, Russ got serious about the military. It wasn't until his friend's father encouraged him to consider signing up, followed by intense soul-searching, that Russ joined the military.

It was late May 1917. He told his parents over Sunday chicken dinner with many of his mom's relatives there. To his surprise, his pop was proud of his move and his mother was thrilled and in tears. He neglected to mention that he had turned to Kline for help and fatherly advice, and he made up his mind that he would go to his grave without ever telling that secret.

Little did Russ know that the results of the tests he had to take would be used to determine his military training assignment. Russ ended up being sent to the Army Headquarters Reserve Division at Fort Dix. He wondered what he had done to himself. He'd joined to catch up with Max, and that just did not happen.

With great reservation, Russell Kaye left to join the war effort through Fort Dix. The mission of his unit was to provide training and support for the 85th Illinois, the 87th Alabama, and the newest unit in Edison, New Jersey, at Fort Dix. Their tasks were to ready the reserve component of those units' personnel and mobilize them.

His unit supported training exercises within the brigade and discharged technical missions as guided by headquarters. Their goal was to enhance the combat skills and motivation of soldiers and units. All troops assigned to this division went through intensive training and were combat-ready and prepared for any mission to which they might be assigned. Russ, on the other hand, was sent for training as a cook and baker to support those troops, and because of his family background, he easily slipped into that job.

Like Russ, some soldiers were a little resistant from time to time and had to be disciplined. It was far better to straighten soldiers out at Fort Dix rather than on the front lines, when other lives could be in danger. At one point, Russ was full of piss and vinegar and let his mouth go without engaging his brain. He had a problem with women outranking him, but some women had earned significant roles in American history before women could even vote.

For example, Harriet Quimby was the first licensed female pilot in the United States in 1911. In addition, few people know that Katherine Wright, sister of the Wright brothers, had as much to do with the first flight at Kitty Hawk as did her brothers. Women were military pilots during WWI, including Princess Eugenie Shakhovskaya of Russia, the first woman military pilot, and Helene Dutreux in France. However, there were no official female military pilots in the United States military. A few female American pilots volunteered, but the military did not take them seriously, even though they were officers. Russ was no exception, as he didn't seem to be able to take military women seriously either.

Three female pilots and a few military nurses were at Fort Dix for some training during the same time Russ was stationed there. As Russ came out of the mess hall one evening, several of them were coming in, and Russ looked away rather than acknowledging them. One female officer said, "Private, don't you salute an officer when you recognize one?"

Russ looked straight at all three of the women pilots and said, "Yeah!"

They then asked in unison, "Then why didn't you salute us?"

Russ, with no emotion on his face, said, "Because one, you are all only ninety-day wonders; and two, you're women and should be at home making babies and cooking for your men."

Russ soon found himself court-marshaled and before a judge. When asked how he pleaded, he said, "I guess I'm guilty of being a man and standing up for what all men should instead of being candy-ass pussies cowering down to wenches. We let them get away with all this bullshit when they don't even have the right to vote. Keep them in their place: barefoot and pregnant."

Russ lost twenty dollars in pay and was ordered to spend seven days in the brig. Because he was only an E1 to begin with, he couldn't lose rank.

When the judge asked what he had to say for himself, he looked at the judge and asked him, "Do you sit down to pee? I just wondered since you seem to be one of them, the way you protect those women." This outburst cost him orders to the front lines the next morning instead of seven days in the brig and an additional twenty dollars in fines. The judge also said that he would see to it that Russ was still an E1 at the beginning of the next year.

As the MPs were taking Russ out of the courtroom, the judge said, "By the way, Private Kaye, I'd like to remind you that I'm a *judge* working in a courtroom, while *you* are going to cooking and baking school. Now who is getting domesticated and acting like he has to sit down to pee?"

Russ spent the night in lockup thinking that the judge would change his mind and he would not be shipped out as soon as he was released. In the morning, he was ordered to undergo additional training in another area of expertise while still cooking in the mess hall. Russ was sure that the turn of events had something to do with the judge.

After Russ's basic combat training and cooking and baking school, he was sure that cooking was his military niche—until his courtroom stumble. Then everything started to change. Russ found himself being trained on how to mobilize and maximize the combat readiness of the troops for deployment. No one was saying when that would happen. With the training behind him, Russ could work in a mess hall cooking food for the troops or be pulled into combat matters at a moment's notice.

Advanced Tactical Training (ATT) was where he learned the skills to perform yet another army job. He received hands-on training and field instruction to make him an expert in the ATT field. He gained the discipline and work ethic to make him effective no matter what path he had to follow.

Some of his advanced training bordered on military intelligence. However, in no way was Russ worthy of a top secret or even a secret clearance. He could gather general intelligence learned during army missions. He also could find himself out front, providing essential intelligence to others and in many cases saving the lives of soldiers fighting on the front lines. He wondered why that judge would have made such a move unless he was hopeful that Russ might be killed.

Russ thought he really had it all figured out when it came to the training for gathering intelligence from enemy subjects using interview techniques and physical methods. He did very well carrying out those tasks. Russ also had a knack for preparing intelligence reports, with the exception of his spelling, which was atrocious.

The school's mission was to transform civilians into disciplined killing machines, with the intent of sparing women and children. They needed to have certain essential skills, instincts, fitness, integrity, self-assurance, a sense of obligation, and the combatant spirit to be an adaptive and flexible warrior ready to accomplish the mission. During the training, Russ was part of a combat team that learned to use small arms, grenades, bazookas, and other firing weapons.

In June 1917, in the midst of training, it was announced that the Big Red 1 Infantry Division that Russ was assigned to was leaving from Governors Island, New York, later in June. Russ recalled from that announcement that they were told the division would consist of four infantry divisions and three artillery divisions. Russ was assigned to the one of the infantry regiments of the division. He was one of about twenty thousand men getting ready to ship out to France within days. The division picked up the nickname of the "Big Red 1," or the "Bloody 1," which became the unit's shoulder insignia.

It was ironic that Russ enlisted after Max, yet if the judge had his way, Russ would be in France before Max would. Russ wondered whether there was a hidden meaning in that or if his lack of self-control propelled him out of the States so fast. Russ and the rest of the Big Red 1 Infantry regiment, along with the other three infantry and three artillery regiments of that division, were transformed into soldiers overnight. Russ still had a bit of tarnished armor and a bit of an attitude, but he was a soldier nonetheless.

When they arrived in New York, Max realized for the first time that the army was much bigger than his unit was. He saw thousands of soldiers in his path as he walked the streets of New York City over the thirty-six hours they spent here. While they were waiting to ship out, more troops from several other military bases arrived hour after hour.

Max and some of his buddies went to a film called *The Beast of Berlin*. It was a movie of hateful propaganda toward the Germans, featuring an extremely malevolent kaiser. A Belgian family, whose father was a blacksmith with several children, finds themselves at the mercy of the Germans. In the movie's final scenes, the war ends, the Allied forces win, and the kaiser is turned over to the Belgian people as their prisoner.

Many soldiers sat on ships writing long letters home to loved ones, while others like Max wrote brief notes home to avoid passing on confidential information about their departure. All letters were being censored, so there really wasn't much to say. Guys like Max spent their free time partying while others explored the glamour and glitter of a big city for the first time ever.

Meanwhile, a spit-shined and polished 314th Infantry Regiment, 79th Division, boarded trains for New York from Camp Meade. This regiment was heading for the area of Paris where there were several air bases, and they were assigned to those units as support. Among the ranks of this regiment was a man named Jack; he would soon make a big difference in Russ's life.

Soldiers swarmed the streets of New York like ants on a picnic lunch. Because of the confusing layout of the town, many of them became as lost as a nut hidden away for winter by a squirrel. Most streets seemed to lead to the picturesque waterfront. The clear summer evening gave way to seagulls gliding through the air and city lights twinkling and dancing across the water. Soldiers stood on the docks, in the streets close to the water, and in the parks at the waterfront, taking in the beauty. Those who were conversing were in total agreement that the sights were as delightful as the photos they had seen in advertisements and magazines.

Many soldiers on docked ships would go topside to stand on the deck and look out over the water. These were the kinds of guys who didn't buy into the bar scene or spend time with seedy women like some others in their unit did. They would tell you that they were keeping themselves pure for their wedding night with Marguerite, Gertrude, Lillian, or Edith—if they were lucky enough to make it back home. If not, they would meet their maker as virgins. Other guys were out to drink with a goal of having their way with seventy-two or so virgins on this side of heaven.

Ships embarked from the docks with thousands of men who did not know one another except for the dozen or so men closest to them. Even the hundreds of soldiers on each individual ship would have no idea who 95 percent of the folks on their transport vessel were. Days passed like flashes of light, to the point of making it hard to keep track of days or dates. There was a storm at sea, and waves rolled over the bows of the carriers as if they were toys in a tub. After several stormy days in a row, the quarters reeked of vomit, as most of the soldiers were incredibly sick. Most who were silly enough to try to consume food simply regurgitated, often at their feet, shortly after swallowing it.

The best entertainment soldiers found some days was watching the ships on either side of them taking on water from the massive waves slapping up and over the bow, their own ship included. The ships were tossed about on the waves like little leaves from oak trees scampering about atop a babbling brook on a windy day.

When the ocean was calmer, small groups of ground soldiers would get half-hour workouts running around the ship's deck and up and down staircases. They also did physical workout exercise sessions on the deck. On the warmer days that brought sweat to their faces, and breathing in the ocean mist and feeling it on their skin provided a unique cooling sensation that they almost enjoyed.

As the seemingly endless days of their journey passed, the sounds they heard continuously were seagulls, their own voices, and the creaks and groans of the ship as the waves slapped against it. From time to time, they cringed as they heard the cries of fellow soldiers who were not able to take any more and jumped overboard when occasional huge waves washed up over the bow of the ship.

As they neared their destination, strange sounds came from the starboard side as the ships hugged the eastern shore of the bay. To the west were more of the same coal-black skies they had experienced during their journey. However, this night was different. There wasn't a single visible star to use as a navigational marker. The moon was nonexistent. The only light was from the occasional flickering of open fires off the starboard side of the ship as their sparks rose and crackled toward the heavens. At the front and on the starboard side of the ship, crew members from the signal corps were lowered to man their small lifeboats. It was their job to carry torches to keep the ships far enough off the coast and to guide the ships from getting lodged on a sandbar or damaged by rocks.

The peculiar darkness coupled with the strange sounds drove several of the torch-carrying soldiers on board to surrender their torches and return to the lower deck to fold their shaking hands in prayer. They asked God to guide them safely through the dangers of this mystifying blackness. They had already forgotten the dangers that the past few weeks had confronted them with and didn't give any thought to the fact that the ocean they just crossed could have swallowed them up in a mere second, without allowing them to see so much as the first sunrise in France. The exhilaration of arriving in the land of battle had vanished and was replaced with fear.

The first United States troops, including Russ, Max, and Quentin Roosevelt, the son of a former United States president, hit the ground in France on Monday, June 25. Ships began docking immediately, and the soldiers were off-loading to enter the country of battle. These masses of men would be going in different directions based on the orders for their units. Russ was immediately sent to Bordeaux. Not much time was wasted, as this was a large gathering of thousands of green soldiers in one area. It was best to get them moving out and marching off to war before they had a chance to stand around with idle time on their hands, making them a perfect target for the enemy. When Russ got to Bordeaux, France, he went to work in the mess hall, preparing food for the throngs of soldiers.

Soldiers moved out on foot, passing through little villages and towns every few *klicks*. A klick is equal to one thousand meters, or .62 miles. The eeriness started to filter through their brains when they realized that there were no young or middle-aged men to speak of in these areas where there was little populations. Only very young and elderly men were there, which seemed haunting to the young soldiers. Fear struck as the Americans wondered if the Germans had killed them all. Their fear created blinders that did not allow them to realize at first that the young French men were off fighting the same war that they were walking into. As nightfall came upon them, they occupied empty homes in these very villages. As they marched along to their ultimate destination, they came across villages that had large gardens in the backyards of the homes, with crops that became free food to the hungry soldiers.

The language barrier was their next challenge, unless there happened to be a soldier in the unit who could speak the local language. Max's unit had a guy in it who could speak French, which came in handy for others like Max. Some of them were only worried about learning just enough French to get them into one or two beds of ladies who were missing their men. Others, thinking about more important matters, got information from these people, like where and when (if at all) the townsfolk had last seen the enemy.

It soon became clear that such questions had to be asked and the thoughts of personal pleasures needed to be put aside because of the reverberation of big guns somewhere not far in the distance. Sometimes the sounds were coming from the northwest, while others sounded off from the southeast. It appeared that Max's unit was walking right into a gunfight. It seemed as if it was going to be hard to go anywhere without someone shooting at them.

No sooner had they gotten into serious discussions with the townsfolk of a little village than the skies lit up like the Fourth of July. Those who didn't wet themselves were the ones diving for cover first. Explosions burst around them like mousetraps snapping mice necks. Max was on a detachment of the brigade command and consequently was away from the company for a while. The company was about a mile away from him on night patrol. There might have been twenty of them. They decided to look for a shorter way back across the open fields. On the way, they were pinned down. All of them were positioned dangerously and under machine gun fire.

Until everyone was out of danger and the skirmishes were over, four US soldiers were dead and seven others were wounded. Two men in Max's detachment were lost; one of them died as Max was trying to care for the soldier's wounds. The brigade officer speculated that inexperience was the reason they headed through the open fields. He also told the commanders to be aware that in his estimation, they were pinned down and all but dead. Several of the Catholic boys crossed themselves and looked up to God as if they were quite sure that this was their last stop.

That was until Joey St. Patrick outfitted himself with two machine guns, plenty of rounds of ammo, a chest full of grenades, several clips, and a pistol. He flanked out to the right through the standing corn to a tree line. He was beyond hearing range within a minute and out of sight within five rods. Not more than five minutes had passed when they heard another nasty firefight break out. That took the pressure off and allowed the unit to move on the enemy's position.

The enemy was overtaken, and Max moved toward Joey, calling out to him. When Max found him, Joey was bleeding from at least a dozen wounds. Joey reached out to Max with bloody hands, giving him a letter to be taken to his wife and children. Max and Joey had gone through training together, and Joey was from Selinsgrove, Pennsylvania, about thirty-five miles from Max's hometown. Max cuddled Joey in his arms and prayed to God over him, even asking Jesus to bless Joey, which is not a Jewish thing to do. Max told his commanders, "You need to know that Joey saved our lives by setting up that firefight all by himself. Please make sure that his wife and children are told that too. They need to know what a hero he was."

CHAPTER

LIFE CHANGES FOR RUSSELL

U ntil now, Russ could barely keep himself out of jail at home and out of the brig in the military. As a soldier in France, Russ was likely to find himself in even more serious situations. The question was whether he could rise to the occasion and become the man God wanted him to be.

Theodore Roosevelt was enraged at America's continuing indifference to Germany's war actions. Starting in May 1915, Germany sunk a British passenger ship, the *RMS Lusitania*, and 128 Americans drowned. Roosevelt campaigned unsuccessfully in 1916 as the Republican presidential nominee. Wilson was subsequently reelected on the Democrats' platform, which included neutrality regarding the war between Germany and European countries of England and France.

After the United States of America declared war two years later, Theodore Roosevelt wired Major General "Black Jack" Pershing, asking if his sons could go with him to Europe as privates. Pershing accepted the request. However, because of their training, Archie was commissioned as a 2nd lieutenant, while Ted Jr. was given a commission as a major. Quentin thought his skills were in the area of mechanics and would surely be useful to the army. Accordingly, he dropped out of college to join a newly formed army aviation unit. He trained on an airfield on Long Island.

Like Roosevelt with his "Rough Riders," Pershing was a no-nonsense kind of a guy. That is probably why these two men got along so well. It was reported that a handful of years before WWI, a number of Muslim terrorists attacked United States forces in the Philippines, so Pershing took matters into his own hands.

Pershing ordered his troops to capture fifty Muslim terrorists. In preparation for their execution by firing squad, Pershing had his men butcher several pigs in front of the terrorists and soak bullets in pig blood. Muslims detest pigs because they feel that pigs are filthy animals. They believe that touching any part of a pig prevents them from entering paradise. Forty-nine of the terrorists were executed with those bullets while the fiftieth Muslim watched. The executed terrorists were buried with the butchered pig remains, and then the fiftieth terrorist was set free. As fortune would have it, Pershing's actions put an immediate stop to Muslim terrorist attacks in the Philippines.

When Quentin finally arrived in France as Lieutenant Quentin Roosevelt, his first assignment was helping to set up the main USAS training base at Issoudun. He was initially a supply officer. As all things go in combat situations, Quentin Roosevelt quickly earned a field promotion and ran one of the training airfields. Eventually, he became a pilot in the 95th Aero Squadron, part of the 1st Pursuit Group. The unit was assigned to Touquin, France, and on July 9, 1918, they became part of a squadron in Saints, France. He was a hot dog pilot who always seemed to be in the middle of everything good, bad and indifferent. One might think he wouldn't fit into barracks life in the military. After all, he was Teddy Roosevelt's son and had lived in the White House.

Those who met him for the first time expected him to be an arrogant and uppity little monster. This was far from the truth. When Quentin arrived at a get-together, it was almost as if someone had let a party animal out of his cage. Like the best of partygoers, he had a love for life and merrymaking. Once people got to know him, they wanted to socialize with him, not because of who he was but because of the festive atmosphere that always surrounded him. It felt good to escape for a while from the war and the gloominess of their surroundings.

The German advance began in late June. They were near Rheims on the Vesle River by July 6. Major highways and railroads were held by the Germans. South from Soissons, German trenches ran for several dozen miles to the banks of the Marne River. From there, the trenches followed along the edge of the river to provide protection for the Germans.

By the approach of a twenty-square-mile wall of German forces, there was a threat on Paris for the first time. This thread included the Château-Thierry, which lay on the north bank of the Marne River. The United States and France had a stronghold south of Paris itself. Like a late night poker game, the Germans went "all in" with a strategy to destroy US and French forces in the theater. Back in Germany, the German military stripped factories and businesses of men to add as many soldiers as they could to their forces. Unfortunately for the Germans, the result of that decision was the beginning of the end. By losing so many factory workers, the manufacture and distribution of supplies to the German troops slowed down drastically.

Along with others in the 94th Squadron, Quentin received orders to shift from Toul to the Château-Thierry sector. Their assignment was to defend against German fighting squadrons that had already left the vicinity of Verdun-St. Mihiel-Pont-à-Mousson. They were to take observing and photographing personnel with them to gather intelligence on the area.

The observers lucky enough to go airborne to snap photos were able to get great ground footage of prisoner camps and shelled-out buildings. Overall, the photos documented the same story the newspapers did, just from different vantage points.

Suddenly, they got something they were not expecting. The day evolved into a day from hell. They quickly realized that the elite of the

German fighting squadrons had arrived. The sky was as crowded as the gates to a Phillies game in a good baseball season. The observers snapped shots of a real-time dogfight in the sky. They got pictures of enemy Fokker planes and bullets racing across the sky toward them, with a few shots of the plane markings, such as the number of kills painted around the cockpits, right down to a few close-up pictures in which the intensiveness on the faces of the pilots in the enemy planes was visible.

The 94th, 95th, 27th, and 145th squadrons had fewer than eighty planes in the skies. The Germans outnumbered them by about four to one. After four years of war in their country, France's morale was low at that point. The air service of France had been depleted so severely that they were pressing men from infantry, cavalry, and artillery into the skies. Unfortunately for France, the under-trained pilots were simply not measuring up to the task. Consequently, the few American squadrons were abruptly plunged into the thick of a ferocious conflict at Château-Thierry. They found that they were overwhelmingly outnumbered, poorly supported, and lamentably equipped, in both machines and experience.

While occupying this sector at Château-Thierry over the thirty days leading up to that afternoon, thirty-six American pilots were either captured or killed. Quentin Roosevelt got his first kill on July 14, 1918. Two days later, he was part of a five-plane formation from the 95th Squadron, which advanced across the enemy lines east of Château-Thierry. As usual, the sky was loaded with enemy formations. On the ground below them, both French and American troops were totally entrenched in battle with the Germans.

Within a few moments after passing over the enemy lines, the more timid 95th Squadron, with but five planes, took on a Fokker formation of seven planes at a low altitude. The 95th accepted the Hun challenge for combat. As they jockeyed for a better position for a kill shot on one another, Quentin realized that several red-nosed Fokkers were approaching. In keeping with his personality, he withdrew and flew right at the oncoming Fokkers. His other four wingmen were unaware that he had left the formation, as Quentin was in the last rear position on one of the wings.

All of a sudden, the leader of Roosevelt's formation saw a Nieuport spiraling downward in a ball of flames right in front of him. Having no idea that another formation was in the area, he could only speculate that the Fokkers he was engaged with were not the only ones in the area. He decided that he was getting out of the area before he lost any of his planes. Signaling the others to follow him, they broke away from the dogfight and headed home. When they landed back at the base, the leader realized that Quentin Roosevelt, flying Nieuport #28, had not returned with them.

Later that evening, a message came from the Germans, reporting that President Roosevelt's son had been shot down by Sergeant Thom at Chamery, near Coulonges-en-Tardenois. Thom was a German Ace with twenty-four kills to that point. Further information was received that Quentin was buried with military honors due to his death that was caused by two bullets to the head by the Germans. As the news spread worldwide, the Germans in the field gloated about the news of Quentin Roosevelt's death.

Quentin crashed close to the front lines, where there were not a lot of resources to work with; the Germans used two pieces of basswood and wire from Roosevelt's Nieuport to create a cross for his grave. For propaganda purposes, some Germans in the field took photos of the plane and Quentin's dead body so they could produce a postcard.

Even though Quentin was the enemy, that action met with astonishment from people all over Germany. Germans generally held Theodore Roosevelt in high regard, and they were awestruck that his son died in active duty and disappointed that their troops would take such a picture for a postcard.

Of course, there were reports that Quentin was not actually dead. Other reports stated that he was wounded and had been put in the Château de Beynac as a prisoner of war. This left an unsettled feeling back home, not only for the family but also for the country as a whole.

This flicker of hope brought forth orders for search parties to look for young Roosevelt. Quentin was never found as a prisoner of war.

The British Flying Boat was an American-made plane with several firsts attributed to its name. Made in 1913, they were the first cargo planes to make a trans-Atlantic flight. These planes were mail/cargo carriers between England and America. Thereafter, they were used for international air travel. Because of the flying boats' abilities, they were quickly put to work by the American and Royal Navies as a patrol and rescue plane. Each had four .303 (7.7 mm) Lewis Guns and carried four one-hundred-pound bombs to defend itself in the sky.

Three British Flying Boats with Nieuports as wing cover took off on July 16, about forty-eight hours after Roosevelt went down on a search and retrieve mission. The 95th pilots, weakened to just four Nieuports, had seen Roosevelt's plane go down and had an idea were to search for Quentin. So they became the flying boats' escorts and wingmen, two on either side of the three bigger birds.

They got into the area of the front line, almost at the same bearing where the 95th was when they met German resistance earlier that week. This meant that they were only moments away from the spot where they were when they met the Fokkers, close to where Quentin must have crashed. The Germans were starting to lose their position on the ground and were patrolling a less-crowded sky than two days ago.

Within seconds, they were flying over the area where the dogfight with the Fokkers had started, just moments before Roosevelt took off on his own after another squadron of Fokkers. They were doing general reconnaissance, looking for a new grave site as the Germans described it in reports. On their third pass, they got unwanted visitors when seven Fokkers came from the direction of Germany. The four Nieuports split away and took on the seven Fokkers. The dogfight was vigorous, as the 95th was trying to take out a few of the Fokkers to even up the score a bit. The Flying Boats seemed to be in the way of the much smaller and speedier fighters. They rolled as hard a possible away from enemy lines to get out of the way.

One of the Fokkers broke away from its formation, dropped in behind them, and started firing relentlessly. One of the flying boats started smoking out of the top-mounted engine. The crew knew they were on the way down. The pilot focused on a highway that seemed lightly traveled at the time and locked it in as a potential runway. Off in the distance, the crew in the plane could see a convoy of German vehicles. They believed they could land, vacate the plane, and take cover or get back over the imaginary line that divided the forces before the Germans could get near the plane. The second flying boat was shot down, and it crashed to the ground before the first one could even land.

Meanwhile, a dogfight ensued in the sky. While it appeared that the remaining flying boat was just getting out of the way, in reality it did a 360-degree turn and went after the German plane that had chased them and shot down the second plane. The German ace seemed to have no idea that the flying boat had turned and was pursuing him. Now he was in the sights of an unconventional fighting machine, and seconds later the Fokker was spiraling down in a ball of fire.

Once the dogfight was over, the Americans retreated to fight another day. They lost another plane from which the two-man crew of Hakes and Weaver floated to the ground behind enemy lines in their parachutes. Their burning plane crashed through the roof of a building. From the perspective of those in the sky, it looked as though someone was putting a signal flare (recently invented by Martha Coston) into a campfire.

The flying boat that was hit had a rough landing, for the landing gear did not lock in place. It was like a bobsled running on a red brick road with no ice or snow. Sparks flew about twelve feet away from an engine that was smothering from a small mechanical fire. The plane was still skidding down the road while those in the plane were getting out of their harnesses. All the passengers got free and jumped from the plane. Just as the pilot was in midair from his leap, the plane went up in flames following a large explosion.

Captain Leffler fell lifelessly to the ground. The copilot, Lieutenant Witcomb, and the others crept on their hands and knees under the wing of the burning plane to pull Leffler out. They got the lifeless body out to safety and labored to revive him. Maybe they should not have revived him. At that point, his wailing from pain was horrifying. He was bleeding from the mouth because several of his front teeth had been knocked out. A large piece of metal from the wing was stuck in his flight jacket and had blood oozing out of it. He appeared to have broken his leg, rendering him unable to walk.

They were still trying to give aid to Leffler when Germans quickly surrounded the four of them. There was no sense in trying to hold them off; they had a few service revolvers, but they were looking eyeball-to-eyeball with at least thirty armed Krauts.

The Germans started yelling, "Werfen Sie Ihre Waffen und legen Sie Ihre Hände auf den Kopf."

As everyone looked at one another as if confused, one of the observers from the plane said, "He wants us to toss our weapons away and put our hands on our heads."

The Germans wasted no time and said, "Tun Sie es jetzt oder wir leiten Sie zu töten, wo du stehst."

The observer from the plane, Jack Earl, spoke and understood German. He tossed his pistol and yelled out to the others, "He said to do it now or they will kill us where we stand."

Leffler said, "I can't get my left hand on my head."

Almost as Leffler said that, the American yelled to the German, "Die Verwundeten kann man nicht seine Hände auf seine linke Hand auf den Kopf."

The German yelled out to him, "Fein, aber was ist Ihr Unternehmen fliegt über dieses Gebiet."

He said, "Captain Leffler, you are fine if you get your right hand up."

Almost without hesitation, the German said, "Wir taten eine Fliege durch feine Lieutenant Quentin Roosevelt Grab Seite."

Witcomb, a crew member from the plane, yelled to the translator, "What the hell are you two talking about?"

He said, "He wants to know why we were flying up and down this area. I told him we were doing a flyby to find Lieutenant Quentin Roosevelt's grave site to prove to our people and his family that he is dead."

The Germans rounded up the four, put them on a truck, and headed out. Within minutes, they were looking at Roosevelt's grave site, which a German soldier was guiding.

The German officer came to the back of the truck and said to the translator, "Wollen Sie gehen über zur Bahre ist der junge Roosevelt Sie wissen, der Boden ist der Verlust, und es ist ein neues Grab?"

The translator said, "He asked if any of us have the need to go over and touch his grave." All the time he was pointing to an unimpressive grave site.

They all said no.

He looked at the German officer and said, "Nein danke, aber danke der Nachfrage." Essentially, he said, "No, thanks."

They started out on a rather long ride until they came upon an enormous castle that appeared to be built into the clouds. In fact, it was built on top of a large cliff. When they got out of the truck and entered the courtyard, the prisoners wondered where they were. The interpreter asked, "Was ist das und wo sind wir."

The German officer said, "Château de Beynac in Dordogne, France."

PICKING UP AND DELIVERING THE PACKAGE

Though Russ was assigned to a quality unit, he was at best short of a good baker and had proven himself to be a screw-up in the mess hall on many an occasion. He was certainly not ever going to hold top secret clearance and work in the White House, so he was considered expendable. First Sergeant Adam Corbett had noticed that Russ never seemed to lose a fight and could use good judgment when he really needed to. Corbett had a great way with words and decided that Russ was his man to make a sure-death mission. He made it sound as if only Russell Kaye could do this job right.

Two aides to the first shirt showed up at the mess hall and asked for Russ's supervisor. They explained that they were taking him with them, as he was being reassigned. Anyone who had been through the military gamut knew what was happening, but for Russ, the excitement of the unknown brought out that edge of arrogance in him.

While walking across the compound, Russ said to one of the aides, "I hope you guys have a good reason for this crap. I've got work to do in the mess hall."

"All we know is that we were given orders to take you to the first shirt's office," said one aide.

"Well, I'll give him a piece of my mind," Russ said. "That fat jackass could afford to miss a meal or two."

Laughing aloud, the other aide said, "I don't think I'd let my mouth overload my ass if I were you, joker."

"Well, you just watch me, teddy bear," Russ said.

Moments later, Russ was in the first shirt's office.

"Kaye, I've been asked for a man to go on a special mission, and I've picked you," said the first shirt as he handed him a Tommy gun.

"What's that for? I'm a cook," said Kaye.

"Soldier, you are going to put down that paring knife and spud picker. Your country needs you. Besides that, along with this Tommy gun come two more stripes for your sleeve. You're now a buck sergeant," said the first shirt colonel.

Russ's chest started to swell, and the words that so rarely left his mouth barked out as if he were an evangelist in a chapel: "Sir, yes, sir!"

Sergeant Corbett knew in his heart of hearts that once he left Jeffers's office, the chances of his living through the next ninety-six hours were about the same as a woman or a black man being elected president.

The reality was that they were sending Russ and two others to the Château de Beynac, where the flying boat prisoners had been taken. Unbeknownst to them, Russ and the other two were being sent there as decoys (more like sacrificial lambs). At the same time, other soldiers, which they called the "A Team," would be dispatched from a more advantageous direction to the Château de Beynac. Intel had reported that several other American prisoners were also being held there. The hope was that by giving Russ and a few other men a couple of Tommy guns, a pocketful of grenades, and a little direction, they would draw the enemy fire while the A Team slipped in and out with the prisoners without being detected.

"Kaye, you're going to be doing a mission for the intel department, but you will be assigned to the 1st Army. You'll receive instructions once you get over to them. You are not to go back to the mess hall. Just get yourself ready to move out," barked Corbett.

Kaye, who normally entered and exited a room lazily and halfheartedly, suddenly acted like a West Pointer. "Yes, sir, I'll make you proud, sir." He slung his Tommy gun over his shoulder and stiffly marched out of the room.

One of the aides who had brought him to Jeffers's office was in the front office sipping from a cup of two-day-old coffee. He looked up from the cup with a sarcastic grin and said, "You really gave him a piece of your mind, didn't you, jerk?"

Kaye looked at him and said, "You damn well better watch what you are saying. I outrank you."

The other aide said, "Tell me that in a week." They both laughed because they knew where he was headed, and that he would probably be dead within a week. Russ walked out scratching his head and wondering what they meant.

That evening, Kaye wrote a letter home, telling them his news. He wrote about his promotion, the special mission, and the fact that he no longer would be getting up at the crack of zero dark thirty to scramble eggs for thankless people. He told them that he probably was going to have normal hours, working with high-ranking officers and attending important meetings. Because he was given a Tommy gun, he even speculated that he was going to be a bodyguard for one of them.

When the letter got home, his papa would have to read it. Like his father, Russ's spelling and penmanship were terrible, and his mama just could not figure it out. His papa had to soften the language and the content a bit for the sake of his mama because she was a God-fearing Christian woman and didn't like what she referred to as "bar room language."

Several Kaye and Rodgers family members had fought in the Spanish-American war nineteen years earlier, in 1898. They had come home talking about military strategy. Pop easily figured out what might be in his son's future, which was long past by the time the letter arrived at home. They could well be waiting for a complement of soldiers to be coming to the front door within days, and he didn't want his wife to be sitting in a chair staring out the window, waiting for what may not come.

Russ left the barracks the next morning with his duffel bag and gear in hand. A horse-drawn taxi from the motor pool pulled up, driven by a black corporal. In his callous manner that made him liked by few, Russ said, "Boy, to the headquarters of the 1st Army." Russ continued showing his ignorance as he got in the taxi he said, "Be a good colored boy and get my bag."

As the corporal exited the taxi, he said something under his breath, and Kaye said, "What did you say, boy?"

The corporal said, "My name is Tyrone Carver. You can call me Carver, but I am certainly not your damn boy. That was settled some fifty years ago. If you say or do one more derogatory thing about my people, I will pull the pin in that grenade hanging on your vest and walk away. Furthermore, get your own damn bag," he added as he climbed back in the taxi.

Russ climbed out of the taxi and loaded his bag, wondering why this guy was such an ass. He treated all black folk like that back home, and it was no big deal.

The ride to the headquarters was a bit awkward, so Russ tried to make things a bit less tense by saying, "Where are you from?"

Carver said, "Philadelphia."

"You an Athletics or Phillies fan?" asked Russ. "The Phillies are my favorite team. I live, die, eat, and sleep Phillies."

"Yeah! I'm an Athletics fan myself," said Carver. "But neither team is worth a tinker's dam."

When they got to the headquarters of the 1st Army, Carver parked the taxi to the left of a side entrance. As they got out of the taxi, Carver said, "Colonel Jeffers is the third door on your left."

Russ entered and walked down the hall with the pride of a lone rooster in a hen house. With a certain swagger, he strutted into the office and asked for the colonel as casually as if they'd been drinking in a bar together the night before.

"Colonel, I understand you have a mission for me," Russ said.

"Yes, soldier," Jeffers said. "There is a situation I need your help with. You may have heard that Teddy Roosevelt's son Quentin was shot down near Dordogne, France. We flew in to try to find him, only to have more planes shot down. Some of our soldiers are being held as prisoners of war. Now we need to send someone in by foot to get our men back. That's where you come into the picture. With you having some training in the intel division at Fort Dix, Sergeant Corbett recommended you out of many choices. He gave many accolades about your demeanor that made you surface to the top of the list of possible soldiers to carry out this mission. You are the patriot needed for this important operation because of your love of country."

Jeffers continued along this path for several more minutes, and soon Russ was thinking that he was the only soldier in the army who could march through the gates of hell in his birthday suit and put out the fire without even sweating. Then he told him more details of the assignment.

Jeffers said, "We had two bombers go down over enemy lines. Somewhere in the neighborhood of nine crew members were taken prisoner. We have sent in an extraction group and lost communication with them, so we are aware of about twenty-three men missing in all. We do not know how many are still alive, but we need to get them out. Our French intel tells us they are being held in Château de Beynac. We are calling this mission Lionheart, as that is the castle where Richard the Lionhearted was killed in 1199.

Jeffers continued. "We will get you and your two men as close as we can to the castle via train. You'll be about ten klicks, or six miles, away, but you'll be on your own to get over several fairly open farm fields with mature corn growing and then up the hillside to the castle. You will be dressed as a German soldier taking two American prisoners into the prison. You will be carrying a fair amount of weight, as you will have their weapons and extra ammo. Once you get over the wall you'll all work together."

Russ was thrilled with the assignment and asked when he was going to meet his men.

Jeffers picked up the interoffice radio and called to his liaison for the other two invaders to come into the office now that he had given Russ the basic assignment.

In walked Corporal Tyrone Carver and Private Benji Greene. Both were strapping black men, and they were as wide-eyed as Russ's mouth was at that point. They could only stare at one another.

Benji exclaimed, "Shiiiiiittttt! Colonel Jeffers, you gotsta be kiddin' me, man. He is a white man's white man! Not only dat, but I thinks he's a bigot. Wouldn't prize me iffen he wore white sheets and da hood. Dis hunky gets ta tell us what's ta do, sir?"

Colonel Jeffers said, "Now in order for this to work, you three must pull together as a team," all the while thinking that they could probably put on a show that would be as good as a Marx Brothers routine. At the start of the war, the Marx brothers performed using ethnic accents. Leonard developed the Italian accent, whereas Chico Marx, being Jewish, used a Jewish accent. That made for a great skit until the war, when being Jewish was dangerous to your health. Chico convinced some bullies at a show that he was Italian, not Jewish, and took off on it. With his red hair, Adolph became an Irishman named Patsy Brannigan. Groucho was the smooth, silver-tonged trickster. Julius Marx's character was an ethnic German, so he put on a German accent for the stage. After the sinking of the *RMS Lusitania* in 1915, he had to change it up depending on the crowd. The public eventually started to detest the Germans, so Julius dropped the accent and developed a fast-talking wise guy

If the three men standing before him continued to fight one another every step of the way, Jeffers knew the plan was not going to work. He gave them their exact orders and told them as much information as they had to know to make it seem as if they were the team expected to complete the mission based on the intel received from the French.

After evaluating the three men standing before him, Jeffers was sure his words and instructions would not be remembered.

He told them, "Going both in and out of Château de Beynac, stay away from the south wall. You will see why ten klicks out on the train. It's straight up and down for about fourteen rods. Your best way in and out is from the southeast, where it is more wooded and there is farmland. A large abandoned yellow farmhouse sits about seven rods, or one hundred feet, back from the railroad tracks. Are you with me so far?"

Russ said, "Yes, I'm with you," but he was thinking, *I have to carry their stuff,* and thinking that back home they'd be carrying his stuff. *If they make one comment about me being their boy, I'll . . .*

Jeffers said, "Kaye, you look like you have something on your mind. Are you with me?"

Russ said, "Yes, sir. I've got it." Looking at the other two, Russ said, "You two on board with this so far?" The other two just ignored him and had disgusted looks on their faces.

Jeffers said, "Once you get to the abandoned farmhouse, you will find climbing gear, a stash of pistols, and grenades for those in the prison, all planted by our friends from France. You are going to want to rest until about twenty-two hundred hours and then make the climb. It is most imperative that you use your compasses to stay on the east side of the mountain. Are you with me?"

The three nodded, and Russ responded, "Yes, sir."

Jeffers continued, "From the top of the mount, the French tell us that up at eighty degrees latitude and sixty-two degrees longitude, you can drop into what is called the bird's nest. It's no more than a small levee where, even in the darkness of night, you'll be able to see the castle. The tall tower to the southeast corner will have four guards. They change guards every two hours, starting at twenty-one hundred hours, all night long. You will have precisely seven minutes to get to the base of the wall with no eyes on you. If you stay within a rod of the edge of the woods, about fifteen or sixteen feet, they will not see you. This seven-minute window is when you have to get out of the woods and run about nine rods till you get to the castle wall."

Russ asked, "Okay, once we get to that point, what do we do?"

Jeffers said, "Stay close to the seven-foot wall and you will move undetected going north away from the river and railroad tracks. Once you are mid-span on the bridge, about two and a half rods from the tallest part of the castle, you will scale the wall and drop down into the courtyard. Staying close to the wall, go toward the main building. You'll see a doorway right in front of you; enter there. The guard's room is almost immediately on your left. I suggest hand-to-hand combat if you have to do anything so as not to make noise. Now, what questions do you have to this point?"

Carver said, "Long walkways are shown in this picture. Are guards stationed there who could see us in the courtyard?"

Jeffers replied, "Good question. If you scale the wall at the halfway point, any noise you make is far enough away so they shouldn't hear you. You will see when you move close along the wall that if you stay within a rod or so of the wall, they shouldn't be able to see you. Any other questions?"

Russ said, "No. Let's just keep moving on."

Jeffers said, "Once you enter the castle and pass the guards' room, there is a 13th century set of steps right in front of you. I mention the age because they are cut into the earth with inlaid stones, so not only are they unlevel, but they are also anywhere from twenty to about twenty-four inches wide and the risers are anywhere from eight to fourteen inches high, so it would be easy to fall down them if you're not careful. When you get to the lower level, you are in the horse stables. That's where we believe the prisoners are being held."

Russ asked, "Once we get the package, how do we get out?"

Jeffers said, "The Germans are likely to assume that you will go out the same way you went in because they know that you would probably not risk running across the drawbridge. They will not expect you to go deeper into the castle. A window at the end of the stable leads to a rickety staircase. Follow that to the noble meeting room. You'll know you are in the right place because the room is all stone, including the rounded ceiling that is some twenty feet high. The room is about two rods long, with a floor-to-ceiling fireplace at one end. Halfway down the east wall is a short doorway down a few steps. That leads into the ceratodus drain field going away from the castle. That is your way out.

"The downfall is that you have to run through the field that is under the tower on the front of the castle. The advantage you have is that you are in the woods in five to seven rods. However, if you are spotted, you know they will track you. You need to be in and out in less than thirty minutes if there is any chance of making it work. Unless you have any other questions, I would suggest you relax today. Write home to your families, eat a good meal, and get some rest; your train pulls out at nineteen hundred hours."

"We are to meet where, sir?" Russ asked.

Jeffers told them that transportation would be picking them up around 18:15 hours and taking them right to the train.

After the meeting, Russ wrote another letter home to his folks to tell them what he could. He thought this might be the last thing he would ever send home to them, so he asked a soldier who had been well schooled to help him use good grammar and spell words correctly. Russ took particular care to write legibly.

August 26, 1918

Mama and Pop,

It is time to write again, as I do not know when I'll get another chance. I feel rather uneasy about the days ahead and don't know what they hold for me. I will proceed with as much detail as I can.

As I told you in the last letter, I am now a Buck Sergeant with the 1st Army and will be leaving on a mission this evening. Orders I received from the post brigade office put three of us out on an important mission. Can you believe my luck? It's me and two colored boys. I mean, they are Americans, of course. We have quite a challenge ahead of us, and it has nothing to do with cooking. I cannot say that it will be so pleasant. If we are here a few days from now, I believe it is more than they are expecting.

Oh, yes, speaking of cooking, the three of us had a good breakfast this morning, with fried eggs, steak, french toast, and grits—along with oleo, strawberry jam, bread, and coffee. We are all guessing that something dangerous is up. That seemed almost like the last meal before an execution. We each get to choose a meal for our dinner. I only wish I could eat like that every day. I really hope it doesn't mean the end is near.

Colonel Jeffers was very interested in a hand-drawn map of our mission and explained in detail what is expected of us. We took that big map, studied it and talked until we couldn't talk anymore. I wish I could tell you more, but I can't. Pop, you probably can wrap your head around this and figure out the story.

I've had a letter from you week after week until now, but I don't know when I will be back, and I can't get my mail as I should. It will come to my old company and then be forwarded to the new company. Then I will get it when I get back from this mission. You will need to send my letters directed to the First Army, PO 77th Division. If it changes again, I will immediately let you know.

Well, it is getting close to dinnertime, and I must go for my center cut pork chops, candied yams, and creamed corn. We will soon be picked up for the mission, and I want to savor my meal. I must get moving or I will miss out on the good grub. After all, I need to be well fed if I have to put up with the colored boys.

Tell me all and everything that you possibly can when you write, as I sure love to read your letters more than anything else. Good-bye for a little while to my loving parents.

With love,
Sergeant Russell K.

*   *   *

A few hours later, at the train station, the conductor leaned from the platform of the train and yelled, first in French and then in English, "All aboard! All aboard to Bordeaux, Angouleme and Poitierl. Last call! All aboard!" He waved his flag. The train whistle blew. Smoke puffed sky bound, and slowly the train rolled away from the station.

The three spoke with one another very little for the first hour of the ride. Then they put their heads together to go over the plan.

Russ finally broke the ice by saying, "Dordogne is the location of the castle, which is on the southwest side of France. It's in the Aquitaine region, between the Loire valley and the High Pyrénées. Dordogne is the great river that runs through it." He continued by asking them, "Either of you know much about the city or area?"

They both said no.

Russ laughed and said, "I only found out one thing about the area and its involvement in war issues over the years that we want to stay away from."

Benji said, "What did you find out?"

Russ laughed again and said, "In 1870, days after France was attacked by Prussia, a young aristocrat, Alain de Monéys, was tortured by a crowd of about five hundred people. It happened in a public square in the village of Hautefaye, after which he was roasted on a pig spit. At some stage, the victim died. It was said that the leading participants appeared to have been drunk. Later, four individuals were identified as the ones involved in the murder, and they were condemned to die by guillotine. The sentence was carried out in the same public square on February 6, 1871."

Carver said, "Is that what you are wantin' for us, man?"

Russ looked at Carver and said, "I promise you this, Carver, and you too, Benji: Though we walk different paths in life, and though we have our differences, I do not wish that for any of us. We will all go home or none of us will go home. If anything happens to either of you, I'll carry you out myself. You will not be left behind."

Just before the train stopped at a steam station where the three jumped off, they all agreed that nobody would be left behind. They quickly hid in the brush near the tree line on the opposite side of the tracks away from the river.

After the train left, they moved quickly downriver, watching the giant wall beneath the castle in front of them with the help of some moonlight. The castle was larger than they had imagined, and it appeared to be peering down on the city as if it were the self-appointed guard over the area.

They soon arrived at the yellow house and were safely hidden away in a tiny valley. From that vantage point, they could not see the castle, but they knew it was a little over a klick up the side of a cliff. They rested in the yellow house and went over the plans one last time.

Russ got dressed as the German soldier packed on all the weight of Carver's and Benji's weapons and grenades to take the American prisoners to the prison. They moved away from the river and into the valley to the backside of the mountain.

Meanwhile, the A Team moved out from the other end of town. They were progressing toward the base of the lower cliff at the west end of the castle. There was a second castle named the Marqueyssac at the top, on the ledge of the lower cliff. The mission of the A Team was to scale the lower cliff, slide in behind the second castle, enter the lower courtyard area, and head to the doors of the horse stable of Château de Beynac. They expected Russ, Benji and Carver to draw German fire away from them to enhance their probability of a successful mission.

The sacrifice of three enlisted men to save the lives of a dozen or so pilots and trained intel, half of them officers with confidential information, was considered a fair trade-off.

Each group was moving toward the castle without knowing the other was even in the area. The worst part, however, was that the United States did not know that one of their sources, with whom Jeffers openly discussed the A Team mission, was a spy. The Germans were lying in wait for the A Team as both groups neared.

At the same time Russ and his duo slipped into the bird's nest, the Germans opened fire on the A Team. Russ realized that there were no bullets raining down on them or crackling through the woods; they were not the ones being fired on.

The four guards in the tall tower on the southeast corner were firing relentlessly toward the opposite end of the castle. There were others firing from the other smaller towers. Nonetheless, Russ and the others were able to run free because all the German attention was focused on the other end of the castle.

Russ looked at the other two and asked, "Are you two spiritual?"

They both nodded, and Russ said, "Let's join hands. I'd like to pray if I may."

Without a word, the two of them interlocked their black hands with Russ's tanned caucasian hands. Russ said, "God, of all three of us, You know I don't pray very often and I only come to you when I need help. I'm sorry for being so selfish like that. You know why I'm praying to you tonight. Help us survive and forgive us for breaking the killing commandment if we must kill some Kraut bastards in there. Help all three of us to get through this and to be there for one another as we get the prisoners out to safety. We're asking for your help. Amen."

As they gathered everything they were taking along, Russ felt the need to say one more short prayer. He looked at the heavens and quietly said, "Lord, I will do whatever you ask of me in the future if you help me now."

Seemingly from nowhere, the sky became an angry deep purple that cast a brown haze over what had been a beautiful yellow crescent moon moments earlier. The wind wailed and howled so much that mature trees twisted in the squalls and bowed toward the ground like saplings. Suddenly, three jagged bolts of lightning struck, seemingly surrounding the castle. Fire leapt straight back into the sky, high enough to be seen over the walls of the castle. The flames appeared to be sucked back into the dirt as if the fire were going back to hell. The lights all went out and the castle went dark.

Because of the weather, there was no need to wait to move out until the top of the hour for the changing of the guards. It was so dark that the trio could make a dash for the corner of the taller part of the castle and the seven-foot wall. They scaled the wall and moved northward undetected, away from the river and railroad tracks. They dropped down into the courtyard, staying close to the wall going toward the main building. They were focused on getting in the doorway without being seen.

Russ said, "Remember that there might be guards in the room almost immediately to our left, just past the door. We'll take them with hand-to-hand combat if we need to. Don't make noise if you have to engage them."

All three of them were seeing action for the first time, but ironically, they were behind the enemy line. They scaled the wall of the castle, and in the snap of a finger, they were down in the courtyard, only a rod or so away from the doorway they needed to enter. Some of the castle's lights flickered and came back on, but the castle was still only dimly lit. Russ gave the thumbs-up, and away they went.

When they slipped in the doorway, they heard a sharp, harsh, snapping voice speaking in German. It sounded like an interrogation rather than a conversation was going on. With that said, the three of them did not speak German, so what was being said could just as well have been Greek.

The three stepped into the room, guns pointed at two men. Russ put his finger to his lips, motioning and mouthing, "Don't make a sound." Then he took off his German uniform shirt. Russ pulled out his own uniform shirt from Benji's pack and put it on while Carter and Benji moved toward the German to take him captive. The American soldier appeared to be unconscious from a severe beating to the face and head. Blood was dripping from either his lip or nose. The German put his hands in the air and stood motionless. The quietness within the room made the American prisoner look up. Realizing the Americans were about to move to the center of the room, the American put his hand up to halt them. He held one finger in the air with his left hand and motioned with his head toward another doorway in the rear of the room.

Russ continued to hold the gun on the German and moved close to the American. He motioned for Carver and Benji to approach the German in the other room. They took control of the second German in a fearful way as he was leaning back in his chair and sleeping with his feet on the desk. They quietly entered the smaller room and stood on either side of him. Carver reached out and shoved the German's shoulder toward the floor. He went tumbling to the ground and was scrambling toward Carver ready to fight when he met the butt of Carver's machine gun on the side of his jaw, only to go down again.

Russ closed the door to the hall to muffle the noise from the smaller room. Pointing the other German to go into the smaller room, Russ and the American prisoner followed him and shut the door to that room, too. Looking up from the floor toward the four Americans, the blooded German said, "Du sollst nicht töten uns, bitte."

Russ said, "What?"

The American prisoner said, "He's pleading for his life. 'Don't kill us, please,' is what he said."

Carver, with his eyes as wide as saucers, asked, "Russ, are we killing them or bringing them along?"

Russ said, "Neither. We'll tie them up."

Carver said, "Oh, let me do it. When wet rawhide dries it tightens, and I got plenty of it. See, in a pinch you can eat rawhide." Carver reached down and picked up the chair from the floor. "Should I get another one from the other room?"

Russ said, "Yes, but be careful that no one sees you." He turned to the American. "By the way, what's your name?"

The beaten American soldier said, "Jack . . . Jack Earl." Carver set the other chair several feet away from the first chair. Then Jack looked at the Germans and said, "Setzen Sie sich wertlos Schwein."

Russ looked at Jack as the Germans both sat down. "You speak German?"

Jack said, "A little."

Carver soaked some rawhide in a nearby bucket of water. Russ had Benji hold a soft cloth over each of their mouths and had Carver tie wet rawhide around each one. Each had an airway to breathe, but his ability to yell was hampered. He then held their arms behind their chairs while Carver tied them up. Then each man's legs were tied one by one to the legs of his own chair. Carver did as he was told, plus he added a touch more on his own. He cut the ankles on each of the man's legs ever so slightly, just enough to draw blood so any rats in the area could enjoy some good old human blood and flesh.

"Now," Russ said to Jack, "I'll take another chair."

Jack did not know what to think about what was going on. Nonetheless, he went to get the chair. They were all about to leave the room when Jack looked at Russ and said, "Could I have a minute?"

Russ said, "I guess so. What's up?"

Jack looked at Carver and said, "Can I have a piece of your leather?"

Carver handed Jack a piece of leather about a half-inch wide and twenty-four inches long. Jack promptly wrapped it around his hand, stuck it in the bucket of water, and walked over to the guard who had just been interrogating him.

Jack looked at him and said, "Sie stinken bastard. I hoffen, dass die Hölle Ratten fressen Sie Gesicht, nachdem ich mit dir fertig bin."

49

With that, he beat the guard's face until 70 percent of it was covered with blood and both eyes were swollen shut. Benji, Carver, Russ, and the other guard watched in shock.

When he was done, he walked over to the other guard and said, "Sie hätten ihn aus, mich zu schlagen zu halten." Jack then hit him with the wet rawhide about five times.

Carver asked, "What did you say to them?"

Jack pointed to the first guard and said, "I told him he's a stinking bastard and I hope the rats eat his bloody face, and the other one was just for good measure because he could have stopped his comrade."

Russ looked at Jack and said, "Damn. My friend, do you feel better now?" He dragged the chair toward the door of the small room on two legs, twine tied around it. When Russ and the rest of the Americans had gotten out of the small room, the chair was close to the inside of the door. When Russ had to pull his hand out of the doorway to go any farther he yanked on the twine and the doorknob both at the same time, pulling the top of the chair tautly up under the knob on the small room side of the door. Now the Germans were tied up behind a door that nobody could open except the two Germans guards who were tied up.

Russ looked at Jack and said, "Do you know where the rest of the prisoners are being kept? We are here to get you out. How many of you are there? Is Roosevelt with you?"

Jack said, "They're keeping us in the stables, and the horse stalls are our cells. There are thirteen of us total; and no, Roosevelt is dead. I have been to his grave and seen what is left of his plane. Follow me."

They headed out the doorway, turned to the left and went down the irregular old stone steps. Jack whispered to his followers, "Quiet! There's a guard right inside this doorway." Benji stepped forward, pulling a knife from a sheath on the center of his back. Russ signaled to Benji to snap his neck instead of cutting his throat.

Benji just grinned like a Cheshire cat and slipped through the doorway as quiet as a church mouse. He snuck up behind the guard, and as quickly as the snap of a mousetrap, he reached around the guard's neck, twisted, and snapped it like a twig, bringing him to the ground swiftly so as not to be recognized. With the exception of those behind him, only two prisoners saw him. Thinking rapidly, the prisoners went fist to cuff with another guard to draw the only other guard to their makeshift cell.

The guard leaned over the stall gate yelling, "Stop, stop, you dumb Esel jetzt aufhören Oder ich gezwungen, Sie zu erschießen."

Jack whispered to the others, "He's saying, 'Stop, stop, you dumb asses. Stop now or I'll be forced to shoot you."

With the guard totally unaware of him, Benji couldn't pass up the temptation or wait for orders from Russ. He crossed the open stable, pulling the blade once again from the sheath. Wrapping his forearm across the guard's head, he pulled it back and sliced the guard's throat wide open like carving a Christmas turkey. The blood pumped from both of the jugular veins in his throat like geysers of red oil.

The prisoners were excited at the demise of the guards, which had just played out before their eyes. They became even more elated when the other three Americans entered the stable area.

Russ said, "Okay, okay. Listen up! We have no time to waste. There are about five minutes to get out of here and a twenty-minute run to the river. We are to catch a certain barge that leaves in about thirty minutes. Stay close together; we have a limited number of weapons."

A captain said, "What's all the shooting outside? Are we safe without more weapons?"

Russ said, "The shooting is in the opposite direction from where we are going. I'm not going to lie to you. We will be leaving the castle right under a guard tower, so we might pick up some fire before it's over and done. There are about five to seven rods of open, unprotected area we will have to run across. We were told there were no more than nine of you to get out, but we will all be leaving so move your asses. Carver, as you remember, over there is the window that we all need to go through. You and Benji lead the way. I'll stay back with Jack. Everybody listen. The wooden staircase you'll be taking isn't safe; watch your step. Those stairs lead to a large stone room with a rounded off ceiling. Immediately and quietly head for the small doorway halfway down the room on the left and then go down a couple of stairs. Benji, get your pig sticker ready. I'd rather you cut their damn throats than to fire even one shot if possible."

Benji smiled and said, "No problem with that, Skipper."

Jack said, "I know exactly which doorway you are going toward. If you're afraid of bats, rats and spiders, you don't want to go through that door."

Russ said, "We have no choice." Looking at everyone, he said, "If you have a problem with this plan, either suck it up or stay here. Let's go now!"

As promised, the staircase took them into a large room with a high ceiling. Just as they started toward the open doorway, a German soldier walked right into the open arms of Benji, who drove his picker straight through his chest. Carver reached quickly to cover the German's mouth. They slid him into the doorway, making him a floor mat that everyone had to walk over. Two other guards were in the room with their backs to the group.

Carver signaled to Benji that he would go for the one on the left; Benji was to take out the one on the right. They headed out, and just as Carver was reaching for one guard, the other guard caught a glimpse of him. He turned to shoot Carver but saw Benji bearing down on him. Carver took his guy out with a quick twist and snap of his neck, but Benji had to throw the pig sticker at the other German guard because he already had his gun out. The pig sticker was a perfect bull's-eye in the center of the guard's chest bone. The problem was that the guard got one round off before collapsing, and it blasted a large hole in Benji's right kneecap at close range.

The prisoners had all swiftly entered the large room by then, and Jack simply pointed at the short doorway.

Russ looked at the two largest prisoners and ordered, "You two, get Benji. You will be responsible for getting him out of here and getting him some medical care."

Carver took the lead. He was followed by several prisoners, then Benji and the two helping him. A few more escaped through the door before Russ and Jack brought up the rear. The thing Jack neglected to mention was that if you were claustrophobic or had a weak constitution, you might as well stay behind. Once they went down the few steps and got into the ceratodus drain field leading out of the castle, they had to crawl through a twenty-four-inch pipe that had water, slime, algae, and human feces floating through it. The rats, bats, and spiders were just an added bonus to the adventure. That was their only way out.

If that wasn't bad enough, the escapees had the long run in the open before being hidden by the woods, especially if they were spotted and shot at. The saving grace was that the tower guards were in an altercation with troops at the opposite end of the castle at the time.

They had to jump about three or four feet down to the ground from where the pipe ended. Three men at a time ran across the field, hiding about two rods deep in the woods until everyone got there. The group before Russ and Jack started catching gunfire. One guy went down, but the other two made it into the woods. Russ and Jack scampered across the field dodging gunfire, and Russ slowed to stoop over and grab the fallen soldier by his ammo belt. The soldier was dead. By now, it sounded as if the sky were raining lead down on top of them through the branches and leaves of the trees.

They heard Germans yelling at the tops of their lungs, and Jack asked, "Which way, Russ? There're coming after us."

Russ said, "Our barge is in the middle of the river; it's the one with the flickering light. Run across the bridge and jump down onto the barge." Russ put the dead soldier over his shoulder and took off after the rest of them.

A few minutes passed in the darkness of the woods, and suddenly they were all in the streets of the town. As they neared the bridge, Russ noticed that the two bigger soldiers did not have Benji with them.

Once on the bridge, Russ called out to the two of them. "Soldiers, where is Benji, the injured soldier I put in your care?"

One of them responded, "Dead weight slows you down! We left him at the top of the hill, and we're getting the hell out of here."

With a dead soldier on his own shoulder, Russ punched the guy right in the mouth. Even realizing he had just punched a captain, he said, "You're a son-of-a-bitching coward. That man risks his life to get you out of there and the best way you find to thank him is to give him to the enemy."

The captain said, "You just lost your rank for striking a superior officer and—"

"Go to hell," Russ interrupted, walking away from him. Russ then said to Carver, "Get him on the barge," flopping the dead body out on the bridge.

Carver said, "Skipper, where are you going?"

Russ looked at Carver and said, "You're in charge of this portion of the mission now. If the captain gives you any lip, you can knock him off and I'll back you to the hilt. I made you two a promise that we would all die here or we would all go home together. I'm going back for Benji, and I'll bring him home or die trying."

Jack asked, "Do you want company, Russ? I owe my life to you. They were probably going to beat me to death earlier in that room, all because of that self-important, coward of a captain. He is a pilot, and they rightly questioned him as an officer. To get out from under their interrogation and the abuse, he told them I was a reconnaissance specialist spying on their troop movements. The skunk did all that just to save his own keister. He told them that although I was an enlisted, I certainly had more intel information than he would ever have. You saved my life."

Russ said to Carver, "Set Jack up with weapons he might need to get safely through the rest of this mission. Once Jack and I move out, you get the skipper of the barge to move out. All of you need to get in the bottom of the barge to be out of sight. The skipper knows where you are going. And I want that son of a bitch court-marshaled for his actions."

CHAPTER

5

THE LONG JOURNEY BACK

When Russ and Jack started back across the bridge, the barge floated under the bridge and downriver, in the direction from which they came. As they got back into the town, they heard voices of German soldiers coming from the north end of the street. They slipped into an alley, crawling under a porch of a badly damaged house. They rested there for about five minutes before continuing down the alley, away from the German patrol.

Within a few minutes, they were at the edge of town, a few rods from the woods. From where they were, they could see the castle way up on top of the cliff. Spotlights on the turret lit up the town below. The guards looking out of the castle windows appeared to be only inches tall from that distance. This told Russ and Jack that they had a long climb ahead of them.

Russ chuckled and said, "That damn cliff reminds me of the one on the east side of the river just north of Harrisburg, where I hail from."

Jack asked, "Do you mean Harrisburg as in Harrisburg, Pennsylvania?"

Russ responded, "Yeah. Have you ever been there?"

Jack said, "Sure have, maybe ten times. I'm from Montoursville, Pennsylvania."

Russ said, "Well, holy hell. Are you an Athletics or Pirates fan?"

Jack laughed. "If I say names like Topsy Hartsel and Socks Seybold, does that give you any idea? I'm an Athletics fan all the way. Do we have something in common?"

Russ said, "Nope, but those were the better two-thirds of the Athletics' outfield. Do you remember for a couple years when Socks played first base?"

"Yeah," Jack said, "but those two never lit the boards up offensively."

"That's for sure," Russ said. "Well, are you ready for the long climb to the top of the rock wall that is France's version of Peter's Mountain?"

They started up through the mountain, and not far into the hike, they saw several large puddles of blood. It appeared that the blood trail went down the path used to escape.

Jack said, "Russ, do you think Benji was trying to get out on his own?"

Russ said, "I hate to follow the blood trail to a dead end and then have to backtrack to the top again. He is probably in need of some quick first aid."

Jack looked at Russ and asked, "Do you know what he would do? Does he have what it would take to stay put and run the risk of becoming a prisoner or would he try to move on? After I saw what he did with the pig sticker, I don't think he is the type to lie down and die."

Russ smiled at Jack and said, "Well, you whistle prick, I have only known those two for three days and hardly know anything about them. Here you met them a few hours ago and are telling me what Benji would probably do. So okay, where would he be headed?"

Jack said, "Think about it and you tell me based on your conversations with them."

By now, they were walking back down the trail, following the blood drops to the right side of the path, about knee high, where incidental blood had rubbed on branches, leaves, and twigs. The blood trail abruptly showed up on the left side of the trail and into the woods. It became easier to notice going through the woods, where there was no trail to follow. They came upon an area where it was obvious that someone had rested for several minutes, as there was a large pool of blood and a bloody shirt. There was some stripping of leaves and bark as though someone was making a trekking pole for a tourniquet.

Jack looked around and said, "Damn, whoever we're tracking— hopefully it's Benji—has done a great job with a tourniquet. I can't find any blood beyond here."

It was as if a light bulb went on all of a sudden. Russ said, "Holy hell, it is Benji, and I know where he must be."

Jack looked at him and said, "Do tell."

Russ pointed away from the direction of the castle. "He's headed toward the house where the French hid our weapons and other necessities for the mission. We were there just a few hours ago. We agreed to meet there if we were separated. I told them we would all go home or all die together."

Jack looked at him and asked, "Are you for real? You made that type of a promise to two men you never met until three days ago? You agreed to die with them or get home with them and not leave them behind?"

Russ chuckled and caught himself saying, "Old leathernecks are not the only ones that can say Semper Fi." Then he broke out in laughter and said, "I don't believe I said that either. Not so many months ago, I was sitting in the neighborhood barbershop telling an old kike back home to shove his war as far up his ass as he could. I was not going in for any reason. My life was all about notches on my belt all right, but not for German kills. I wanted different lassies in the sack, so the game we played was that twice still only counted as one. It was the TDT. Now here I am putting it all on the line for a colored boy."

Jack looked at him and asked, "TDT? What's that?"

"Oh my God, man, don't tell me you're a virgin! TDT is the Two Date Theory. If you don't nail her in two dates, you go on to the next girl. If you got her on the first date and she was worth a second date just for the experience, do it again. Then she was gone no matter what. Hell, some girls I have been with lived on the other side of the river and went to Lemoyne High. We never even bothered to get their names. After all, they were just conquests."

Jack just shook his head and said, "You, my friend, are foul. My new name for you is the Foul One. I am in a committed relationship with Winifred Jadite."

Russ said, "Winifred? How in the hell will I remember the name Winifred?"

Jack laughed and said, "Most people call her Winnie." He continued by saying, "Inevitably, once we get back, you will get on to doing your thing and me to doing mine. We may never see each other again. Then someday forty years from now, I'll be bouncing my grandchild on my knee, and he'll pass wind. I'll look at him and say, 'Boy, that was a foul one,' and I'll remember this very day."

Russ said, "Yeah. Foul One. You're an ass. I think I'll be calling her Winnie."

At least I've had a relationship that lasted more than the ten minutes it takes to have your way with someone."

Russ wasn't sure whether he'd pissed Jack off or if Jack was just punching back with the same amount of smart-assed comments. He couldn't read Jack's facial expressions. "I think we should move out," he said, changing the subject. "However, if you don't mind, I'm going to sit over there for a minute. I want to thank God for getting us out of the castle and ask for His continued guidance."

Jack said, "That, my friend, is fine, but you can sit right here if you want. I'd be honored to share in the prayer with you. I pray a lot."

Russ said, "Well, that's fine with me, but you never know anymore, and I didn't want to be offensive."

Jack said, "As I said, I pray a lot. In fact, I was praying when you walked in the door back there in the castle. I had just finished asking God to send me an angel to take me out of the mess I was in, and I promised that I'd be a good steward for Him and do whatever He asked of me."

Russ laughed, which made Jack look at him with somewhat of an offended look on his face. Russ said, "Don't take my laughter the wrong way, my friend. It's just that you must be a better Christian than I am, because not more than fifteen minutes earlier, I said almost the same words in a prayer to God. I said it just before climbing the walls of the prison, and right afterward, the skies opened up and the thunder and lightning blasted the castle without a drop of rain."

Jack said, "Well I'd say God helped us both in His own way."

Russ smiled and lowered his head in prayer, as did Jack. After about two minutes had gone by, Russ said, "Oh, Heavenly Father, bless us and keep us safe as we journey in this treacherous, unsafe land and keep us out of the hands of the German army as . . ."

Jack quickly reached out, placing one hand on Russ's wrist and the index figure of his other hand to his lips as Russ looked up. Russ then heard a German patrol in the distance, coming up the trail they were just on.

"Schauen Sie Blut leding off in die direction."

Jack looked at Russ and whispered, "Shit, they see the same blood that brought us over here. So far I've heard three voices."

Taking the high ground, Jack and Russ quietly moved farther off the trail and hid behind two large boulders. They got in place just in time to see the three men coming on the trail. Though Russ and Jack had more firepower than the three German soldiers did, the castle was only about half a klick away.

The Germans stood there in conversation, and one of them said, "Der Weg endet hier, woher zum Teufel er von hier aus?"

Jack whispered, "He said, 'The trail stops here. Where the hell did he go from here?'"

Another German with his back toward them said, "Lassen Sie die bastard sterben Ich denke, wir sollten zurück zum Schloss und vergessen Sie ihn."

Jack whispered, "The one with his back to us is telling the others to let the bastard die. He thinks they should go back to the castle and forget about the blood trail."

The German officer laughed and said, "Wenn es jemanden gibt, hier draußen, und sie sind in der Nacht Zeit Blutungen des Wolfs haben Abendessen."

Jack smiled and whispered, "The officer is a damned pessimist. He just laughed and said that if there is someone out here bleeding, by nighttime the wolves will have dinner."

The Germans stood around smoking Zigaretten, or as Americans knew them, cigarettes, and chatting about their dominance over the American military. At one point, the officer said that Oberste Heeresleitung, their supreme commander, was a dumme Esel, or a stupid jackass, and Jack was taken aback to hear an officer calling the supreme commander a dumb ass in front of enlisted men. In sharing this with Russ, Russ simply whispered back, "We've got some dumb asses running our army too, in case you hadn't noticed."

The German officer then said, "Sie müssen weg oder werden, würde oder sollte mitgebracht Gelächter der dumme Esel Amerikaner hav."

Off in the distance, they heard, "Wer ist da draußen, Freund oder Feind? Brauchen Sie Hilfe? Komm heraus wi Ihre Hände in die Luft und lassen die Waffen hinter sich. Wir haben für Sie."

The major yelled out, "Zum Diteman Hölle Es ist Dur Hiram Swavley, kamen mit unseren Waffen und einer von euch, dass ich pesonally töten schießen. Wir sind schlecht hier unter einer Zigarettenpause." The Germans all laughed and walked back out on the trail.

Russ looked at Jack and quietly said, "What was all of that gibberish?"

Jack said, "In a nutshell, one of them said that he knew no one was out here or they would have laughed at his story. Then the guy calling out from the distance said he was planning to shoot if the guys by us did not surrender. The German officer, Hiram Swavley, yelled back that it was just him and a few others smoking cigarettes. What a name that is—Hiram Swavley! Then Swavley yelled back to the patrol that he would kill anyone who pulled a trigger. They yelled back and forth, 'Who's out there, friend or foe? Do you need help?' 'Come out with your hands in the air and leave the guns behind. We have you covered.' 'Go to hell, Diteman. It's Major Hiram Swavley. We're coming out with our weapons, and if any one of you shoots at us, I'll personally kill you. We're back here taking a smoke break.'"

After several moments passed, Russ and Jack were sure that the immediate threat was gone. They continued out to the edge of the mountain ridge for another two or three klicks. Before long, they came across Benji, who had collapsed with the yellow house less than a quarter of a klick away. They went to his aid. He was very weak.

Benji looked at Russ and whispered due to a lack of strength. "Russ, you came back! You kept your promise and did not leave me behind. Thank you."

Russ threw Benji over his shoulder like a sack of potatoes and carried him into the yellow house. Jack took the lead to be his eyes for anyone acting hostile. They got to the yellow house quickly. Russ laid Benji out on the kitchen table and tore open the leg of his pants.

He knew by looking at it that his leg would need to be amputated. The bullet hole, though a relatively small wound going in, appeared to have annihilated every bit of bone structure behind it and snapped the ligament to the outside of his leg. The flesh that was once the side and back of Benji's leg was missing large chunks of flesh, and the edges of the wound looked similar to a battle-worn, ragged, torn, and tattered flag, only it was soaked in blood. Adding insult to injury, two hours earlier he had been dragged through an active sewer pipe.

Russ quite honestly had no idea how Benji had been able to walk at all, let alone the distance he had gone before he collapsed.

Russ went to the shed out back of the house and fetched a jar of turpentine to dump over the wound, knowing it would clean the crud from the open wound and stop the bleeding. He figured he would have to hit Benji to knock him out. Otherwise, he'd scream so loud he'd bring every German in the town down on them. Russ looked at his injured companion and had to close his eyes before he hit him, as Benji looked so sad and frightened. Russ gave him a left hook that rendered Benji unconscious. Russ quickly took the tourniquet off, and Jack took Benji's pig sticker and sliced his pants from ass cheek to ankle in one swift motion. It was as easy as cutting through butter for your corn on the cob on a hot, sunny day.

Jack said, "Good God Almighty! That pig sticker is like a Japanese katana used by the Samurais in the 1600s; it cuts like a razor blade slicing through paper. Maybe we should name it katana the banana."

Both Jack and Russ laughed a bit, but they went right to work before Benji woke up. Russ took the pig sticker, wiped it off with turpentine, and scraped away the dried blood, leaves, dirt, cloth and Lord knows what else from the sewer pipe journey away. It started to seep out blood again until Russ took part of a clean area of the tablecloth, soaked it with turpentine, and all but stuffed it in the wound. Even though Benji was still passed out, his leg jumped about on the table, putting one in mind of a chicken jumping around the yard after her head is chopped off. Russ worked like a pro, wrapping the jumping leg as if he had done it a time or two before.

Benji was either in shock or sound asleep from total exhaustion from the day's events. Between Russ and Jack, they got Benji's leg cleaned up and bandaged. They discussed making a litter to carry Benji on so they could more easily get out of there. They started looking around the house for items that could be used to make one.

Russ said, "Jack, I'll be right back. I saw some awnings and posts of some sort in the outbuilding when I was out there earlier. They should work to make some sort of litter to carry him in."

Just as Russ walked toward the door, he saw two Germans approaching the house. Jack was still in the kitchen, and Russ slipped back into the room with his friends and signaled to Jack that two Germans were coming toward the front door. Jack picked up the pig sticker, went over to the doorway, and handed it to Russ while he pulled out a bayonet. When the Germans walked through the doorway, both of them shoved the knives completely through the Germans' bodies.

Before they even hit the floor, Jack began speaking. "Well, it will be easier to move around behind the enemy lines with these uniforms." He continued looking at Russ and pointing to the outbuilding. He said, "Let's not waste any time. I'll start stripping the Germans out of their uniforms and hiding their bodies in a closet while you get out there and find the stuff we need for a stretcher. Now get your ass in gear and stop wasting time."

They both stopped and looked at one another and started laughing. Russ smiled and said, "Are you in an adrenalin rush or are you taking control of the mission?"

Jack laughed and said, "Sorry, Russ. I guess I'm worried how many friends these two have and I want to get out of here."

By now, it was 16:30, and Russ was thinking that it might be more sensible to move in the dark and lay low during the daylight hours. He had not shared that with Jack yet, but Jack's comment became his first clue that he was not going to like that idea. When Russ shared his plan with Jack, it was obvious that Jack wasn't interested in hanging around the yellow house any longer than they needed to.

Russ said, "It will be sunset in four hours, dark in five hours. We will move out then. In the meantime, we'll get the stretcher made, raid the house for supplies and food, and try to get an hour or so of shut eye."

Jack said, "Maybe you'll get some shut-eye, but I won't sleep until we are far away from this place."

They went about their business of getting prepared for their next move. Jack looked around the inside, and Russ went to the outbuilding. Russ got not only the canvas they needed but also found a few tools and galvanized piping that could be made into the stretcher frame. Jack grabbed medical supplies to care for Benji, and he found a futon to put on the litter for Benji's comfort.

Thanks to the people in the house before them, there wasn't much in the way of food left. They found some fruit preserves, canned vegetables and one jar of meat that probably was not a favorite and that was why it was still there. It appeared to be a mix of pickled tripe and pigs feet. Let's face it. It's not one of those Pennsylvania Dutch favorites that you want for your birthday dinner, but when military food rations are all you have had for weeks, almost any change of diet is welcome.

Russ was working away on the litter. In passing, Jack looked at it and asked, "You're dragging <u>Benji</u> around in that? I haven't slept in anything that nice in months."

"Wait a minute," Russ said. "I hear you boys in the Air Corps have the best of everything: good food, great women, and thick mattresses with silk sheets."

Jack laughed and said sarcastically, "Yup, and it's because the Air Corps is one step down from the White House, whereas you ground pounders are one step up from a jail cell. By the way, I found some food in the coal cellar. Do you want to eat some real food?"

Not at all thinking of what he might be getting into, Russ simply said, "Well, hell yeah."

Jack smiled and dished him up what looked like canned olives, shallots, fennel, leeks, and white beans, plus a large helping of pickled tripe and pigs feet with a side of cherries and pears.

Russ took one look at the meal set before him and went on a lengthy cussing binge about what it looked like on his plate. In short, he really said, "This doesn't look anything like good old-fashioned Pennsylvania Dutch pork pot pie with dumplings, and that salad doesn't look anything like red beet and apple salad. The only thing that looks worth eating is the cherries."

Jack told him what the food items were. Russ wouldn't even try the tripe and made some crude comment about it. However, once he tried the fruits and vegetables, he ate every bite and even went back for seconds. As they were eating, a unit of about a dozen German vehicles and two dozen foot soldiers marched right past them, within five rods of the house.

"Damn it, Russ," Jack complained, "we should have left an hour ago. This is nerve-racking waiting around until dark."

With anger lines and veins popping out on his face and a tone that Jack wasn't sure about, Russ said, "Think about what the hell you just said. Had we left and hour ago, we would have walked right into them outside of town. We are better off here, trust me. If we get any German visitors stopping by the house, we'll be getting one or two guys at a time like we did earlier. Now, Jack, if you are questioning my abilities, you are welcome to walk out there on your own. Be my guest. No, I didn't think so. You stayed inside to look for food while I was outside looking for supplies. Now you just relax and trust me. Are we good?"

They just sat in the house quietly, watching the yard to make such they were alone for a while and finally started to relax a bit. They slumped down with their backs against the wall in complete silence for a few moments, and finally Russ said, "Montoursville, huh?"

"Yep, up the river a bit from you."

Russ said, "You said you'd been down my way a few times?"

"Every Christmas season since Pomeroy's opened, my family went to Harrisburg by train on a Saturday in December after deer season. We enjoyed shopping at Fourth and Market."

"Did you ever go to Hershey Park?" asked Russ. "I hear tell it's one of the top-rated parks in the country. It opened to the public back in 1907 to give workers a relaxing place to go on lunch breaks. The rest of us started using it because there was a playground for the kids and benches for adults to sit around on and talk."

Jack laughed. "That would never happen in my family. My father thinks I had a horrible work ethic because I worked at Indian Park up near home. I'd never get him to travel over two hours to go to a park in Harrisburg."

Russ said, "What the heck is Indian Park? I'm talking about a park that opened in the early nineteen hundreds and was originally a sitting park with some swings for kids. Over the years, a dance pavilion, an amphitheater, bowling alleys, and a carousel were added. They also built a miniature railway to transport guests around the park."

"Your Hershey Park sounds nice enough, but it's bush-league," Jack said. "Indian Park is over the top. I operated the merry-go-round, which is a grandfather of a carousel—and it's electric. Some days, if I got to work early, I'd be given the job of working on the largest roller coaster in the east. You haven't lived until you get a go on that monster. In the winter months on weekends, I was a soda jerk at the Indian Park Theater. For this, my God-fearing father said I had no work ethic, and I know he thinks I'm going to hell. Between that and being consumed with wanting to fly planes, he has had fits with me."

Russ said, "It sounds nicer than anything we have in the capital city. Maybe when we get the hell out of here, I should visit you in Montoursville rather than you coming to Harrisburg."

Jack grinned and said, "Yeah, but let's not get ahead of ourselves. We both know there is a thirty-five percent chance that one of us will not make it home. Besides that, what's the possibility that we'll ever see one another again? When it's all said and done, one of us could end up in Boston and the other in San Francisco! Who knows?"

Russ said, "Well, one place I will never live again is in my pop's house. I'll never be able to go back."

Against his better judgment and the resistance he was putting up, Jack's eyelids were starting to get heavy. He looked at Russ and said, "So, Foul One, I'm getting sleepy. Can you watch for an hour or so? Wake me and then I'll watch for you before we get out of here." Almost in the same breath, and surely not quickly enough for Russ to respond to his question, Jack said, "Let's pray." Jack immediately started saying a protection prayer about keeping them safe, and then they said the Lord's Prayer aloud together.

Before they finished, a third voice in the room began chiming in, the voice of Benji. Russ reached out and grabbed Benji's hand, not missing a beat or a word. When they were done, they both looked at him and welcomed him back.

Benji said to Russ, "You som'bitch. What in the hell did you hit me with?"

Russ said, "Man, I'm sorry, but we knew that you'd be screaming. We couldn't risk alerting the Germans that were here. Now we're getting ready to move out. If you're hungry for some real food, I'll get you some grub to chow down. Found some in the cellar."

As Benji winced in pain, he asked through gritted teeth, "What is it? Pickled pig snout or something?"

Russ gave out a fake laugh, like ha-ha-ha. "Close. But the vegetables and fruits are good."

Jack glanced at Russ and said, "I thought I did a good job preparing dinner."

Still through gritted teeth, Benji said, "Didn't take you long to get to know him. I didn't really believe he would come back for me two days ago . . . I think it was two days. How long have I been sleeping?"

Russ smiled and said, "Okay, Benji, remember the pig sticker? That wasn't even a day ago. Now, if you'd like, we can leave you behind."

Benji said, "No, no. You are my lifesaver, and I will always be in your debt. But right now I think I will try to eat a little."

Within a half hour, Benji had eaten. They got him out back to relieve himself in the bushes and then secured him to the stretcher. The plan to nap was forgotten and they started on their way. It was an extraordinarily starry night, and they were able to travel rapidly through the woods just off the road, moving east with the northern star at their left shoulders. They traveled roughly eight hours before coming to a tiny French community. It was nothing but a crossroad leading in and out of the town with a few shops. Several farms dotted the landscape in the outlying areas.

Russ left the other two behind to rest and went down to a fencerow, where he talked to a Frenchman who was tending his crops. Then Russ went back to collect Jack and Benji. Russ said, "Thank God he spoke a little English. We must gather ourselves and meet him at the edge of the road in a few minutes."

When Russ took control, there was no questioning his actions, as Benji knew and Jack had quickly realized the day before, when Russ told him they were staying at the yellow house until dark. Jack realized that Russ had good battle sense and stopped questioning his thinking after all the Germans marched by.

The Frenchman was there as promised, with his young son, teenage daughter, and an open mule-drawn hay wagon. They put Benji in the middle of the wagon on his stretcher, with Russ and Jack on either end of him. The farmer covered them with hay and rode right into the barn at his farm. At one end of the barn in a stall, he stored harnesses, bridles, and a feed trough that was on hidden hinges. Once it was swung open, wooden steps were exposed, leading to an underground shelter. There was a sign at the bottom of the steps: "Chemin de fer Souterrain de l'Amérique."

The French girl spoke fairly good English and translated for her father. He chattered on a mile a minute, talking even faster with his hands than his mouth.

Russ looked at her and said, "Honey, what the hell did he say?"

She said, "In a nutshell, as long as you need to stay, you can. There are several drums of goat milk cheese, dried beef, and pickled pike over there. He is sorry, but all our fruit has turned into wine . . . but help yourselves to it. Do not drink bottles with green labels. It is spoiled, and he gives it to the Germans when they pass by and want to buy wine."

They all laughed at that, even Benji, who was much worse for the wear after the eight-hour hike. When they laughed, the old man knew what the laughing was about. He gave a thumbs-up, winked, and laughed himself.

Russ said, "Tell him we are very grateful."

"I'm Danielle, Danielle Aimèe," she said, "but you can call me Dani. If there is anything you two need me for, just let me know. By the way, I'm seventeen."

Russ smiled at her and said, "Well, Dani, I'll keep that in mind."

As she started to walk away, Jack asked, "Dani, what does your sign at the bottom of the steps say?"

"Hope the colored boy doesn't take offense to it," she replied. "It says 'American Underground Railroad.' Remember, Russ, I've got my eye on you."

Russ said, "Well, you aren't that hard to look at either, with your raven hair and sky-blue eyes.

She swung her hips up the steps like a gate in a yard during a windstorm, and Russ undressed her with his eyes, simply saying, "*Grrrrrrroooowwwwwlllll.*"

"Foul One strikes again," said Jack.

Russ looked at Jack, and as innocent as an acolyte in a Catholic church, he said, "I was simply responding to her generosity and would not know what you are inferring."

Benji said, "Do you think she said 'you two' because I'm colored or because I'm wounded?"

Russ and Jack looked at each other, and Jack said, "More than likely because you are colored and your people used the underground railroad in America."

"Thanks, Jack," Benji said. "That makes me feel better."

That evening, they relaxed as they had not been able to in weeks. They feasted on real food and got to know a bit more about one another. It gave all three of them time to think about home. Russ entertained them by sharing stories about himself and his brother, Cal.

Jack told a story about his childhood, when he was all boy and so rambunctious. He said, "In my attempt to never let any grass grow under my feet, I jumped off everything—like the bunk bed, tables, the front and back porches, and out of trees—all in feeble attempts to fly."

He continued, saying, "My heroes, Orville and Wilbur Wright, were at least a day-long train ride or even farther away. Do you know about the Wright brothers? Once they made their historic first airplane flight on December 17, 1903, all I could think about was being in an airplane in the sky, with a destination of the wild blue yonder. I wanted to go wherever a plane could soar . . . and beyond. I believed I was destined to be a pilot some day and nothing or no one would ever stop me or change my mind."

"Jack, around the Christmas of 1903, Max Kline and I were dating the Holsum twins, who weren't—wholesome, I mean," Russ said. "I remember those Wright brothers you speak of because the Holsum twins and the news about flying were the only things that were right in my life back then, if you get my drift."

Jack laughed at him. "You are so foul. You must think I'm nuts to believe that. You weren't even seven years old then."

Russ looked at him and said, *"Well."*

Benji laughed, and Jack said, "You're as full of it, and you know what I mean, as a Christmas goose."

The three were sleeping within half an hour of putting makeshift beds together. They slept for an extraordinary number of hours, as they knew they were safe for the first time in days—and in Jack's case, weeks. The morning brought its own set of challenges. Benji had a raging fever. They uncovered the bandages on the knee.

Russ took one look at the knee and said, "Good God Almighty. Jack, go get the farmer and his daughter down here now."

Jack made his way up the steps and into the barn. In the barn was the son, who had just finished collecting eggs from under the chickens and was getting ready to milk the three cows. Jack asked him, "Where are your papa and your sister? Can you get them? We need their help downstairs."

The boy looked at Jack and said, "Oui, Oui," handing him a half dozen eggs and nodding his head yes.

Jack said, "No, no. I need your papa and your sister."

The boy said, "Oui," this time handing him a dozen eggs.

Jack said, "No." He turned and went to the doors of the barn, and as luck would have it, Dani was coming to the barn with homemade French pastries. Jack told Dani what was going on, and she went to the house and got medical supplies and her papa.

CHAPTER

BENJI'S EXODUS

In the underground shelter, Russ was looking at a completely swollen leg with yellowish-green puss covering the wound area. It made Russ realize that black men were not black on the inside. The injured leg was obviously inflamed, hot to the touch, and most probably infected. Gangrene was likely to be close to setting in. Benji was shivering and whining in agony.

Benji said in a shallow tone, "Russ, I feel like I'm dying."

Russ responded, "Stop talking like that. I'm going to get you out of here safe and sound. Come on, have a little faith in me."

Benji said, "Russ, let me talk. I need to say this. You did something for me that no one else ever has. When you came back to find me, you became part of my family. If I die, and this is only if I die, I want you to pray over my casket, and I also want you to take and carry the pig sticker."

Russ gave a nervous laugh. "Jack suggested that we change the name of the pig sticker to katana the banana."

Benji grabbed Russ's wrist with all the strength he could muster and said, "Jack can call it what he wants. You named it pig sticker, and you are my brother. You and no one else will have the pig sticker."

Russ looked into Benji's eyes, now so deeply sunken into their sockets and less focused than before. His eyes were beginning to look as if they were glazing over. He drifted off into a semicomatose state. Just then, Jack walked down the steps with Dani, her papa, and enough supplies to care for an army. As everyone looked at the leg and saw that Benji was totally out of it, the consensus was to save his life. The leg would have to be amputated and cleaned up. Even then, it wasn't clear whether there was any hope of saving Benji's leg—or even Benji for that matter.

There was no time to waste. They placed some sawhorses in the middle of the room and put an old barn door across them. They took him and the futon off the stretcher and placed Benji on the table. Transferring him and shifting his position woke him somewhat. Dani took that opportunity to hold him up under the shoulders and give him two opium pills and a dash of wine to get them down. She used her apron to wipe the sweat from his brow, kissed his forehead, and laid him back down gently. She whispered something in his ear, and he forced a smile.

Benji looked at Russ and said, "She's mine now, and she hopes you're jealous."

Russ chuckled. For the first time since meeting Jack, he had not a clue what to say, so he said nothing.

The Frenchman was busy starting a fire in an old potbelly stove. It vented up and through the wall above it and connected to the ductwork that went into the same wall of another stove above it so as not to draw attention to the hidden room. He began boiling and sterilizing rainwater needed for the upcoming surgery.

The only question now was who was going to do the surgery. Everyone looked at Papa because he was the senior person there. However, Jack nudged Russ and pointed to the old man's shaking hands. He apparently had early onset of Parkinson's disease. They agreed with their eyes that Papa would not be the best candidate to be the surgeon.

Jack said, "And not the brother. He'll just hand you eggs."

Russ finally said, "He's my responsibility. I'll deal with it."

Jack said to Dani, "Look, where I come from, the cook stove was only in the kitchen, and the kitchen was Mama's job. Your papa is doing a great job with the stove. Tell him his job is to man the fire. I'll handle everything on top of the stove, and you work as Russ's nurse at the table. You should both enjoy that, and it also gives you something nice to think about instead of the blood and the infection."

Dani jumped on that idea. The first thing they did after washing their hands was put a clean cloth between the leg and the futon. As they lifted the leg, a smell permeated from the wound, and it was the most pungent odor imaginable. Little lice-like looking worms crawled out of the leg wound, and puss resembling greenish-yellow volcanic lava bubbled and oozed seemingly from all sides of the wound.

Dani turned from the table, took a few steps away, and vomited.

Russ looked at her and asked, "Can you continue? We're going to have to amputate his leg and clean up the puss. We may need to cauterize the areas that start bleeding once we start working on the leg. Will you be able to handle all of that?"

Dani, "I'm with you," she said. "If you wish, I'll get my brother working on this as well."

Russ asked, "What can he do . . . or understand to do."

Dani smiled at Russ and said, "So long as I speak in French, he is good to go. You just need to trust that I'm not going to hurt Benji."

Russ said, "Go for it. Just tell me what he's doing."

Dani got her brother's attention and told him what she needed. He opened a box that had a red cross on it and started to make a paste. She said to Russ, "He's making a nerve surgery paste for numbing the area around the amputation—it's from the sixteen hundreds. You apply alcohol to the area where there are nerves in the stump to disinfect it. Then the suture needle and thread are soaked in a mixture of red wine, rosemary, and dried crushed rose petals. You sew the stump together. Olive oil is then applied several times a day, and then Benji will need to stay in bed with his stump in traction for a few weeks, disinfecting it daily to prevent more damage."

Jack said, "That's wonderful in theory, but I can't imagine us being here more than a few more days."

Russ nodded in agreement as he continued with the surgery. He took some sheep sheers that Jack had held in the fire and cleaned them with lye soap and hot water. He then wiped them down with corn whiskey. Russ cut away at the flesh and then cut through the tendon. The lower leg dropped to the table. Blood started running out of the upper leg. Russ used the lower leg as a prop to elevate the stump and to get it higher than Benji's heart. Jack turned and handed Russ a red-hot branding iron to cauterize the bleeding areas.

Russ looked up at Dani and said, "The operating room at Harrisburg Hospital is a bit cleaner than this lovely room, but nonetheless, we've got this operating thing down. You did a great job."

Dani said, "I hope the hospital workers aren't using sheep shears to cut or branding irons to cauterize."

Jack said, "No, they're in the big city, and they got it together in both the Harrisburg Hospital and the Poly Clinic. I'm from Montoursville. Our hospital is a lot dinkier, but we have it just as well at Williamsport Hospital. We even have a nursing school there that I could get you into with my fiancé if you want to immigrate to America."

Jack and Dani's conversation continued as he gave her a verbal tour of central Pennsylvania. He covered many things: hospitals, crops, the railroad, religions, and the communities between Jack and Russ on the Susquehanna River. Neither of them realized that Russ was silent. He washed up and left the underground shelter.

Russ went to the rear of the barn and cracked the barn doors so he could sit and look into the midst of one of God's miracles, the woods. Russ reached into his left-hand shirt pocket and pulled out his military prayer book. He started to look for a prayer to help him cope with his feelings of despair.

Suddenly, Russ noticed a man approaching through the pasture. As he came closer, Russ's hand found the handle of the pig sticker. When Russ saw a Bible in the stranger's hand, he felt somewhat relieved. Still, for the sake of safety, Russ called out, "Halt! State your name and reason for being here."

The man froze in his tracks and said, "I'm family and a lay person from a local church. My nephew who lives here told me there is a fellow here that needs to be prayed over. I see you are using your prayer book. May I pray with you?"

Russ said, "You have yet to give me your name."

He said, "Forgive me. I am Francois Lambert DesChamps. Trust me, I come in peace and mean you no harm."

Russ ordered, "Turn around slowly so I can see if you are packing a pistol."

"I am not here to harm you," Francois assured him, "but in case you haven't noticed, things around here aren't as they are in your country right now. Allow me to put my free hand on my head. With my Bible in the other hand, I can use that hand to hold my shirt up, exposing my weapon, and then approach you."

"Okay."

When Francois entered the barn, he dropped his free hand and extended it to shake Russ's hand. They agreed to sit in the doorway and pray, both laying their weapons an arm's reach away in front of them until they felt more comfortable with one another.

They prayed for several minutes, and then Russ asked him, "What do you do for a living?" Russ thought it strange that someone of Francois's age wasn't fighting the war.

Francois said, "Well, if I weren't ill, I'd be fighting a war, but since that's not in the cards, I do God's work. I pray with troops for protection against perils, for His mercy on one's soul, and for His guidance. I also bless troops' ammunition going into battle and pray that the souls of the bodies it destroys may know God's love. I pray for those who are homesick or missing loved ones, for those mourning the loss of fellow troops, ministering to the sick and wounded, those dying, and those who have died. I give communion, and I guess you could say that I'm starting my own church. It has been my dream for years, ever since I became ill."

Russ was struck by the calmness of this man's demeanor and said, "What denomination do you follow?"

Francois said, "I truly do not know; it is still more like a Francois denomination. I strongly believe in devotion to peace through prayer and meditation, more so than any of today's denominations."

Jack had also left the underground bunker, and he walked up behind Russ to make sure he was okay. He saw the stranger talking with Russ and said, "Sounds like my father is with us."

Russ, startled by Jack's voice, turned and asked, "How's that? Oh, by the way, meet Francois. He's related to Dani and her family, a layperson who is not fighting in the war because of illness. Francois, this is Jack. He's been traveling with me. Now, Jack, what were you saying about your dad?"

Jack said, "One time I was giving him some crap about going to church, and he put me in my place. He said to me, "Okay, since you know all there is to know about church, religion, and God, you can stay home. I don't care if you stay at home today for a break, but if you are staying home, you will be helping me with a little project before you sit around reading about those flying death traps that you insist you want to get involved with."

Russ said, "Oh good Lord, I see one of those parent lessons coming; and I thought it was only Pop that did that kind of bull crap."

Jack chuckled and said, "I was reading a magazine about the Wright brothers when my old man described the project to me. I was to write his lay sermon for church the next week. He wanted a sermon as to how my planes that soar in the skies with his angels relate to one another. He told me I was to use, verse by verse, the book of Revelations."

Both Russ and Francois laughed. Russ even forgot about his woes for a moment. "This should be good. How did that go for you?" Russ asked.

Jack said, "Oh, it was good stuff all right. Dad continued by saying, 'Oh, son, by the way, this sermon will be written out of text from chapter two, verse one, to chapter twenty-two, verse sixteen, between which angels are mentioned sixty times. I want a thorough contrast and comparison of each mention of these angels and your planes. Do not think that I don't know the book. And I *will* review your work."

"Holy Lord Jesus, what in heaven's name did you do?"

"I complained, and he told me that if I didn't wish to do that, I still had time to get into my church clothes. But we'd be leaving in the next three minutes."

Russ smiled. "What did you do then?"

"Well, you can say it temporarily put me in check and cooled my heels for a few months, until the fall of 1908. By that time, I was about eleven, and I had become what both of my parents considered to be out of control with my ongoing babbling about flying. For the first time during this period in my life, I strongly resisted going to church."

"That's funny because it was about then when I wanted to go to church all the time," Russ replied. "I ran with a kike named Max Kline, and he went to church with us all the time. I went to Salem UCC with Mama. My brother, Max, and I were always trying to hook up with girls. The whole time Mama thought we were serious about learning religion. She was learning about the women of the Bible, inside and out, in a ladies' group. Pop was home getting drunk."

Jack said, "Now you have come up here, I'm sure, because of the outcome of the surgery. You, my friend, are moved because of what you had to do. Are you feeling like you failed Benji because of the outcome?"

"Yes, but I'm also wondering if Carver already got back safely with the others."

"I'm sure they're fine, but let's ask God for their safety. Then we'll go down to check on Benji, hit the wine cellar, tie one on, and relax the rest of the day."

Russ laughed and said, "Well, that sounds good, but Dani might have other plans for you."

"In your dreams, bucko. It's you her roving eyes are all over."

Francois said, "You seem to be feeling better, Russ, so why don't we go to see and pray with Benji before I head down the road again."

*   *   *

During the next few days, Russ and Jack made plans to leave once Benji was a little stronger. They decided that they would not be heading back to the western coastline first because from where they were, it was closer to get to Montpellier, France, and the Mediterranean Sea, where the navy had the *USS Bridgeport*, a hospital ship, stationed just off the coast. Russ felt that their number one mission was to get Benji to it before they worried about their own comfort. Either way, they would be running into "friendlies."

Speaking of friendly, it became obvious that Jack was right about Dani's interest in Russ. They would spend several stretches of time in the hayloft in the evenings. Though they spoke different native languages, they found a way to communicate their desires about going to the hayloft.

Dani's papa was getting fed up with the animal-like behavior between them. He returned to the farm with a vehicle one morning after a trip to town and said, "Prendre le camion et obtenir l'enfer d'ici."

They looked at him and said, "What?"

Dani's brother said, "Take truck. Get the hell out of here."

"Why?" they asked.

He pointed at Russ and in broken English said, "You and Dani bunkie, bunkie. Pack and go now."

Russ and Jack started preparing the 1908 utility truck to make it comfortable for Benji. They wouldn't be driving at night because they didn't have oil for the oil lamp headlights. Every step of the way, if he needed help from Russ, Jack would ask, "Hey, bunkie, can I have . . ." It was a good laugh between the two of them; even Benji pulled himself together enough to joke about it a bit.

The last thing Russ had done before leaving was to give Dani contact information for his parents' Harrisburg home. Jack thought he was nuts, but Russ said that he and Dani had some kind of connection and thought they should stay in touch.

A little after fifteen hundred hours, they were under way. They headed south to southeast and found themselves on a road that was pretty well shelled out. There were ruts several inches deep, with some even deeper. Many of them were one and a half to two feet wide. The truck was not making the trip much nicer than an old Conestoga wagon would have. The only difference was that a Conestoga was powered by two horses and had a top speed of about twelve miles per hour. The Conestoga driver could navigate around many of the larger potholes. The truck traveled between forty and forty-five miles per hour, and it could not dodge the ruts and holes. The hard rubber tires provided little comfort. They tried to make the 255-klick trip in about four and a half hours, but the condition of the road didn't help.

When they got to the south side of Millau, Benji needed a break. There had been too many bumps and too much jarring around. They pulled into an abandoned Calvinist church and carried Benji in, laying him on the sacrament table in the chapel.

As they walked into the church, Russ thought for the first time in days about the health and well-being of his little brother, Barrel, back home. The thought shot through his head at that very moment that if Barrel knew he was risking life and limb for a blackie, he'd have a baby. However, all Russ could focus on now was saving Benji's life and getting him onto the *USS Bridgeport* hospital ship. He didn't want to fail at this mission.

Everyone knew, including Benji, that he was not ready to be moved when they were told to leave. Russ blamed himself. If it were not for his sins of the flesh, Dani's papa wouldn't have kicked them out, Benji could have recovered in the amount of time he needed to, and they wouldn't be in this fix.

They both saw blood seeping through his bandages; it wasn't there when they'd left two and a half hours earlier. For that matter, his leg had not bled in the last three days. Russ said, "Damn it! We are totally set back to day one." They worked on his leg, cleaning it and wrapping it in fresh bandages. Jack noticed that Benji's voice was barely more than a whisper and his motions and reactions were very weak. His strength was markedly less than it had been during the last several days.

Jack said to Russ, "I think he needs some rest and . . ."

Russ walked away while Jack was in the middle of his sentence. Something had caught his attention. Russ's eyes locked on one of several stained glass windows in the church. He walked toward the pews like a crippled disheveled old man and sat staring at the window, saying, "Dear Heavenly Father, forgive me for my sins."

Jack finally caught a glimpse of the stained glass window that had Russ's attention. It was a small side window with Christ on high, in a purple robe, a saint on either side of Him. They all had locked arms, and their satin robes seemed to flow away beneath and behind them.

He looked at Russ and got a better understanding of who the man was that he had met just days ago. To hear his stories, he was the guy who never walked away from a fight, who did not take orders well unless they came from someone with collar brass, and even then, it was a hard pill to swallow. He certainly played himself to be a racist and a sexist. His bad mouth and foul thoughts involving women had to do, or he would have you think, with a total disrespect for the Lord and for women. The list went on. This scrawny shell of a man had tears in his eyes as he sat silently staring at the window. It told Jack all too well that Russ's foul actions were a front to make an insecure fellow feel more like a man.

Jack knew that he had to get Russ's mind back on track and get him to stop feeling sorry for himself, so he grabbed an informational brochure on the church. He made sure that Benji was resting comfortably and went over to sit with Russ.

"Do you know anything about the Calvinist faith?" Jack asked Russ.

Russ asked with a forced smile, "Are you going to tell me it's named after my little brother?"

Jack said, "No. It's named after John Calvin, a chap from the Reformed Church. That would be funny, though. What's your brother's middle name?"

Russ was now chuckling. "He got in his share of fistfights over that name. His full name is Calvin Leslie Kaye."

Jack said, "Good Lord, why didn't they just name the poor kid Sue? Where did the name Barrel come from?"

"Well," Russ said, "it's like this. Mama lived by a barrel factory, where her father and about ten of her brothers worked, and Cal was shaped kinda like a barrel when he was born."

Jack smiled and said, "That's neat."

"Pop wasn't so kind. He called Cal 'lard ass' and me either 'WR' or simply 'mistake.'"

"What's WR? Or don't I want to know?"

Russ lowered his head like a scolded child and in a mousy voice said, "Without rubber. You can see why there's no love lost there. Max Kline's dad has been more of a dad to me, and he truly doesn't like me because I always got Max into trouble."

Jack shook his head. "Anyhow, Calvinism is the Reformed Church and is summarized under the five points of Calvinism in this brochure."

"Oh yeah? What are they? Does it say?"

Jack said, "The main idea of these principles is that God is able to give salvation to every person upon whom He has mercy, and that His efforts are not exhausted by the unrighteousness of man. They are total depravity, unconditional election, limited atonement, irresistible grace, and perseverance of the saints."

"Okay, I'm a reformist, and I know I didn't really have church on my mind when I was there, especially when Susie Spencer was in Sunday school. But what all does that mean?"

"Well, total depravity means that we all are born enslaved to the service of sin when we serve our own interests, as you, my friend, did with Dani," said Jack. "We as sinners reject God. God knows that we are not of the mind to love Him, as it is easier to believe in something you can touch and see. The unconditional election is that God has chosen from eternity those he will bring to His home, not because of what we do during life but because it is His unconditional mercy for us."

Russ looked at Jack and said, "So the life that I've lived may not have given me a direct ticket to hell?"

Jack smiled. "No, Russ, and believe it or not, maybe not even your pop."

Russ said, "Huh? That surprises me."

"Limited atonement is about Jesus' crucifixion, how its purpose was accomplished and is sufficient for all who believe in Jesus as their Lord and Savior. The irresistible grace is the redeeming quality of God and is therefore all of those He is going to save. This overcomes our resistance to obeying God's word as we sin. If you are one of His chosen children, you will be saved. That, my friend, is why you will be with Him in the end, because I do not see you as a black person."

Russ asked, "Are you saying that you don't believe colored people like Benji will walk with Him?"

"No, I'm not saying that. I'm not talking about people who are black in skin color. I'm talking about those who are black in the heart."

"Yes," Russ said, "but my actions with Dani have jeopardized Benji's life. How will He forgive me for that?"

Jack said, "Well let's talk about the fifth point, the perseverance of the saints, which is us, Russ. We are set apart by God although we are not exceptionally holy. God is sovereign, and man cannot disrupt His will. Those He has called into His fold will be with Him in the end. I believe, Russ, that the stained glass window that brought tears to your eyes was a sign from God that He is with you. He is telling you that though tarnished, your actions over the past several days are saintly, and they are beating Satan away from you."

Russ started crying like a child. "Jack, I try to be the tough guy all the time and show my strength. I never back down from a fight, and I don't lose many, because I would get beat with my pop's size fifty-six belt if I lost. I have to tell you that breaking into that prison was the scariest thing I ever did. The thunder and lightning just as we charged the wall was so amazing. I was sure we were going to die."

Jack smiled and said, "You aren't going anywhere soon. God has plans for you. You are one of His chosen children, and He has plans for you."

"You have made your daddy proud," Russ said. "I have gone to church many times, but you have explained things to me better than anyone else has."

Jack said, "Well, let's just say that if I were Susie Spencer, you wouldn't have heard a word of this."

*　　*　　*

They had no plans of being there overnight but hid the utility truck since most of their supplies were in it. They ate some MREs and drank some wine they'd brought from Dani's wine cellar. The two of them checked on Benji one last time after deciding that they should stay and get some sleep after all. They made themselves comfortable, bunking out on pews to get some shuteye.

Before dawn, as clearly as the minister on a Sunday morning, Benji bellowed, "Russ, help me! I need your help!"

Russ ran to his side to find that blood and pus were oozing out of the bandage like grease poured through cheesecloth after frying ground beef. It was running across the table like spilled chicken gravy.

In the relatively dark chapel Benji said, "I think it's the end. I see bright lights and angels. Russ, I'm going home."

Russ said, "No, no, you are not."

As Russ tried to tie the tourniquet around his thigh, Benji murmured, "Russ you need to let me go. I woke you to share the beauty. Grab my hand."

Russ didn't take his hand. He lifted Benji by reaching under his shoulders and held him to his breast. Russ kept saying, "Stay with me, Benji. Stay with me."

"Russ, take my dog tags with you and get them to my mama. She's at nine nineteen South Sassafras in Philly. I want you to keep the pig sticker." Jack was writing the address down.

"I don't want you to leave me, my friend, but if you must, let me read to you from the *Army Soldiers Book of Prayers*," Russ said. He pulled it from his pocket and stumbled through a section, as his reading abilities were weak. "'Fear ye not. Stand still and see the salvation of the Lord which He will show to you today.' Now, Benji, I'm going to read a prayer."

Benji said, "Russ, I have to go. Jesus is in a beautiful purple gown telling me to come. He's with my grandparents."

"Hear this prayer as you drift away, Benji," said Russ. He read, "'Unto God's gracious mercy and protection we commit you. The Lord bless you and keep you. The Lord make his face to shine upon you, and be gracious unto you. The Lord lift up his countenance upon you and give you peace, both now and evermore. Amen.'"

Benji went limp in Russ's arms. Russ looked into Benji's wide-open eyes and noticed the smile in his face. He was aware that Benji had left this world with contentment in his heart.

Russ bowed his head and said, "Father, receive Benji's soul and praise this hero, as he has fought this miserable damn war and served you well. Amen."

Jack gave Russ some quiet time as he started getting ready for the next leg of the journey. He drove the utility truck to the front of the church, put some of their belongings into the truck, and brought the map into the sanctuary. He also found an eight-foot ladder in the storage building and brought it in. He walked by Russ, who was sitting quietly, and picked up the pig sticker. He then set up the ladder near the stained glass window that Russ liked so much. Jack removed it from the window frame to give it to Russ one day. Jack loaded it in the truck without Russ ever noticing what he did.

Russ sat in a catatonic state with tears in his eyes, feeling that he'd let Benji down. Jack had everything loaded, including Benji. He sat down with the map and plotted out the trip back to Bordeaux, France. It was about 440 klicks, or a nine- to ten-hour trip. Jack got Russ to respond to him, and he said, "We're ready to roll. I've worked out a map route to get over to Bordeaux now that there's no need to get to the hospital ship."

Russ said, "Yes, but we must get Benji in the truck."

Jack smiled, patted Russ on the back, and said, "It's okay, my friend. I've worked around you for the last hour. Benji is in the truck covered with wet cloths and wrapped in a canvas tarpaulin and bed sheets to keep him cool during the heat of the day. We need to get to Bordeaux today so they can get him in a morgue before he starts to decompose."

The ride was quiet for the first three and a half hours, as Russ simply stared out the window. Every now and again, he blamed himself and then called the Germans everything but human. They eventually stopped to water a few trees on the opposite side of Toulouse, France. Russ was ready to drive now, but they first set out to find a bite to eat. They found a farmers' market and got a slab of cheese, a small loaf of round bread, some fruit, and a carafe of red wine. They got on the road and ate while they traveled.

Russ said, "I'm sorry for being so quiet, but I had to process the whole thing. My thoughts went to those evenings with Dani, and had they never happened, would Benji be alive right now?"

"You're your own worst enemy about this," said Jack. "If it weren't for my relationship with Winnie, Dani would have turned my eye as well, and then we would have been fighting over her and not taking care of Benji at all."

Russ laughed and asked, "How much of a fight do you think that would have been? How many fights have you been in?"

"Do you mean other than the constant fight I was in with my parents about the Wright brothers and flying? Ah, let me count them. None."

"Who are the Wright brothers? Are they buddies back home?"

Jack looked at Russ as if he were the green cheese man that lives on the moon. "Are you kidding me?"

Russ said, "What are you talking about? Am I supposed to know them?" Russ obviously did not recall his claim about remembering the Wright brothers because of the Holsum twins.

For some dumb reason, Jack had a feeling of superiority over the man who saved his life, and he started to tell Russ about the Wright brothers. "They have been in my life since just before my eighth birthday. On October 4, 1905, Orville took his forty-sixth flight, covering almost twenty-one miles in a little over a half hour. Their first passenger flight occurred shortly thereafter. I was awestruck and could talk of nothing else. Every now and again, Mama clipped my wings and handed me my Bible for some verse studies."

Russ said, "Do you mean those guys from . . . I think it was Kittychop, South Carolina?"

Jack laughed loudly. "You're close. It's Kitty Hawk, North Carolina. In 1909, President Taft invited the Wright brothers to the White House. To the *White House*, I say. I could not imagine how important they must have felt to be invited to meet the president. I believe that for some, not for me as a child, reality struck when the United States Army bought the rights to their plane. What would that mean for the history of aviation? Our country now had the ability to put planes to work in our military."

"So you're telling me that early in the twentieth century, those two men changed the look of a one-hundred-and-forty-year-old army?"

"I'm not saying they solely did it," Jack responded. "They were the inventors of the plane, but Taft had a lot to do with it. Also, think about your question. The Wright brothers had nothing to do with other modes of transportation such as the one we are in as we speak. So alone, they had very little to do with the change in the look of the army. However, I knew from my perspective, at eleven years old, what I was doing with my life. I was going to be a pilot in the army. My mother wanted to hear nothing of such nonsense."

Russ laughed. "It sounds to me like we both had problems with the parents in our lives—you with parents who wanted you to do what they wanted you to do; and me with a father who was a drunk and made himself feel better by hurting me, my brother, and Mama, who lives her life walking on eggshells."

Jack agreed with Russ in theory, but he said, "Yes, but the difference was that all my mother could imagine was me crashing and dying in one of 'those contraptions.' She tried to convince me that the ministry needed spirited people like me. If I could have been a swearing man in that house without the wrath of God coming through the ceiling with lightning bolts, I would have had a mouthful right then and there. I was certainly biting my tongue pretty hard at that point."

"You never heard your parents swear once?" asked Russ.

"Once my mother dropped a sack of flour on the rug, and the words that rolled off her tongue were ungodly," Jack replied. "Some words were ones that I had never heard by an adult up to that point; they were words I had only ever heard from kids. For hours afterward, she was repeating 'Hail Mary, full of grace,' and we aren't even Catholics."

"Other than the story you told me about your planes and the sixty angels in the book of Revelations, what did your father think of you wanting to fly?" Russ asked.

Jack laughed and said, "You might say I was a disappointment to the *O holy one*. My father told me to stop talking about such tomfoolery. He wanted me to start focusing on real life, not this fantasy world I was living in. He told me, 'Most boys your age are out working to help support the family, as you soon will be. Right now, however, we cannot put you out there to work, as I have a reputation in the community of being a sensible man and an insightful spiritual leader. You and your childish stupidity would shatter all such opinions of me.' He followed it up by telling me that I had exactly one more year, until my twelfth birthday, to grow up, stop chattering about flying, and start taking responsibility."

Jack laughed and continued as if Russ had given him a "get out of jail free" card in the game of Monopoly. "My twelfth, thirtieth, sixtieth, and even eightieth birthday came and went, and my commitment to not follow in my dad's shoes had not changed. I became even more determined to fly. I was driving my father to his wit's end. That good Christian man was to the point of having to say that he and his boy had very little in common with each other."

Russ said, "I think it's safe to say that our mothers were typical wives of twentieth-century homes. They are good women but have no voice because of the dominance of strong-willed men. In a perfectly good house that is controlled correctly, a good wife has three main jobs: take care of the house and children, cook fitting and proper meals for their men, and perform admirably in the bedroom. That's what Max, my brother, and I called the big three."

"Well, doggone it, that's a concept I never thought about in my whole life. I thought my mother only ever did the nasty three times— resulting with Harlow, Perry, and me."

They both started laughing at the thought of any of their parents doing the nasty, and Russ said, "I don't know if Pop has been sober long enough to in the last nineteen years since Barrel was conceived. However, whether they ever have done it isn't important right now, because if we don't stop soon and water some trees, my back teeth will float out of my jaw."

With that, he swerved off to the side of the road and stopped. They both did what needed to be done, and Russ took the opportunity to light a Pall Mall, because Jack didn't like the smoke in the truck. They realized that they were about a klick or so outside of Langon, which was only about forty klicks away from Bordeaux. Getting to Bordeaux would require about two more hours on the road. They would soon be back to where Russ had started his two-day mission ten days earlier. A lot had happened in that time.

As they stood there resting and stretching their legs, Russ said, "Where is your duty station? Where are you going to end up when this is over?"

"Dijon Air Base. It was established in 1914," Jack said. "It's located approximately two hundred and sixty-six klicks southeast of Paris. That is, of course, if the Krauts don't capture or destroy it during their push."

Russ said, "You'll like this base we're going to. It's approximately two hundred and sixty-six klicks southeast of Paris. It will kind of remind you of Montoursville. Both are on the west bank of a river, with the mouth of a creek as one of their other borders."

Jack said, "Sounds like you know a bit about my hometown. Did you know the original village was built around the mouth of Loyalsock Creek and the west branch of the Susquehanna River? It was an important layover for missionaries who spread the gospel throughout the wilderness areas of Pennsylvania in the 1740s. Montoursville wasn't an incorporated town until 1850."

Russ lit another cigarette and said, "Well, I don't know much about the start of Harrisburg. I think Mama told me once that some guy named John Harris built a trading post about 1710, where Paxton Creek and the Susquehanna River merge. Also, I know that the first church, a log building, was built in 1720 and was named the Paxton Presbyterian Church. It was rebuilt in stone in 1740. I went to a wedding at that church just before I left for the army."

Just then, from the southeast, they heard a lot of rumbling approaching on the road. Russ and Jack stepped back off the road and into the tree line until they determined that the noise was being made by friendlies. They stepped out into the open to see what was causing all the noise. There were about ten trucks, with eight to ten German prisoners in each truck. Three Italian motorcycles led three staff cars with military officers in them. The trucks followed behind.

They stood and watched the makeshift parade. As the officers' vehicles approached, Jack stood straight and in proper form in his filthy, disheveled, torn uniform and snapped a salute that would make

President Taft proud. Russ looked as unkempt as Jack did. He simply planted the sole of his boot on the bumper of their truck, bending his leg at the knee and resting his butt on the back of his boot. Pulling the cigarette from his mouth, Russ tilted his head toward the heavens and blew smoke rings, one after another.

From the corner of his mouth, Jack said, "You are an ass, Russ. No matter who's in those cars, they outrank you. Salute them."

Russ said, "Oh, I'm so sorry. Did those yahoos put their lives on the line like we have in the last ten days? Did they lose a good man like we did? Do they ever get their hands dirty? Furthermore, do they put on their pants differently than I do? They can all kiss me where the sun doesn't shine right now."

"Man, I hope you get it together before we have a debriefing in a few hours. Are you up to driving the last leg of this journey? I'm sleeping on my feet."

Russ said, "Yeah, I've got you covered."

They jumped into the truck, and Jack was true to his word—he was sound asleep before they went through Langon, France. It gave Russ two hours of solitude to think about many parts of his life. He realized that in many ways, as much as he wanted to be different from Pop, he was Pop.

No, he was not drunk every day of his life like Pop was. However, he had the tendency to tie one on every now and again. He started many fights and looked for fights to get in the middle of, always walking away and never being carried away. Disrespectful to most anyone he felt was subservient to him, he also didn't give respect automatically to many superiors unless he felt they had earned respect by his own standards. Certainly, women had no real importance in his life except for the big three, as Max, Barrel, and he called it. He believed those in charge of every firing range in the army had something against him personally because of how he carried himself. Oh, yes, he always got marksmanship ribbons one after another, but because of his temper, every attempt to become a sniper was stopped before the ink was dry on the paperwork.

He wondered how he could change things to become someone who was more respected. His mind kept wavering back and forth between these thoughts: *I can do this* and *The hell with everyone.* There was so much wrong with him, where in the hell would he start? Then he struggled with the idea that having spent so much time thinking about everything that was wrong with him, what about the things that were good about him? He spent the last half hour of the journey trying to get that list started. When he finally got to the base, he was hard up, still with nothing on the "good" list.

Russ shook Jack's shoulder and said, "Jack, wake up! We've finally made it back to the starting point, my starting point. It's time for you to meet some folks."

CHAPTER

NEW ASSIGNMENTS

T hey pulled up in front of the command post and hopped out of the truck. They entered Colonel Jeffers's office and walked up to his aide's desk. With his back to Russ and Jack, the aide held his finger in the air as if to say *Just a second*, as he was clearly trying to finish something he had been working on.

Russ said, "Hey, you damn darkie, turn around now, boy."

Carver came flying out of his chair yelling as loud as he could, "Russ, oh my God." Carver threw his arms around Russ as if he were a long-lost relative.

Colonel Jeffers walked to his door with one hand in his pocket. With the other hand, he was spinning his glasses around in a circle by an earpiece. Jeffers said, "Well, I'll be a monkey's uncle! Come on into my office."

"Benji . . . Where is Benji?" Carver asked.

Russ reached out to Carver's hand and placed Benji's dog tags in his hand. He said, "As I promised my friend, we will all come home. He's in the truck, and I wish I weren't the one to tell you this, but he needs to go to the morgue. Unfortunately, we lost him about zero five thirty this morning. We had to do what virtually amounted to field surgery to remove his leg several days ago, and he survived until this morning. He asked that we return his dog tags to his family when we get home. I'll do it if you wish, but I didn't know if you would want to. I'm sure the colonel will be writing a letter . . . so they'll know long before any of us get home."

Carver looked as if he could have been knocked over with a feather. He said, "Russ, I can't do this. He was with you." He handed the dog tags back as tears welled up in his eyes.

Jeffers said, "Carver, take Jedadiah with you, son, and show him where the morgue is. On your way back, stop by the chow hall, bring the boys some solid food, and let Sergeant Corbett know that Russell Kaye made it back. Tell him to see me ASAP about where we go from here. If you need some time to reflect, do so, son. Take an hour or so in the chapel if you wish. Just bring the food back and have Jedadiah bring it in with him, and then you go if you need to."

Carver said, "Thank you, sir." He turned to walk away but then turned back to Russ and said, "The day I met you, as you may remember, I wanted to kick your white ass. Now I think of you as one of us; you are my brother. Thank you for believing enough in Benji and me to treat us with dignity. You are one of the few whities who would do that. Thank you . . . and thanks for being a man of your word and bringing Benji home."

Russ was speechless. Until this moment, he had been accused of being a racist in almost every sense of the word, and a black man had just complimented him. Was this the first thing he should put on his list of things that were good about Russ? Not knowing what to say or do, he just reached out to shake Carver's hand.

Then it was just the three of them—Jeffers, Russ, and Jack—in the room. The introductions were made between Jeffers and Jack, and Jack was assured that he would get back to his unit as soon as possible. When Jedadiah returned, he telegraphed Jack's unit to let them know Jack was safe. Jeffers had countless questions for Russ as to how the mission went as well as many questions for Jack so his answers about the security and manpower within Château de Beynac could be passed on to intelligence.

The conversation continued for almost an hour over hot pork roll sandwiches, potatoes, and summer squash. Dessert was real goat's milk, coffee, and some unidentifiable fruit pastries. Whatever it was, it went down a lot better than MREs or wine and cheese in Dani's barn. It was hot food. Putting up with the long conversation with Jeffers was worth every second in exchange for hot food.

Jeffers finally said to Russ, "Take Jack to supply and get him some clothes. Go back to your barracks and find him a room with an empty bunk. Take showers, get a good night's sleep, and be back here at oh nine thirty. Then we will see what's next."

They followed his orders to a T, except that when they arrived at the barracks, Jack told Russ that he had to find the truck to get some of his personal things. Jack insisted that Russ just settle in to sleep while he went to the truck. Jack was back shortly and wasted no time getting into his bunk. Once their heads hit their pillows, neither of them remembered anything until reveille at 0630. They were to meet up with one another in the morning at 0730 to go to the mess hall for breakfast, but Russ was out front ten minutes earlier to have a smoke. Jack arrived with a wrapped package in his hand.

Sergeant Corbett was on his way out of the chow hall when Russ and Jack were entering. Russ said, "Morning, Sergeant. How are you?" Sergeant Corbett said nothing at all to Russ, which Russ thought was a bit strange.

Russ looked at Jack and said, "Wonder what's eating him. That's my mess hall sergeant."

Jack said to Russ, "If the army knows what is best for them, they won't waste your talents by working you in a mess hall." With that, he laughed and added, "After all, last night Carver made you bi-ethnic. You are now even more important to this man's army."

"I thought for a second you were paying me a compliment, but here you are, just milking a duck at my expense."

Jack gave Russ a sly smile. Many people could go a lifetime and never interpret the look on Jack's face. He ever so slightly lifted one side of his face into a slight grin and let the twinkle in his baby-blue eyes gleam. Then, like a mischievous schoolboy, he said in a matter-of-fact manner, "What you did on that special operation mission is the stuff heroes do, not the work of stupid cooks. Here, take this." Jack handed the package to Russ.

As Russ quickly unwrapped it, tears came to his eyes. It was the stained glass window from the abandoned church where Benji had died. Russ couldn't think of anything to say, but his face told Jack all he needed to know; the gift was appreciated and would be with Russ for the rest of his life. When he regained his composure, Russ thanked Jack, tucked the window in an embrace, dried his misty eyes, and entered the chow hall with Jack.

Many of the guys at the mess hall were happy to see Russ—or so it would seem by the reactions and comments when he walked in. Many had questions about the mission that he, of course, was not allowed to answer. Everybody wanted to know the story of the stained glass window. Russ and Jack finished breakfast and left the chow hall, slowly meandering to Jeffers's office. This gave Russ time to brace himself for whatever would come next.

When they arrived, they were asked to wait while Jeffers finished a meeting. Carver said to Russ, "I reenlisted for two more years, so I am rotating out and will be heading back to the States within a week, to the operations office at Fort Ord, on Monterey Bay Peninsula in central California. I'll be in Philly for two weeks before going out there."

Russ shook his head and said, "Oh my God. Did you know that when we went out there on the suicide mission from hell?"

With eyes as wide as saucers and huge white teeth beaming through his smile, Caver said, "Well, I had been thinking about it for a few weeks 'cause I know this kinda work ain't for me. However, that mission made up my mind overnight. I got back here and told Colonel Jeffers first thing the next morning. Jedadiah is my replacement."

Russ laughed and said, "Think it would work for me when I walk through those doors? I thought Jedadiah was a stand-in for Benji till he got back."

The doors to Jeffers office opened, and out walked Corbett. The baking Russ had done over the months was not doing Corbett's waistline any good. On the other hand, maybe it was from sitting around exercising only the index finger on his right hand. Hooking that finger into a coffee cup or pointing it in peoples' faces was the only thing Corbett did other than ratcheting his jaw telling other people what to do. His belly hung over his belt, and you could tell that he would exhibit a flabby plumber's crack in the back whenever he squatted.

Corbett noticed the men sitting there, and the smile on his face turned quickly into a snarl when he saw Russ. He shot Russ a look that could have killed him quicker than mustard gas if he would have had any longer to stare at Russ before walking out the door.

Jack said, "I sense you made him mad once or twice."

"You're lucky you're my brother, least for another week or two," Carver responded.

Russ and Jack laughed. "Carver," Russ said, "you and Benji, God rest his soul, are my brothers—and don't ever forget it. Now I'll have a place to stay when I'm on vacation in California! Lord knows if I spend the money to travel across the country, I won't have the money to stay in a motel."

"Tell us what you did to make that man that angry, Sarge," Jack said to Russ.

"I just put him in his place a few times about his lack of knowledge. He was given the position he has in that kitchen because of his age. I went to school for cooking and baking, while he was a plumber before he went in the service."

Carver laughed and said, "It's best if you keep your mouth shut about this tidbit, but Corbett said to send you out to get those prisoners because you were expendable and he didn't care if you returned or not. Guess what. You're back! It's best to drop it because of what's in store for you."

"What is it?" Russ asked.

"The old man will tell you soon enough."

The door to Jeffers's office opened, and he stepped out, saying, "I hope I didn't hold you up. Did you and Carver have a chance to catch up? Did he tell you his wonderful news?"

Russ nodded his head and said, "Yes, he's told us a little about what's up for him. Are you going to make us the same offer?" They laughed as they entered Jeffers' office. Russ and Jack looked at one another in awe as the "old man" held out a wooden box of expensive cigars and said, "Cigar, boys? Can I interest you in a snifter of brandy?"

Both agreed to the brandy, and Russ accepted the cigar, whereas Jack just held up his hand in a "no, thank you" manner, shaking his head to confirm his lack of interest in the cigar. However, they exchanged a look that said, "What the hell is this about?"

Russ bluntly asked, "Sir, are we in trouble for something or another? Is there a problem with something we did? Does this have anything to do with the captain I wanted court-martialed?"

"No, Russ," Jeffers said. "Lighten up. In fact, your actions with the captain worked in your friend Jack's favor if he wishes to take advantage of it."

Jack asked, "How's that? He did what he did, and I said nothing. So how did he help me?"

Jeffers responded, "Well, I personally spoke with your commander from Dijon Air Base, and during the last several days, everything in your base has been retreated to the Paris base, as Germany is making a major push for Paris. They now have a wall going from Piave, Marne, Amiens, Havrincourt, and Hindenburg. Dijon is now behind enemy lines. To get you there, we'd need to go through enemy lines, and there is no sense to that."

As Jack slowly sipped on his brandy, he said, "So, sir, what is it you are saying or suggesting to me? My specialty is reconnaissance from planes. Nothing personal, sir, but I don't see planes or an airfield on this base. Staying here does nothing for me."

Jeffers frowned slightly and rolled his eyes. At the same time, he lifted his eyebrows in a look of disapproval regarding the comments

Jack had just made. "Soldier, let me ask you a question. Were you not trained in the area of supply? Wasn't reconnaissance a secondary fallback?"

Jack said, "Yes, sir, but—"

"So why would you drink my brandy and sit in my office and try to make me think reconnaissance is your field of experience?" Jeffers asked.

Jack sat up a bit straighter in his chair. "No, sir, I was not trying to make you think anything of that sort. I was truly of the opinion that since I was taken from supply and put in reconnaissance, it was a permanent thing."

Russ was sitting back listening to the conversation and sipping his brandy while enjoying the finest quality cigar tobacco he had ever smoked. His mind wondered back to those days when he was a child smoking corn silk out of a corn cob pipe and blowing smoke rings. He choked on the smoke rings he was making as his mind tried to compare the difference in the quality of then and now.

Jeffers grinned and asked, "My Lord, Sarge, is that the first cigar you ever smoked?" He turned back to Jack and said, "As to your thoughts regarding reconnaissance versus supply, nothing I was told this morning by your superiors from Dijon led me to believe you are reassigned away from supply. Here, however, are the options on the table. We are sensing that the German army is weakening. You could be back with your unit within weeks or you could leave on a ship going back to Norfolk, Virginia, in the States. From there, you can transfer to the 480th Intelligence, Surveillance, and Reconnaissance Wing [480th ISR Wing], which is headquartered at Langley Air Force Base, Virginia. There, you would serve as an army instructor for the duration of your tour."

Jack looked at Russ and then at Jeffers and said, "I'm going back to the States. When do I leave?"

Jeffers said, "Jedadiah will pick you up tomorrow morning at oh nine hundred hours. He will bring you by here, and I'll give you rotation orders. Then he will take you to the docks. The ship leaves for the States at thirteen hundred hours. Do you have any other questions for me?"

Jack said with a large smile, "No, sir. I'm as ready as I'll ever be."

Jeffers dismissed Jack, went back behind his desk, and sat down. He said, "Now for you, Russell. Your tour is about to change as well."

Russ asked, "Am I going to head home too?"

Jeffers laughed and said, "If you wanted to go home you shouldn't have done such a good job out there over the last couple of weeks. I'm in the same boat. I would love to get back to my happy home in Hope, Maine, but they keep telling me they need me here. The good news is that you're not going back to the chow hall again except to eat."

"Okay, so what is it I'm going to do from this point forward?" he asked.

Jeffers said, "As of tomorrow morning, you are assigned to the intelligence department. You will need to report to Captain Randall Henderson in the Pasadena Building at zero eight hundred hours. You will be working on collecting intelligence about the large offensive the Germans are pushing right now and working with the French to determine a strategy to save Paris."

"Yes, sir, I'll be ready in the morning."

*   *   *

A twenty-one day battle started on July 15, which was the Second Battle of the Marne. Unbeknownst to the Germans, it was their last offensive on the Western Front, and it was fruitless for the Germans because of a strong counterattack by the French.

Within six or eight weeks of Russ, Carver, and Jack returning from the mission, the war made a major shift. On September 12, 1918, the Battle of Saint Mihiel started when approximately three hundred thousand American troops, under the explicit command of General Pershing, hurled themselves into the midst of the German lines. Within thirty-six hours, the Americans took over thirteen thousand prisoners and captured 466 guns. The Americans killed and wounded five thousand Germans, while the Americans suffered seven thousand casualties. By September 30, Bulgaria signed an armistice with the Allies.

Lieutenant Colonel Thomas E. Lawrence was a British Army officer renowned especially for his role during the Arab Revolt against Ottoman Turkish rule earlier in the war. Lawrence was deeply enmeshed in the buildup to the capture of Damascus in the final weeks of the war. Much to his displeasure, after all the work he had done to prepare for the submission, he was not present at the city's formal surrender on October 1. He arrived several hours after the city had fallen. It seemed the war was quickly gearing down throughout the theater. On October 20, Germany continued to lay down their weapons of war, and they suspended submarine warfare. On November 3, Austria and Hungary signed an armistice with Italy, which was effective November 4.

With Germany actively seeking an armistice on November 9, 1918, and a German revolution threatening, calls for Kaiser Wilhelm II to relinquish command grew in intensity. Wilhelm was less than enthusiastic about making such a sacrifice. He expressed a preference to march his armies back into Germany from the Western Front. His military advisers informed him that it would not be prudent to do so because his own troops might very well harm him. Wilhelm abandoned the notion.

Then finally, on November 11 at 6 a.m., Germany signed the Armistice of Compiègne, which ended all fighting, effective at 11 a.m. that morning. Then, last but not least, after many troops had already begun transferring back home, on January 18, 1919, the Treaty of Versailles between the Allies and Germany was signed, and the Peace Conference opened in Paris.

CHAPTER

STATESIDE AGAIN

Jack's ship got into Norfolk, Virginia, on a Saturday afternoon, October 19. Walking on land was a bit of a challenge at first, as he was still trying to use his sea legs. The smell of salt air, fish, and the sea was strong around the docks that day. The gulls were swarming around the sailors as they came down the gangplank, crying out and begging for the smallest bit of food to fight over. There were wives, girlfriends, and lovers, to say nothing about children of all ages, waiting for some of the soldiers. An olive green bus was there to take the rest of them to the base near Suffolk. Jack wished he were in the arms of Winnie instead of heading to a beat-up old bus.

Nothing much was going to happen until Monday morning because it was the weekend. For Jack, there would be a lot of sleeping in a musty old bunk room that smelled of stale cigarettes, thrown-up booze, rotten food, and dirty socks and drawers. If he wasn't in the barracks, he was hanging out in the chow hall and calling home when he got around to it. Jack had an idea for what he thought would be an incredible article for the *Stars and Stripes* so maybe he'd get the urge to start on the first draft.

Saturday afternoon, Jack found himself walking into the social hall. There were several guys sitting around playing cards, eating snacks, drinking, telling jokes, cussing up a storm and listening to a college football game between Virginia Tech and Belmont AC on the radio. It was the first game of the season for VT. Jack did not recognize any of the soldiers. Someone noticed him in the doorway and invited him to join them.

By the end of the first quarter, money was flying around the room like when the gold rush was in full swing in 1849. Those were the days when gold meant disposable income. Jack watched and thought that history should have taught men at least one thing from the taverns during the gold rush. When there is money and booze in the same room, there will be people looking for ways to relieve each other of their money. When miners or soldiers patronize an establishment where there are spirits, there will there be gaming. The only thing missing was attractive women willing to pleasure these men and separate them from more of their money.

Early on, the Georgia Tech, 11th Cavalry, and the Oklahoma, Arkansas games started to get out of hand, and money started being bet on them, as they both looked like runaways. Jack was astounded to see guys jumping into as many as a dozen pools at a quarter apiece, popping quarters into used beer cups. Wagers were being placed on numerous different betting categories for three different games.

Jack thought this was ridiculous, as everyone in that room, including him, was making only thirty dollars per month. Those who were away fighting the war like Jack were making an extra six dollars for hazardous duty pay. Jack could only scratch his head. Every bet you could think of was going on in that room, like which team out of the four would score the most points, how many total touchdowns there would be, total points in each game, total passing yards, rushing yards, turnovers, total receptions by the winning team, offensive time on the field by the winning team, and so on. They even had a dollar pool on picking the closest total points scored in all three games without going over.

Jack was truly shocked that Georgia Tech won 123 to 0, while Oklahoma won 103 to 0. In the game they were listening to on the radio, Virginia Tech beat Belmont AC 30 to 0 in yet another shutout.

After getting into Norfolk on Saturday of the weekend, Jack spent a few days at the army base in Suffolk, Virginia, before getting on a transport bus to Langley, Virginia. Part of the time at Suffolk was spent debriefing, having a physical exam, getting his orders for transfer, exchanging foreign money, and taking care of banking issues. Once the midpoint of the following week arrived, Jack was ready for the next leg of his journey.

The two-hundred-mile trip was about an eight-hour bus ride, with stops scheduled at several posts and bases. Spending some of the time sightseeing out the bus window, Jack was feeling thankful that he had made it back to the States safely. The bus ride from Suffolk took him to Petersburg and then to Richmond. Scooting up Route 95 to the nation's capital city, Washington, DC, was the last leg of the journey.

When Jack wasn't daydreaming or sightseeing, his mind drifted away on a long journey back overseas to the war front. Had it not been for Russ, Carver, and Benji, he would have never made it back. He felt sure that he would have died at the hands of German guards in a faraway land.

He started reminiscing about the perfection of the whole break-in and breakout. He started jotting down notes of his memories to use when he wrote an article about being saved by a Harrisburg doughboy. He also started penning a letter home to let everyone know he was back in the States. He never finished it because he decided he would call home before a letter could get there. At the stops along the way, he got out to stretch his legs and use the latrine. On the road again, he felt safe enough to close his eyes and nap.

It was about 11 p.m. on October 23 when the bus pulled onto the United States Air Service training camp at Langley, Maryland. Though it is considered an airfield, the navy and army were both at this base because of its close proximity to Washington, DC, which was only nine miles away. Like the weekend before, Jack arrived at the base during off-duty hours. This was going to be another night in the overnight lodging area, where late arrivals were assigned to stay just to get some sleep.

Jack's mind was set on one thing. He made one phone call before turning in, and that was to the nighttime operator, Barbie Sumac, in Montoursville, to ask her to ring him through to the Jadite house. He just wanted to let Winnie know that he was safely back in the country.

Barbie answered the phone and said, "It's late, sir. I don't like putting calls through after nine thirty unless it's important."

Jack said, "Ma'am, this is Jack Earl, Winnie's fiancé, and I just got home from the war. Ring me through now, please."

Barbie had been in Winnie and Jack's high school class. She had been overlooked by most guys in Lycoming County. People steered clear of her because she did the unthinkable. Barbie married a Mexican at one point, and it didn't work out. Jack thought, *Of course it didn't work. None of those crossbreed marriages work.* Then he thought, *No, that's not fair to say. Russ walked into my life for two weeks and changed my whole way of thinking. How is that possible?*

Barbie had at least one other flaw. She did not laugh; she cackled. She was a bit hefty for a short girl. She had reddish hair and light washed-out-looking skin. The only thing she had going through the eyes of any warm-blooded male in his twenties was that she had a nice personality. Of course, that is not what a guy in his twenties is usually looking for.

Just then, Jack heard a voice from home for the first time since he joined the army. Winnie's mama said in a sound-asleep voice, "Barb, what is it? Who in God's name has the nerve to be calling at this hour of the night?"

Barb replied, "Ma'am, it's Jack Earl calling for Winnie . . ."

Mrs. Jadite retorted, "You tell that boy that he dare not call at this hour . . . Wait a minute, wait just a doggone minute. It's my Jackie calling from France! Put him through!" she screamed at the top of her voice to wake the whole family. "Jackie is on the phone all the way from France!"

Jack was wondering if he was going to be in trouble when she realized that he was only 225 miles away. Jack said, "Mama Jadite, I'm home from the war! I arrived in Norfolk and was brought to

Washington, DC, by bus. I just got here moments ago. I made it through the war and was a prisoner of war most of the time I was there. That's why you haven't heard from me."

Mama Jadite said, "It's wonderful you are back. I'm so glad! Winifred wants to talk to you now."

Winnie grabbed the phone from her mother's hand and almost took Jack's head off because he hadn't written to her in well over two months. She followed that up with, "But I still love you. What do you have to say to that?"

Jack laughed and responded, "I'm glad to hear your voice too."

She said, "Honestly, Jack, I thought you hooked up with some French floozy and forgot all about me."

Jack thought momentarily of Dani and her silky long raven-colored hair. Then there were those incredibly inviting bright blue eyes and the smell of vanilla perfume that he had never consciously noticed until that minute. Oh, yes, it was to cover up the horrendous hygiene conditions that everyone had to deal with, but it was there nonetheless. He remembered the sweetness in her come-on voice and then came back to reality, remembering that he'd yielded her to Russ because of his love for Winnie.

Jack said, "Winnie, our plane was shot down behind enemy lines on July sixteenth, and we were all taken prisoners of war. If it weren't for Russ Earl from Harrisburg and two colored fellows from Philadelphia coming in and breaking us out of prison, I'd be dead right now. I had no time for French floozies."

He figured he could get away with saying that because Dani would not be considered a floozy by any measure. Even poor dying Benji got a certain jolt in his blood pressure when he looked at her. For the next fifteen minutes or so Jack, continued telling Winnie about being a prisoner and his savior and the team that got all of them out. Talking to her made Jack want to get home and see everyone now that he was back in the area.

After they finished their conversation, Jack went back to his room and jumped into the sack but could not sleep. His mind had taken off in a million different directions. He realized that he'd lived through his ordeal, and he was home and safe without getting shot. It bothered him that Winnie was just 225 miles away but he wouldn't see her for some time to come. He wanted to write his story and wondered what was next for him at Langley.

He knew that he wasn't going to be able to sleep anytime soon so he went to the desk and found a Bible, tablet, pen, and envelopes that had been put there for the convenience of the guests. Jack started making notes. His notes led into thoughts that were rewritten into paragraphs. Soon he was putting together an incredibly heartwarming story that he called "Dani and the Doughboy." The story was based on the adventures during Russ's and his journey, but he didn't provide too much detail because it was a story about the struggles of the French people, not about American soldiers.

Jack's father would be proud when he read it, and he would know at last that much of what he'd drilled into his son's head was retained after all. Jack included Bible verses based around the intolerance of man in Matthew 22, the challenges of testing the integrity of man in Psalm 101, the importance of loving parents as talked about in Matthew 1, and making the right choices for our actions as stated in Proverbs chapters 18 and 19.

He included many other Bible verses and wrote another compelling article about the need for the country to take care of the children in France left without parents due to the war-related devastation in their country or because they were maimed by being in the wrong place at the wrong time. He also introduced the concept of a fund to provide for the children fathered by our servicemen who moved on with or without even knowing they were leaving children behind. Jack's point was that we had a certain responsibility to stand behind these children, while gently recognizing the additional need to do something for the children in the United States who had lost their fathers.

Exhausted, Jack finally fell asleep for an hour or two and then was wide-awake again. There were still several hours before he needed to check into the base. He left his few belongings in the room rather than checking into work with his limp almost-empty duffel bag. Jack did take his transfer orders and his "Dani and the Doughboy" story. He got onto the base simply by showing his ID and his orders, and he headed right to the chow hall. He would find it easy to get used to eating real food after having only MREs for so long on the front. That morning, he ate French toast, eggs, and bacon, also drinking his share of coffee before heading to the command post to be assigned.

Where he checked in, there was a young female civilian aide whose face reminded him of Dani's. Taken aback by her looks, he glanced at her just long enough to read her name tag. He had to take a second look, not for her name but at her face. It had a striking resemblance to Dani's. The only difference was the eye color; Dani's were blue and Elsie's were green.

He said, "Uh . . . um . . . I-I'm here to check in, Miss Elsie Presley, to the 480th Intelligence, Surveillance, and Reconnaissance [ISR] Wing." He studied her face again. She had a coy but confident smile, and it was clear that she was aware of her attractiveness.

She asked, "When did you get in?"

His eyes left her face. "I haven't yet . . . I-I mean, I arrived late last night."

She said with a chuckle, "My friends tell me my face isn't hard to look at."

Jack felt the heat in his ears as his level of embarrassment rose. "Ma'am, I'm sorry. It's just that you look so much like someone I met overseas."

She just smiled and said, "Don't worry about it. I'd worry about you if you didn't look! I am my mother's child. If I am nearly as attractive as my mother when I am her age, I will be happy!"

She told him that there would be a group of five of them processing in within about half an hour, telling him that he could take a seat.

Jack asked, "Miss Presley, where is the communications center? Can I get there and back before the meeting?"

She said, "It isn't far, but they are not known to be quick at customer service. You could stand around for a half hour just to be waited on. Here is a map of the base." With a pen, she marked where they were at that moment, where his barracks was as well as the communications center.

Over the next several hours, Jack received a tour of the important locations on the base: the chow hall, which Jack had already found; base infirmary/hospital; the base exchange; and their barracks. He received his barracks assignment and was told to take the rest of the day to move his belongings into the barracks and get settled.

Jack first went to the communications center so he could get his article wired to the *Stars and Stripes* out in Kansas City. He was issued one more set of fatigues and purchased more underwear as well as one civilian outfit to get started. Then he got his few belongings situated.

The next morning at eight o'clock, Jack reported to the 480th ISR Wing headquarters to begin learning what he needed to know to become an instructor for the duration of his tour. He was told to take a seat and that Command Sergeant Major Arthur Garfield would be with him soon. Within a few moments, a spit-shined older fellow walked down the hall with shoes that looked like black mirrors. Jack thought that perhaps the pleats on his shirt and pants could have been used for a close shave.

The fruit salad above the left pocket of his khaki uniform shirt told everyone that he was a dominant factor in the Spanish-American War. The United States got involved on April 25, 1898, after Spain sunk the USS *Maine* battleship in Havana Harbor in February. The war was short-lived, ending with a treaty in Paris in December of the same year. The result of the war ended any hope of Spain controlling Cuba, Puerto Rico, Guam, and the Philippine Islands.

Garfield's physique told everyone that he had not run any five-mile sprints since the Spanish-American War. His abdomen hid the buckle on his belt from sight. His waistline was larger than average, but he seemed not to even have a butt. His hair was as white as a

New England snowstorm, almost matching the fistful of paper in his right hand. However, most noticeable was the large mug of coffee in his left hand.

He said to Jack, "Morning, Junior. Did you get up today with your hair on your head?"

Jack said, "Excuse me, sir. I don't understand what you're asking me."

With that, the old chap said, "Then, you must have far more between your ears than you show, and you would be advised to say less than you know." He just kept on walking.

Jack looked at the old chap as he walked down the hall. He asked whoever was in earshot and listening, "What the hell was that all about?" Nobody answered.

The aide that had earlier shown him to his seat approached Jack and announced, "Command Sergeant Major Arthur Garfield will see you now. And oh, yes, he does like his title."

Jack walked into the office, and sitting at the desk sipping his coffee was the seemingly confused elder fellow from the hallway. For the first time, Jack wished he were still back in the war. To the man he said, "Let us try this again, Command Sergeant Major. Good morning, sir. How are you?"

Arthur Garfield said, "I may have been better, but I don't remember when. And you, young man? Did you wake up with both ears on?"

Jack said, "Sir, about your jargon—I don't understand it. Where are you from?"

Arthur Garfield said, "I'm from a lot of places, mostly round east overshoe, about three buckles up. To you flatlanders, that really means I'm a Green Mountain Boy and proud of it. How about you?"

"If my history's right, ah . . . oh . . . It's on the tip of my tongue. Oh, oh, ah, dagnabbit . . . Oh, oh, oh, oh, oh, ah, it's about Ethan Allen going back to the . . . crap . . . damn . . . ah, the American Revolution, right?"

"I know you can speak gooderer English than that," Arthur Garfield responded. "Maybe your tang got tongulled around your eyeteeth, and you couldn't see what you're saying. Or maybe it's worse. Maybe you put the em*PHAS*is on the wrong syl*LA*ble.

Garfield continued by saying, "It is Ethan Allen, but the Green Mountain Boys were a militia organization first launched in the 1760s in the region between the British provinces of New York and New Hampshire. It was known as a New Hampshire Grant, but it became the state of Vermont in 1777."

Jack nodded his head and said, "Your ribbons, sir. Are they from the Spanish-American war?"

Garfield continued without missing a stitch. "Sonny boy, just because there is snow on the roof doesn't mean I'm two days older than dirt. What about you? I'm the boss and am becoming an open book to you. Who are you? Why are you here? Where did you from come? Where do you call home?"

Jack sat there thinking, *This crazy man can't even read. He has my records jacket right there in his hand.* However, he politely said, "Oh, sir, I'm sorry, sir. I'm Jack Earl from Montoursville, Pennsylvania. I just got back from France about a week ago now, and I am here to be trained as another instructor."

Garfield said, "Young fellow, you're totally impressive. You passed the test. You must be you, because that's what these papers say. You never know who might wanna be you since you're such a handsome Hector."

Somewhat like an insane person, Garfield shifted from one sentence to another without a pause or even much of a breath. He said, "Montoursville, Pennsylvania. If I remember my geography, it is close to Williamsport, on the west branch of the *mighty* Susquehanna River, about two hours north of Harrisburg, Pencil-tuckey." He flitted his hazel eyes, and his chubby checks broke into a grin. He continued by saying, "Named after Madame Montour, a Native American interpreter and friend of the Brits. She was a welcome sight to the white man as he expanded west, and she also had a great deal of influence with the tribes in the area, if I remember correctly."

Jack said, "Now, sir, I'm the one who is totally impressed. How did you know all that?"

Garfield replied, "I'm not all that impressive. A number of years ago, I knew a young lassie from Williamsport. I was stationed at Middleton Air Field in Middletown, just beside Harrisburg, Pennsylvania. She got away because it didn't have no stamp on her. I took a specific interest in Madame Montour's story because it is my family's story all over again—except they were in Vermont. My great-great grandma was an Indian princess and the daughter of a local Native American medicine man. Her husband, a white man, was involved in the founding of the town of Randolph, Vermont, and she was the person who provided most of the medical treatment in the area. It all reminds me of Montoursville for some unknown reason."

Jack was now intrigued by this odd duck and became totally engrossed in Garfield's general orientation to Jack's future. When it came to describing the job responsibilities and introducing the details of the program they were teaching, Jack was turned over to several others, one at a time, for the remainder of the day. He got more and more excited as he learned where he was going to fit in over the next eighteen months.

Every person he spoke with stated that the next class would not start until after Christmas. In a nutshell, Jack was being turned loose until after Thanksgiving. No one made any mention of wanting to start his training right away. One instructor even mentioned that nothing would be happening until after Christmas, as he was headed to his home in Kentucky on December 15 and wouldn't return until January.

After spending the bulk of the day with others, Jack reported back to Command Sergeant Major Garfield around sixteen hundred hours. Jack knocked on his door, and Garfield said, "Who dat at da door? Who said who dat when I said who dat?"

Jack grinned, shook his head, and stood in the hallway away from the window so as to not be seen. He said, "It's Jack Earl, Command Sergeant Major, sir."

"Youngster, if you dig deep, you will weep. Why are you hiding your face out there in the hall so I can't see you shaking your head *no*? Should I believe that you are really Jack Earl? Whoever you are, come on in if you're good-looking."

Jack wondered to himself if this man had sex with his wife while talking in riddles. He walked in with a smile on his face and told Garfield, "Everyone that I met with today mentioned that training would start after Thanksgiving, and one was even talking about starting after Christmas."

Garfield smiled and said, "Well, if it's worth doing, then it's worth doing right. If you can get a ride home, you take the next several days off and get some downtime with your family. Come back on the Monday after Thanksgiving and we'll find something for you to do."

That in itself sparked Jack's imagination, and all kinds of plans started swirling through his mind. Plans for travel and seeing his family danced in his head, resulting in his getting little to nothing else accomplished for the rest of the day.

Jack had attended many meetings with a number of people throughout the day, but none had been as memorable as those with the old chap with the strange sense of humor. During one of his other meetings, Jack talked a little about his family. He was asked to join the interviewer and his wife for dinner that evening instead of dining in the chow hall all by himself.

CHAPTER

DINNERS AT TWO
HISTORIC TAVERNS

The husband and wife were both teaching at Langley. The husband, Douglas Dalby, was a sergeant as well and would be a co-teacher working directly with Jack once Jack was trained. In the meantime, Sergeant Dalby would be Jack's mentor until Jack could be on his own. Doug's wife, Margo Dutree Dalby, was a SP4 and an instructor in the same building in the Aviation Section, US Signal Corps.

Doug said, "Jack, we're going to a restaurant in Alexandria, about half an hour or so down the road. You are more than welcome to join us if your wallet can handle it right now."

In figuring out his finances, Jack asked, "What does the bus ride both ways cost?"

"Oh, we have our own car," Doug said. "She isn't much to look at, but she gets us around. The wife's parents gave it to us for a wedding gift; I think it was more a way of telling me to bring her home a few times a month. It's a first-year Dodge, made in 1914, and it has an L-head four-cylinder engine."

Jack said, "Gee, that's a generous wedding gift."

Doug laughed. "Ah, it's a seven-hundred-and-eighty-five-dollar car. Her father sells them, and it was two years old when he got it.

Therefore, my guess is that he took no commission or broker fees and the used-car price on it was about three hundred and fifty dollars. I think if I had a daughter and had money, I would do that too."

Jack smiled. "Yeah, I guess I would too."

Doug and Margo were as opposite as cats and mice, as planes and trains, as angels and demons. Doug was tall, every bit of six-five, while Margo would need to stand on an unabridged dictionary to be five-six. Doug's legs outweighed this woman. She looked like the size of his shadow close to sunset. Though he had a handsome side, he was a brute of a fellow. He had a large nose and dark curly hair. In reality, Dalby had a Native American and European heritage.

Margo, on the other hand, was a tiny china doll with crystal blue eyes, perfect white teeth, and an almost painted-on smile that completed the package. As Russ once said about Dani, "She's built like a brick house without any bricks out of place." She had dirty-blond hair that she wore almost to the tops of her shoulders. One could not overlook the dash of natural pink blush to her cheeks that quickly reddened whenever she was embarrassed.

Doug's family was from out near Belcourt, North Dakota. This is a part of the Turtle Creek Mountain Chippewa Indian Reservation. Margo's family claimed to be coal crackers from Pennsylvania. Her Dutree ancestors had come from England and Wales.

The three of them pretty much got to know one another on the ride to Gadsby's Tavern in Alexandria, Virginia. They eventually got to the subject of the restaurant where they were headed. Jack asked, "What's the deal with it? Why travel so far for a meal?"

Margo said, "Oh, the tavern is beautiful and so classy in a rustic kind of way. The waiters and waitresses dress in period costumes, right down to the uncomfortable wooden shoes, knickers, baggy tops, and the little wire rim glasses. They not only dress in period, but they also go into character when they are communicating with you."

As they walked into Gadsby's tavern, Jack felt he was walking back into the mid-1700s. They were seated and ordered drinks while looking at the menus. The waiter came up to the threesome and asked what they would like to order, using thee's and thou's in the thickest Old English accent Jack ever heard. As he walked away, the water and drink waiter was there again for refills, and the bread waitress came next.

They were having small talk over soup and salad before their tantalizing Atlantic Ocean seafood dinners arrived, fresh from the ocean to the tavern. Jack asked the bread waitress the history of the building, and she said, "It was built in the seventeen hundreds and was a favorite establishment of famous folks like George Washington, Thomas Jefferson, John Adams, James Madison, and many other founders of the country. There are two buildings, one of which is being used as a restaurant. The other building to the rear of the restaurant is used for storage but also has a small museum in the front. The museum highlights the importance of its visitors who frequented the establishment over the years, from presidents to authors of the Constitution and the Declaration of Independence."

Jack commented, "When I learned that the restaurant wasn't within a few minutes from Langley, I wondered if the trip was worth the ride. It certainly exceeds my expectations!"

For Jack, honoring the special men from America's history who were so pivotal in the United States' fight for its independence from Great Britain was reminiscent of his and many others' modern-day sacrifices. Now, some 140 years later, men were fighting side by side with Great Britain for France's independence.

Jack said at one point, "Six weeks ago, I was a prisoner of war and close to being beaten to death. Then three men I never met before broke into the prison and sprung over a dozen of us. I will never be able to repay them."

"Do you at least know where their families hailed from so someday you can try to track them down through their families?" asked Doug.

"Yes, the sergeant was actually from Harrisburg, Pennsylvania," Jack replied.

Margo said to Jack, "Speaking of Pennsylvania, Doug told me you are from Montoursville. We go to my parents' home in Sunbury often. We're going up that way for the weekend and again for a bit around Thanksgiving. If you can get away for the weekend, we'll gladly run you to and from Sunbury . . . and again over Thanksgiving."

Jack smiled. "Were you a little bird in the old man's office a few hours ago? He told me to find a way home now and be back to work the Monday after Thanksgiving."

Margo said, "Well, then, if you want a ride this Friday evening, we will be leaving for Sunbury from work. If you have any family or friends up home you'd like to visit and can find a ride home from Sunbury, you are welcome to ride as far as Sunbury with us. Your ride to Montoursville could meet you at our normal meeting place, and then we'd bring you home on the Sunday after Thanksgiving. We do it at least once a month, sometimes twice, whenever you're interested."

Jack said with the warmest smile possible, almost with tears in his eyes, "Yes, my Lord, yes. Where and when would my parents need to meet us on Friday evening?"

"We usually meet Margo's parents for dinner at Penn's Tavern in Sunbury at seven thirty," Jack said. "We'd love to meet your folks. Maybe Winnie could come too."

Overwhelmed at his good fortune, Jack said, "This is too much good news to take in at one time."

"You'll have to be ready when you walk out the door of work, no later than two thirty," said Margo. "There's no time to go back to the barracks for anything if we are to make Penn's Tavern by seven thirty. Do you think you'll be able to get out by then?"

"The old man told me I could leave tomorrow, so I'll be ready. As for my clothing, I'm still waiting on my stuff to get here from Paris. It was shipped home from Bordeaux, France. The Germans took my base in Paris and guarded it with a wall of military personnel around the base and the city. The Germans were trying to crush Paris when I left. All my belongings were in a duffel bag somewhere in Paris or on a supply truck driving around the countryside while trying to avoid the Germans when I was shipped home. Had I not been reissued two sets of clothes in Bordeaux, I'd still be in the same clothes I wore for a solid thirty-three days in a row in the POW prison."

Margo laughed. "Yeah, well, you wouldn't be offered a ride in my car if you had them on" she said. "Poor boy! Just two sets of clothes; we'll have to change that too." She said that with a chuckle, probably knowing that would not happen because of blue laws closing stores on Sundays.

Doug interjected. "Maybe Margo and I will go shopping for an hour or so on Saturday before we come home."

Jack said, "If you are serious, I'll call both my parents and Winnie tonight. By the time I get back to base, I'd have some civilian clothes, and my military clothes would possibly even be back from Paris."

Margo smiled. "Yeah, well, I was just kidding you. We don't have room for you." She saw Jack's face drop in disappointment and added, "Don't act like a jackal. Would we have asked you if you wanted a ride if we didn't mean it?"

Jack, looking relieved, said, "Thank you. Thank you very much." He was choked up just thinking of holding Winnie and his mama, and even the first hug from his father, after all he had endured during the past several months. "Thank you," he said again. "You two are wonderful people."

Their meals came, and the dinner conversation was about work, the job, what Jack could expect during training, and Doug's belief that training would not take long because Jack had done the job in the field. They spent the evening getting to know more about each other and exchanging small talk about this, that, and the other thing. Doug tried to guess when Jack would have his first real class to teach since nothing was going to get started until early January.

Jack hoped he was appearing interested and engaged in the conversation. However, when Doug said that he more than likely would not have a class to teach until mid-May, Jack's mind started to wander. He just wanted to finish dinner, get back to the base, and make the call. He was planning the surprise of a lifetime in his opportunistic mind.

On the ride home from Gadsby's, he told Doug and Margo of his plan, and they were thrilled. They were excited to be a part of his devious plot. All he would have to do was to get his dad, who could not see the need for secrets and romantic surprises, to help. The thought was that if Jack could suck his mother into the scheme, his father would follow her lead because he knew that if mama ain't happy, ain't nobody happy. Getting back to Sunbury on Sunday might be a problem since his father would not miss church for anybody, including a visit from Jesus himself should He return to earth, but he would find a way.

When they got back and dropped Jack off, he was sure to say, "Again, thank you for the wonderful evening and the invitation. I'm going in and getting my folks on the phone right now."

Doug said, "Not a problem. Just let me know tomorrow how you make out so we all can start planning. Remember, it's just two days away." Hearing Doug's words, Jack felt his heart skip a beat in his chest and a lump swelling up in his throat.

"Jack, it was great meeting you," said Margo, "and I'm looking forward to hopefully meeting Winnie."

Jack managed to get past the lump of happiness in his throat to say, "I'm excited about all of this. See you in the morning!"

*   *   *

Jack quickly went to the barracks' duty officer's office just off the great room to use the phone. He felt he had to wait a day and a half, but in reality, he waited about twenty minutes for the two others ahead of him to finish with the phone. He did the part of the call he dreaded, and that was talking with Barbie, the local operator. He enjoyed talking with her just about as much as a warm water and salt enema when he already had stomach flu and diarrhea. He swore to his maker that her cackling laugh from hell was as fake as some of the people written about in the Victor Hammond book called *Freaks and Fancies: 1893-1900.* Nevertheless, like a good soldier, he suffered through the misery and had "Cackles the Clown" put his call through to his mother.

Jack's mom answered the phone, and before Barbie could announce the call as she was supposed to do, Jack spoke loudly over her and said, "Mama, it's me. I'm home from the war!"

His mama started to cry. "Praise the Lord, Jackie. Is it really you?"

"Barbie," Jack said, "you can hang up now so my mother and I can have a personal conversation that the town won't know about in ten minutes."

His mother said, "Jack, that's not nice."

You could hear the disappointment in Barbie's voice as she said hello to Mrs. Earl and told her that she hoped she was feeling better.

When she disconnected, Jack said, "Mama, what's wrong with you?"

"Oh, about twelve or fourteen weeks ago, a feeling came over me that your plane had gone down and you weren't doing well. I haven't been doing well since then. Old Doc Steinman said it's depression, but you know your father. He would not hear of the use of that word in this house. He believes that if you put enough faith in God, those blue feelings go away."

Jack said, "Well, Mama, you were one hundred percent accurate. I was shot down in the summer and was a prisoner for quite some time until three wonderful army men broke into the prison and helped us escape. One of them died from injuries he got during the escape, but they saved us. As we speak, I'm in Washington, DC, so you can stop worrying."

"Where are you stationed?" Mama asked. "Maybe we could come and see you sometime . . . unless you can't have visitors."

"I can do you one better than that!" Jack exclaimed. "Can you pick me up at Penn's Tavern in Sunbury this Friday night? My unit commander is giving me till the Sunday after Thanksgiving off to come home and rest."

Mama started to cry just when Papa walked in and saw her crying on the phone. He feared that the notification she had been worrying about had just happened. He fought back the lump in his throat, he approached his wife and said, "Come here, Mama. It was a damn plane that took him, wasn't it?" He hugged her.

Jack said, "Papa, it's me! Papa, it's me!"

Finally Mama was able to mumble, "Rubin Jeremiah Earl, talk to him. It's your son, Jackie."

Rubin got on the phone, and Jack said, "Papa, that's the first time I ever heard you use bad words."

Papa retorted, "Son, that's how much I hate those flying things you go up in."

"I'm home and in Washington, DC, and will be in Montoursville on Friday evening if you can pick me up at Penn's Tavern in Sunbury."

Trying unsuccessfully to hide his enthusiasm, Rubin said, "Just tell me when, and we'll be there."

They made all the arrangements, including getting Winnie there without letting her know they were picking up Jack. Papa agreed with the scheme but said, "I think it best if Mother handles this because it's something out of my league. Furthermore, Winnie would surely know something was up if I called her. I've spoken to her only a handful of times since you left." Everyone agreed that it was too late to call her that night; Mama would call in the morning.

The rest of the conversation was about catching up with one another and Jack telling an abbreviated story of his prison ordeal. Of course, he skipped over some parts, like beating on two German guards that were already tied up, lusting after Dani, killing a German in cold blood to steal his uniform, and stealing a stained glass window out of a house of God, even though it was abandoned. They finished making the plans for meeting at Penn's Tavern in Sunbury at five thirty on Friday.

The rest of the evening passed with Jack lying around wanting to be home again, thinking how just a few months earlier, when he was leaving for the service, he'd wanted to be as far away from home as he could get. Now he was itching to get home.

His mother tossed and turned in Montoursville, thinking who to have over on Sunday to celebrate Jackie being home, not to mention trying to decide which of his favorite meals to prepare for him. She thought that Perry might even come up since the store was closed on Sundays, but maybe he'd want to wait until Thanksgiving to make the trip. Jack's mind raced for what seemed to be hours that night in anticipation of the coming days, and he was sure his mother's was too.

The next morning, Jack confirmed times with Doug. Having spoken only with Doug and not with Margo, he worried whether that was a bad move or not. After all, Doug was a guy, and we all know that men process things differently than women do. Should he try to track Margo down or trust that Doug would handle it?

Meanwhile, up in Montoursville, Sarah Earl put a call through to Winnie. Winnie came to the phone and said, "Hello, Mama Earl. How are you?"

Sarah said, "Jackie called last evening, and as you know, he's home, or at least back in the States."

With the excitement of a child getting ice cream, Winnie said, "Yes, he called. Every time I think about him, I start getting choked up because I want to see him, hold him, and kiss him again."

"Honey, that's why I'm calling you. Rubin and I want to take you out for dinner Friday evening and have a talk. We are discussing taking a trip to Washington, DC, sometime in the next few weeks, and Rubin thinks we should take you if you want to go. We want to see, one, if you want to go; two, if your folks will let you; three, if you can afford a room; and four, when it will be."

"I certainly can go out with you Friday and would love to get together with you for dinner," Winnie replied.

Mrs. Earl said, "I'll need to speak with your mother about all this."

Winnie protested, saying, "I'm almost twenty now, and I don't need permission to go out to dinner with you and your husband."

Mrs. Earl countered with, "Yes, but if we're thinking of taking you to Washington, dear, I need to speak with your mama about that."

With an almost disappointed and defeated tone of voice, Winnie said, "Okay, Mrs. Earl."

"Thank you, honey!"

Mrs. Jadite came to the phone.

"Caroline, hi; this is Sarah. How are you?"

Caroline Jadite responded, "Hi, Sarah. I'm just fine. What wonderful news that Jack is home!"

Sarah said, "Yes, and that's why I'm calling you. Winnie is very much unaware of what I am about to discuss with you, and that's how Jackie wants it. He'll be getting into Sunbury this Friday evening and wants us to bring Winnie to Penn's Tavern. We asked her to go to dinner on the premise of making plans to get down to Washington, DC, for a weekend around Thanksgiving, and we want her to go along to Washington with us, but we'd need to know that she had her parents' permission. I told her that we want her input about the plans for the trip. Jack wants us to walk in around five forty-five, which is about fifteen minutes after he and the couple that is giving him a ride up are seated."

Caroline looked across the room at her daughter, who was sitting there anxiously, on pins and needles and said, "Sarah, that sounds wonderful. Also, keep me in the loop about the dates you decide you are going to Washington, and so long as she pays for half of her share of gas, food, and motel, we will come up with the other half. But you must give me your word that the children won't sleep in the same room."

Sarah gave a nervous chuckle and said, "Good Lord, you certainly have our word on that! Rubin is so God-fearing that I think he would paddle them both even at their ages if they tried any hanky-panky before marriage, especially on his watch."

Without pausing, Sarah continued. "For now, you can just say yes or no so as not to give anything away to Winnie. I can get with you at another time with more details. Would you and Henry like to come over Sunday evening about five o'clock for a welcome home get-together?"

Caroline said, "Oh, yes, that sounds wonderful."

Sarah finished making plans with Winnie as to when they would pick her up on Friday, and then she got off the phone, as secrets were something that were not kept well in the Earl house. In fact, it was going to be everything she could do on the journey to Sunbury to keep her mouth shut about the secret. Maybe Rubin would have to put a muzzle from the barn on her to keep her from running her mouth and giving away the secret for the duration of the trip. Now the only worry was whether Barbie would keep her mouth shut.

Friday morning came, and for Winnie the hours passed ever so slowly and with fear and trepidation, not so much about an evening out with Mrs. Earl but rather about Jack's father. She didn't know him all that well, but his hard, rugged look with his muttonchops reminded her of General Burnside from the Civil War. She thought that muttonchops made men look scornful and even mean. She never saw him smile other than from the pulpit, where he was an eloquent speaker. Other than during church, she'd never heard the man say more than three words at a time. He had a stocky build and huge muscular arms from working the farm. The odd appearance of the man was further emphasized by his dark facial hair, the seemingly black eyes that were set back in his skull, and his receding hairline, with his hair slicked straight back over his head. Frankly, she was scared to death of him and thus had never really tried to talk with him.

Jack was planning the perfect reunion. He would have Doug, Margo, and her parents sit on one side of a table while he was off watching from a corner. When his parents and Winnie came in, he was going to have the hostess seat them together with Doug and Margo because of prior reservations and limited seating. Then, because of his fear of what his mother might say in all the excitement, he was going to quickly come from behind them to Winnie with a bread tray and ask her if he could interest her in warm bread. He would then lean over her shoulder and kiss her neck.

For Jack, it was going from one gorgeous tavern to another in just a few days. Penn's Tavern is an old gray stone building with thick walls and hand blown glass windows, built in the first ten years of the 1700s. Conrad Weiser constructed it, and it overlooked the east bank of the Susquehanna River, near Fort Augusta. History tells us that William Penn's son, John, was separated from Marie Cox, his wife, when she was taken and detained in the midst of raids by savage Indians down river in Harrisburg. It was in this building that the couple was reunited moments before she died. Over the years, it's been a hotel, a ferry house, a post office, a railroad station, and Penn's Tavern. Dining at Penn's Tavern, just like at Gadsby's Tavern, takes one's mind back to historic events that had happened there.

When the Friday evening reunion time arrived, it was played out in real time nearly as perfectly as if it had been rehearsed for days. There was just one slight glitch with Jack's plan, and that was when Winnie nearly slapped the "bread waiter" when he kissed her neck. When she realized it was Jack, Winnie jumped out of her chair to hug him. The rye bread soared over Jack's head, the Italian bread fell to the floor to his left, the pumpernickel flew to his right, and the Vienna bread was still on the silver tray, squashed between their chests. Winnie hugged Jack with so much gusto that she pushed him until he was sitting on the table. Then she started to kiss him with an equal amount of zeal. Jack could hardly breathe.

Doug laughingly said, "Lordy, girl. Let him come up for a breath of fresh air!"

Winnie let go of Jack and sat down crying tears of happiness. That gave Jack a chance to greet his parents. Sarah hugged and kissed her son and was obviously very happy. Rubin did not want to show it, but he put his arm around Jack's shoulder and squeezed it a little. Jack was very surprised at the amount of affection that his father expressed in a public place, as surely he did not approve of the scene he had just witnessed.

The patrons in the tavern applauded when they realized that Jack was just back from the war. All three of the military servicemen received a free meal of their choosing. The people in the tavern purchased two bottles of wine for them, and an elderly couple came over with a New York—style cheesecake. Presenting it to them, the old-timer said, "In sixty-three, when I was only thirteen, my papa died in the Civil War. My mama went loony and was locked up in a nuthouse. Then my brother and I had to go into the war. I was a flag bearer, and he was a frightin' man. This is our way of saying thank you for your service to our country in this day and age."

The families enjoyed conversation during dinner; it worked out as many do. The parents sat at one end of the table and had "boring" adult conversation about the things old folks talk about. Jack, Winnie, Doug and Margo sat at the other end of the table, getting to know one another and having hopes of many visits to come over the years.

CHAPTER

STUDENT AND WRITER

As they parted company to go their separate ways for the next few weeks, Jack and Winnie made plans for things they wanted to do while Jack was home. On the car ride home, his mother told him of her plans for him, and in several cases, the two itineraries just did not mesh. He had planned to go to church once at their church and once at Winnie's. He also had no plans, at least until that moment, for a welcome home party on Sunday, with half of Montoursville present. Jack had planned to do little things like helping his father organize and clean the garage and doing small repairs around the house.

His number one desire and mission for this time of relaxation was to spend every possible waking minute with Winnie, of course. However, whenever he wasn't with her, he wanted to write another story and get it into the mail to *Stars and Stripes*. He thought that if the story was a hit and the right someone read it, maybe Russ would be recognized for what he did.

He wrote an incredibly compelling 750-word story that was a chilling look at the reality of war. The story quickly took his plane from its rough landing on the road behind enemy lines to his weeks of beatings in prison to the incredible recue by the Keystone state boys. It was also about the heroics of a selfless individual who saved thirteen men. Yet once they were safe, that same man walked back into the jaws of the enemy to save one of his own team who was so severely wounded that he could not walk out. As the team leader, he had promised that no team member would be left behind, and he kept his word.

It read like a recommendation to give Russell Kaye a ribbon for his distinguished service. He mailed it directly to Harold Ross, the editor who was also a roving reporter for the *Stars and Stripes* magazine.

He wondered whether the story, being one of thousands like it that Ross and the *Stars and Stripes* might come across, would ever be printed. He decided he would also send the story to Russ's hometown of Harrisburg. Edward J. Stackpole was the editor of the local newspaper, *Telegraph*. Its office was in keeping with Stackpole's personal style. It was in a newly built seven-story office building at the northeast corner of Locust and Court streets in Harrisburg, not far from Russ's home.

As Stackpole looked at the story, he was thinking that it would be great to have the scoop and be the only paper in town to release it. However, because of his respect for the military and the job they were doing overseas, he sent it to Vance McCormick. Just a year earlier, McCormick had founded the *Evening News*, which published its first issue on February 15, 1917. Jack would not find out for several weeks that the article was published in both Harrisburg papers under the title "City Doughboy Seizes German Prison," with the subtitle "Neutralizes Countless Guards in First Special Ops Mission."

There are many old wives' tales such as "Someone is talking about you when your ears are ringing" and "If your nose is itching, you are either going to have a fight or kiss a fool." However, while Jack was on leave in Montoursville, Pennsylvania, there were a number of conversations about Jack that he never knew about.

Once the leave was over and Thanksgiving was behind him, Jack headed back to Langley with Doug and Margo amongst discussions of what was next for Jack.

The next morning, Jack reported to Command Sergeant Major Arthur Garfield's office. He was shown into a meeting room with the old chap, who said, "Welcome back, young fellow! I trust your leave was suitable."

Jack smiled and said, "I got as much time in as I could with my sweetheart, but my mother insisted that every meal had to be at home. She said she was making me every meal I loved, many of which I'm not at all a big fan of. When I was a kid, I'd tell her what how good her cooking was just to make her happy. All of the meals while I was home, however, were better than MREs."

Garfield said, "Yes, nothing is better than home-cooked meals. After all, if it weren't good for you, your mother wouldn't have made it."

Jack said, "Oh, yes, this is true, but there must have been a gazillion times when I was growing up when it was hard to swallow some of her cooking."

Garfield grinned at Jack. "Youngster, I told you a million times to stop exaggerating."

Jack's eyes widened because he finally recognized one of the old guy's off-the-wall idiotic one-liners that he had heard somewhere else before. *Okay, now we are starting to communicate on a level I understand*, he thought. He said, "Your Thanksgiving, sir—how was it?"

Garfield said, "Wonderful! Christine and our son-in-law, affectionately known as "Fat Cook", put a feast on, and all the kids were in with their families. Food was dandy, sort of like candy, and the adult boys and men played the grandchildren in the annual Garfield family football game. The grandkids won five to three, and it only cost one twisted ankle, three sore backs, and five damaged prides. The fathers and outlaws have to wait a year to try getting the title back and eat humble pie from the crumb grabbers the rest of this year."

He continued, saying, "It appears, however, that you were doing more than neckin' dirty with your lady friend and eatin' your mom's food."

"What do you mean, sir?"

Garfield pulled a folder out of his desk file organizer. "Well, it seems you are a regular Robert Louis Stevenson. I see you wrote your own *The Strange Case of Dr Jekyll and Mr Hyde* . . . or your own personal *Treasure Island.* I have copies of the two articles you wrote to *Stars and Stripes.* Good work."

Jack was puzzled because he had sent both articles to Kansas City and somehow copies were at his new duty station, so he asked, "Who gave you copies of my articles, sir?"

Garfield smiled. "Did you have the feeling folks were talking about you last Wednesday?"

Jack said, "No, sir."

"Well, youngster," Garfield said, "you had company the day before Thanksgiving by some folks from the *Stars and Stripes*, wanting to talk with you about a job as a reporter. They tend to believe you could be more of a help to them than to me. If you wrote these on your own without that little lassie up in Montoursville doing the writing while you talked, I'll tell you that you are gifted."

"Thank you, sir. I wrote them by myself," Jack said. "However, I don't understand how I'd be able to do any substantial writing on a serious basis for them if I'm assigned to you. Did they give you any sense as to what they're looking for?"

"It's like this, Junior," Garfield said, almost as if he were talking to his own son. They told me from soup to nuts what they are after. However, they want to talk with you about this project, and it's not my place to try to interpret what they said. I'm just telling you that before you bite down on the bridle's bit and get started this morning, you are going to be interrupted a few hours from now by the guys from *Stars and Stripes.* We all know that the hurrier we go, the behinder we get. Since you're a writer, I thought you might like to work on a military Christmas card/newsletter until they get here. I want them sent to bases throughout the country."

"Do you have general notes that you would like me to work with for the newsletter stories since I know nothing about your base or department?"

Garfield was almost like a kid in a candy store when he handed Jack a manila folder that he'd worked on all through Thanksgiving. He had even made a rough sketch of his idea of how the card would look. He pointed to a table at the other side of the room where Jack could go to work, telling him to let him know if he had questions. Garfield said, "You make me happier than a pig in mud."

Jack started to work on the card and, being inspired, clipped right along. His first story was about the effect on Langley when they learned about the eleven o'clock on the eleventh day of the eleventh month armistice ending the war with Germany. It sported a cartoon of Santa and the reindeer riding on a German tank that was flying a white flag as it passed through Langley's front gate. Next was a story about the hundreds of men being shipped back to the states to bases even when only limited military jobs were available. Third was a story about older soldiers being given gifts of early discharges to make room for those coming home from the war front. Jack found himself in his element; it was an aspect of himself that he never knew existed until most recently.

Unsure of the expectations of his superior, Jack would check with Garfield for clarity, and the old gent was thrilled beyond expectations. Garfield said, "Son, your writing is so smooth that you could piss off a skunk eating dinner in a dumpster and the end result would be perfume from Paris. Get confidence in yourself, boy; you're *great*."

Jack asked, "Sir, has your family ever written down the Arthurisms you say? It would be fun to write a whole book of them."

"What would we call it, *The Idiotic Blurbs of a Twisted Green Mountain Boy*? Who would buy such a thing?"

"Don't sell yourself short, sir," replied Jack. "Your humor is catchy and keeps folks on their toes. At first, I thought you were losing your mind, but now I look forward to our conversations."

Garfield said, "Don't get used to them. Good things don't last forever."

Jack asked, "What's that supposed to mean? Are you one of the ones being forced out?"

Garfield's aide walked in and said, "Sir, the folks are back who were here last week asking about . . ." With that, he stopped talking and jerked his head in the direction of Jack. He hid his right hand from Jack's sight yet visible to Garfield and pointed at Jack.

Jack stood there looking at the aide with a grin on his face as if to say, *What the heck? Don't you see me standing here?*

Garfield said, "Show them in. Jack, clear the table so these gentlemen can sit down at it."

The aide escorted the visitors in and left the room. Jack did what Garfield asked as the two gentlemen walked toward the table. The captain, Captain Early, looked over his shoulder at Garfield and said, "Command Major, are you joining us? Sergeant Earl is your soldier."

Garfield said, "I'd like that. This will be very interesting."

Captain Early situated himself and asked, "Well, Command Major, what have you told the good sergeant about our visit?"

Jack looked at his watch and said, "About an hour and fifteen minutes ago, he told me that some people were here to talk with me the day before Thanksgiving, and that they were going to be here again today. Other than that, I know nothing."

Corporal Saul Goldberg, know to all as "Goldie," looked at Captain Early and said, "Note this, sir. His writing is superior bar none, and it is detail oriented and organized. He wants things done on a schedule that he doesn't like to have to waver from."

Captain Early said, "Whoa, whoa, hold on now, Goldie. He has no idea who we are or why we are here. He may not even want to speak about this." He looked at Jack and said, "We are with the *Stars and Stripes* magazine, and I would like to talk with you about the two articles you sent in recently, one more so than the other."

"Did I do something wrong?" Jack asked. "Did I offend someone? Am I in trouble for something I wrote?"

Early replied, "No, no, and no—and quite the contraire my friend. You caught someone's, the right someone's, eye. If you know anything, you know that Harold Ross is the chief editor of the magazine."

Jack nodded his head and said yes, simply waiting for the next shoe to fall.

"Ross is hoping to start a program called the French War Orphan Relief Fund," said Early. "His eyes fell upon the article you wrote the other week, and he wanted us to speak with you about a possible position on *Stars and Stripes*. You would take a six weeks' TDY to take a journalism course, though it looks to me that you do not need it. You'd work out of Langley with a two-person staff. The staff will be Corporal Saul Goldberg." He pointed at the other gentlemen at the table and continued. "And the other corporal, not yet back from the front, is Corporal Charles Warren."

Jack asked, "Would I be working a dual assignment, with my duties and responsibilities to my military instructor job along with added responsibilities to *Stars and Stripes*?"

Garfield chuckled. "As soon as you're done with my Christmas letter, I'd release you. I wouldn't mind staying in contact with you to have you do my writing of important stuff. Beyond that, you just need to write my book. Ha-ha! As I told you earlier, we will soon have a large influx of troops coming back from overseas and needing jobs. I see no need to have one person taking two positions. If you take this *Stars and Stripes* gig, you will be transferred to the Army Journalism Corps."

"Let me explain something to you," Early said. "As of today there is no *Stars and Stripes* magazine office in the Washington, DC, area and there will not be one for some time to come. Eventually, your office will be in the American Red Cross Building. That is being built now, and the grand opening will be sometime in May. The three of you will eventually be in a small but adequate office in the Red Cross's new building. You will be on a TDY for a few weeks in journalism school, and then you will be stationed here until our DC office opens."

Jack looked at Goldie and asked, "Are you stationed here at the present time so I can pick your brain over the coming weeks if I agree to this?"

"No, Sarge, I'm not," Goldie replied. "I'm up in New York and will be training under Harold Ross when he gets back to the States. Therefore, once I'm down here, I'll be the office manager and make your life easier. If you agree, we will see one another several times a month because you'll be up there for meetings with Captain Early and Ross. You'll also be up to New York to meet with Warren when he gets back stateside, as well as being at monthly staff meetings and a few special meetings."

Early said, "Yes, you will be attending a journalism course, but you will find that much of what you will be doing will be supporting fund-raising activities. Your audience will include several major newspapers, churches, entertainment events forthcoming, men's and women's groups, and events asking businesses to pass the hat at work on payday, et cetera."

"What exactly am I raising funds for?" asked Jack.

Early answered him. "Ross is introducing his new pet project, a fund for French war orphans. He saw your article about your feelings toward things you saw in France and sensed that it could have possibilities, especially with the inclusion of the young French woman you met. The negotiation is complete, and the venture is between the *Stars and Stripes* and the American Red Cross. It will be announced on December sixteenth."

"No disrespect intended, sir; the intent is swell," said Jack. "However, who will really be the recipients of these funds? Will the children or the French government control the funds? If there is no guaranteed way to get the money to its intended recipients, the government could see to it that only twenty percent goes to the children and eighty percent to rebuild the infrastructure or to some frivolous venture."

"Sir, please wrap this one up and bring him home; this is exactly the kind of guy I want to work with," Goldie said.

Early grinned. "Goldie, relax! Jack, I like and appreciate that question. It says a lot about the character of the man. Jack, I'll share something interesting with you. That is the first factor that Ross addressed when creating this program, thus the reason to build it through the American Red Cross rather than the French. The fact that you think along the same lines as Ross does tells me you would be a good fit for this program."

"If I may ask, what did Harold Ross see or experience that started him thinking about a program like this?" Jack inquired.

"Marie Louise Patriarch was a young girl taken in by doughboys on the front line as their mascot," he began to explain. "Both of her parents had been killed by the Germans, so she went wherever the soldiers went. Several weeks ago, when they got orders to come home, they personally put money in a bank trust at an orphanage, and she will receive it when she comes of age. They went to *Stars and Stripes* and met with Ross to get help from the magazine to raise money back home to send her to college. This started his wheels turning to do the same for all children in France affected by the war. It's to help out children who were fathered by our soldiers or orphaned, ones whose fathers have been left crippled and unable to work . . . or children left crippled or homeless."

Jack asked, "If someone gives money, what proof do they have that it goes to a child?"

Goldie responded, "They can adopt a specific child from the area where their loved one was if they had someone there or just pick any area, any age, or any sex. They will get the child's photo and the history of his or her situation. The American Red Cross will go into their schools and homes regularly and send progress reports about their lives. When the children are old enough, the donor can communicate with them directly. The money goes toward food, clothes, medical care, primary and secondary education, and housing."

Jack looked straight at Garfield to read his face and pick up any clue as to what he was hoping Jack would do. One thing he learned about the old man right then was that he had a great poker face. Jack had to make this decision on his own. In what seemed to be twenty minutes but was probably less than a minute, Jack said, "Okay, I'm in. What's next?"

He saw a smile come to Garfield's face. "Congrats, junior," Garfield said. "Now you owe me a book titled *The Idiotic Blurbs of the Twisted Green Mountain Boy.*"

Early and Goldie looked at one another and then at Garfield and Jack. The captain asked, "Jack, is he saying that you are already a published author?"

Jack chuckled and said, "No, No. A moment before you got here, I was joking with the command sergeant major that someone needed to write a book about his humor. So I guess I just got another job as well."

Early laughed. "You're definitely referring to the witty one among us, the one who comes up with crazy one-liners like 'I've been better, but I don't remember when.' Then there's the first one he ever said to me: 'I'm doing well for a man of my age and habits.'"

Goldie said, "This is the one that had me scratching my head: 'They think I'm two days older than dirt, but I'm a mere child, because when I hit sixty, I shifted out of third gear and put it in reverse. The engine seems to be running finer the younger I get.'"

Garfield said, "If I had half a brain, I'd think you were picking on me. But that would be fine 'cause you'd be leaving someone else alone."

*   *   *

The day was turning out to be so surreal. Jack remembered taking on the role of a salesman with his parents a year or so earlier. He'd tried to convince his religious parents that he wanted to assist France because the Germans were destroying France's countryside, even if it meant personally going there with the military.

It was a hard sell because he knew his father did not approve of any invasion by the United States, either from an economic or from a theological standpoint. He preached that the war was not our business and that Americans should stay out of it. He repeatedly referred to James 4:1 and 2. Using his own interpretation of the Bible verses, Jack would say, "Where do wars and fights come from? Do they not come from human desires for pleasure? They lust t for that which they do not have, they murder and covet yet cannot obtain. They fight and war, yet they do not have because they do not ask." He would continue, trying to make the point that our government needs to stay out of this mistake.

In all actuality, his father's words fell on deaf ears. Jack's eyes were simply blinded by the star struck notion that this was his chance to get into the skies. Jack's salesmanship was focused on the concept of aiding the French men, women, and little children from a missionary standpoint or like a battlefield angel for the American Red Cross, which had been a household name since 1881. When Mama and Father Earl heard the words "angel" and "Red Cross," their minds started shifting. Jack was winning a straight-up nomination for the Nobel Prize for twaddle. He got into the sky for a short amount of time. Now these men walked into his life offering him the opportunity to be an angel and assist children from the war with the added benefit of being involved with the American Red Cross.

Within days, Jack was once again transferred, but this one was a fantastic move for him. They decided to send him to a regular college setting, where there was the active Student Army Training Corps. Jack had no say about the location where he would attend school. Although Jack's hometown and other such information was not known, Jack was told that he would be going to Bloomsburg State Normal School because Captain Early was partial to their program. In a few quick weeks, Jack was to take a full load of five courses, all related to journalism. He would also do some writing assignments for *Stars and Stripes* as part of his formal training and in preparation for his new job.

The school that Jack was to attend was north of Selinsgrove, Pennsylvania. It was originally formed in 1839 as an academy teaching elements of a traditional education. After having several different names, it was currently known as Bloomsburg State Normal School. This is where Early got his formal education, and he had friends on the staff there. The Bloomsburg Bison Battalion military heritage dated back to 1863, when Bloomsburg's student voluntary organization company assisted in halting the Confederate tide at Gettysburg. Their military pride has marched firmly forward, including involvement in World War I and the formation of the Student Army Training Corps.

While attending Bloomsburg State Normal School, Jack found a room in a boardinghouse owned by a Native American Indian squaw by the name of Bubbling Hot Springs. Her white man's name was Carol Helms, and she taught domestic skills in the Bloomsburg State Normal School. She was one of the many Indians gathered up to attend Carlisle Indian School in Carlisle, Pennsylvania, an hour south of Bloomsburg. Bubbling Hot Springs was originally from the San Luisenos Mission in California. After her father died, her mother could not continue to take care of her, and she sent her daughter away. She was several years older than Jack was, as she had been born in 1883. She graduated from Carlisle Indian School in 1904 and registered at Bloomsburg in 1905 for teacher training.

Jack met another interesting chap, John Bakeless, through Carol Helms. He was also a few years older than Jack was, and he was already an up-and-coming journalist at the Bloomsburg Morning Press. John was born while his father was an instructor at the Carlisle Indian School. Later his father became a professor at Bloomsburg State Normal School. John was also working part-time at the paper, and he helped Jack get a freelance job there. The job assisted Jack in meeting his financial obligations, and at the same time, he got extra experience in journalism. It didn't exactly allow him to be at Winnie's beck and call, but in general, he greatly enjoyed this phase of his life.

Jack wrote about Bloomsburg area events for the newspaper and was on the run from one location to another. He also submitted stories to the *Stars and Stripes,* attended classes, and completed homework assignments. He eventually had to explain to his boss at the newspaper how demanding things were and that he would have to slow up a bit so he could keep up with his classes, homework, and other school-related activities. His boss told him he would work with him, as he thought Jack was a good addition to the paper.

Winnie had her hopes set on spending a lot of time with Jack during the time he was in Bloomsburg. They were now only an hour apart, but with his schedule, it just didn't happen. Winnie was thinking with her heart, and Jack was thinking with his head. Teaching aerial military reconnaissance was a field that would keep him in the military. College courses gave him the option of getting out of the military and following a civilian literary career.

He wrote a story about a campus special activity. There was a buzz about a memorial, the pergola at the science hall, donated by the class of 1913. It stopped Jack in his tracks, as it was a memorable addition of seven stained glass windows. They took him back to France and the small side window he took for Russ from the church where Benji died. The stained glass windows for the chapel were in honor of the efforts of Professor Oscar Bakeless.

When writing the story about Professor Oscar Bakeless, Jack not only used interviews with several students, but he also used personal input from Oscar's son, John, to humanize the article. This also resulted in a strengthened relationship with John.

The weeks passed quickly, far too quickly for Winnie, as she was hoping that there would be talk of wedding bells or possibly a ring—at the very least, a hint that marriage was on Jack's mind. However, the subject never came up. Jack found time to be together with Winnie, but it wasn't nearly as often as they had thought it would be. Even worse, all Jack could think of to talk about was whatever article he was in the process of writing. When he wasn't talking about that, he'd be chattering with excitement about his pending job with the children's fund.

At one point, as she stroked his neck with her fingertips and kissed his ear, she said, "I wish I were one of your articles and one of those kids over there so you would get that excited about me again."

Because he was so absorbed in his new life and unaware of what she was hinting around about, Jack said, "Winnie, if I didn't know better, as hard as you're breathing, I'd think that you were having an asthma attack. Do you not feel well? I can go if you're not."

Winnie threw her hands in the air and said, "Good Lord, Jack, you might as well go. You're not here anyhow. Do you even know that I'm in the room?"

Jack looked at her dumbfounded and said, "*What?* What is your problem? You're acting strange. Maybe I should leave so you can settle down. Sometimes I just don't understand your high-strung personality."

This misunderstanding happened the evening before Jack took a journey to New York City to meet at the corporate office of the *Stars and Stripes*. There would be several busy days of meetings in preparation for the coming setup in Washington, DC. Jack's time in New York did not help Winnie's mood either.

Jack had dropped a few subtle hints to Winnie about marriage but did not produce a ring. Nevertheless, Winnie and her mother began to plan a wedding in Montoursville for May of 1920. The wedding wasn't to be within the next month—not even for another year—and it was not even on Jack's radar screen yet. However, when Jack said, "I want to spend the rest of my life with you," when they were in church on Christmas Eve, Winnie had all she needed to start planning their wedding day.

Jack didn't know what to expect, as this would be one of his last meetings before the drop-dead date of going back to Washington, DC. This was to be the meeting where the announcement of cooperate structure was being made.

He wasn't sure the structure was going to end up as Early and Goldie had originally told him. It might not put Jack on the top of the DC office pile. His understanding was that Chuck Warren was still in France, working with *Stars and Stripes*, when all this started out. He was then assigned to the American Red Cross when the program was set up. He was now in New York, training under Hank Ross. What this meant to Jack only time would tell.

He had arranged with Goldie to share a room in a local hotel, the Pabst Grand Circle Hotel, owned by the Pabst Brewing Company. It was a combination theater, hotel, and restaurant at the northwest corner of 58th Street and 8th Avenue. Just the thought of Jack staying at a hotel owned by a brewery put a bur in Winnie's craw and agitated her. She could not believe that it wasn't really a boys' drinking weekend.

When they weren't in meetings, Jack and Goldie were too busy exploring the town to worry about dumping suds down their throats. They went to Times Square just days before Christmas. At the beginning of WWI, Times Square was already the center of the Theater District, attracting many tourists just like Jack and Goldie. It was certainly a great spot for billboards. It was here where many businesses started placing large electric billboards, something Jack and Goldie had rarely seen, and they wanted to take it all in.

However, they had plenty to talk about when they hiked to Times Square. During breaks in the meeting throughout the day, they asked Chuck to join them on several occasions, and he acted as if they were subservient to him. He was now a civilian and placed himself one step ahead of both of them, dressed in their military clothes. Chuck strutted in his navy blue Norfolk double-breasted lounge jacket with oxford-gray pleated trousers. It was highlighted with a white, soft-collared shirt and an oxford gray flat bowtie to match the pants. He was also sporting black-and-white walking shoes.

Jack leaned over and whispered one of Garfield's Arthurisms to Goldie: "Something stinks in Amsterdam, and it ain't a Dutch oven."

Goldie snickered and whispered back, "That sounds familiar. Is it Shakespeare? But what stinking Dutch oven are you referring to?"

Jack surreptitiously pointed at Chuck and whispered, "He dressed to the nines in his civilian clothes, making us look less important than he is. We're talking about who will be assigned to which positions in the corporate structure. Who would you pick?"

Goldie snickered and said, "Oh. I just thought he was an ass. After all, look at Ross's unrefined clothing selections and his demeanor. Oh my Lord."

As he glanced at Ross, Jack had to bite his lower lip to keep from laughing in the middle of the meeting. He was wearing a god-awful burnt orange double-breasted tweed jacket. It was tight fitting over his chest, sported wide lapels and a lighter orange-colored silk hankie stuck out of the breast pocket. The long jacket flared out over his hips. His cream-colored silky shirt had pearl-looking buttons; a floppy bow tie matched his pants. His pants were baggy at the top and slimming from the knees down, with cuffs, all done in chocolate-brown and cream plaid. One could say that the outfit bottomed out with brown-and-white wingtip shoes. All of this was topped off with a sailor's cap, giving the look of "Mr. Used to Have Money" stepping onto the *Titanic* for his last journey.

Jack thought to himself, *How can I take this meeting seriously when the guy running it looks like a clown out of the Ringling Brothers Circus?* Just then, a paper was passed around, with the corporate structure appointing Chuck to head the Washington, DC, office for the collection of funds for the French War Orphan Fund. Jack was to be the assistant. Captain Early was the district representative between the northeast offices. Goldie was just a staff organizer, and there was a young woman that Jack had not met yet, by the name of Francesca (Frankie) Finklestine, not Finkleston. She told everyone that she was Jewish, not German.

Chuck spent some time discussing how the program in France would work. Jack had already written a story of interest about a need for a program similar to this, and what Chuck said wasn't what Jack had been hoping to hear. The fancy clothes and the pompous attitude of the speaker weren't helping much either. Jack figured this must be a side show for what God had in mind for him. As the assistant, he would be flying around a lot. He would have limited time with Chuck, and poor Goldie would have to put up with him every day.

The concern in the back of Jack's mind was the claim flying around town that Ross was a literary fraud. Many thought that anyone who dressed and acted like Ross could only be playing the part of an editor. Though the paper in the United States was already ten months old, many questioned how long Ross could keep it going. His critics said that he could not pull off the rigorous duties of producing a major magazine potentially viewed by all of America's population.

Ross openly discussed the comments of his critics at that meeting and provided them with a resume of his journalistic skills and abilities. Ross had been around print since 1908, when he started writing for his high school paper, the *Red and Black*, in Salt Lake City. As a teenager, he got a part-time job running errands for the sports editors of the *Telegram* and the *Tribune*.

Ross quit school after ninth grade, another reason his critics doubted his abilities. However, at that time, he went to work full time for the *Tribune*. In the summer of 1910, Ross left Salt Lake City, looking for adventure. He took up riding the rails and started as a freelance author, as a "tramp reporter," for newspapers across the country. A year later, he went to work for the Sacramento Union. His adventure took him to Panama City and then to New Orleans and Atlanta. In 1916, he was back on the West Coast, working part time on the *Call* and the *Post*.

Therefore, as one can see, Ross was no stranger to at least some aspects of the newspaper business. Most critics' comments were about his hopping from one job to another. With clothes like those he was wearing that day, no wonder so many people thought Ross was a joke.

As the war dragged on and the United States got involved in the spring of 1917, Ross enlisted in the 18th Regiment of Army Engineers. He was sent to France with the masses, and he quickly found himself working on the *Stars and Stripes*.

When Ross returned stateside, he agreed to settle in New York City to revive the *Stars and Stripes* in the States. He ran the paper, but his main pet project was to use it as a tool to continue to build the fund for French War Orphans. Because of his seemingly singular focus on the fund, there was significant concern about his abilities to cover all the important topics.

The last thing discussed was the fact that though they were working for the *Star and Stripes* magazine, the stateside edition was to be called the *Home Sector.*

Ross did his best to try to convince everybody that he was a responsible, reliable boss, but Jack walked out of the meeting with many of his questions unanswered. He vowed to himself to do his job and to work with Chuck on the French War Orphan Fund to the best of his ability for the sake of building his resume, although he wondered how long the magazine would last. He hoped it would last until he was out of the service in sixteen months, in the spring of 1920.

Jack sat in his office on a daily basis, sending freelance articles to several newspapers up and down the east coast, promoting the mission of the War Orphan Relief Fund. He asked for donations from philanthropic companies, community groups, and individuals. Occasionally he would even be asked to speak at the newly founded Lions Club, which was started by a young businessman.

Melvin Jones, a thirty-eight-year-old Chicago businessman, asked a simple question one day. "What if people put their talents to work improving their communities? What could happen?" In response to such questions, he created the mission of and founded the Lions Club in Chicago. It slowly but surely started to catch on in one major city after another, eventually even in more rural areas.

Jack was given the duty of speaking at many of their monthly meetings in several different locations up and down the east coast, as he was still in the military. It was thought that a man in uniform would help the pitch for donations sound more attractive. He didn't mind, as he was getting both of his passions put together, journalism and flying. To keep him in the air and going to different cities, he took the initiative to seek out other venues to speak at as well. He was often found speaking at meetings of the Chamber of Commerce, Knights of Pythias, and Kiwanis Clubs, not to mention his presentations at several large business conventions.

There was a subcontractor near Baltimore who worked with the American Red Cross and provided air time for them up and down the coast. On March 29, 1918, the ten-passenger F-1 seaplane debuted. It was built as a war plane but the war was over before it came off the assembly line. It was an instant success, but the end of the war destroyed their market. For Jack, however, it was fantastic; all he needed to do was to plan events by a body of water and he could get air flights in that he so desperately wanted and enjoyed.

When he had downtime between trips, Jack was searching for another person important in his life. He had started to think about getting married in a year or so, but he wanted to find Russ first. Jack knew that almost everyone was out of France by now, and that Russ would probably still be in the service for another year.

In a conversation with Ross one day, Jack suggested introducing a section in the paper called "Find Your Old Foxhole Friends." Ross told him that he'd take it under advisement, but Jack sensed that it fell on deaf ears. It seemed apparent that Ross was blowing smoke out of another hole, for it sounded much like one of the many empty promises Ross made.

Jack quickly saw that Ross was a guy who wanted you to do all the work so you'd make his resume more impressive. There were all too many of those people in the world, but before working for Ross, Jack had believed that they were all politicians. He knew that his idea about finding foxhole friends would almost surely not see the light of day because it was Jack's idea. Jack figured that he could just submit the section and then take the wrath of hell if it failed. On the other hand, if it was a great success, then Ross would put out an article thanking soldiers for using his newest idea.

Ross would no doubt take total credit for Jack's idea of a forum to assist soldiers in finding their buddies. Then it would be one more thing that Jack could not put on his resume, as it would be in writing that Ross founded the program. Jack thought long and hard about the idea and ultimately figured the heck with making Ross look good. He'd use his own sources to look for Russ.

CHAPTER

PLANNING A SURPRISE

Jack hit a home run on his first attempt to find Carver. Carver was easy to track down because Jack remembered that he was being transferred to Fort Ord, on Monterey Bay Peninsula in central California. He asked Carver over the phone, "Have you talked with Russ since you have been back?"

Carver answered, "I've done better than that, my friend. He was in Weed Army Community Hospital at Fort Irwin near Los Angeles. I've seen him three times. He has even met my wife."

"I'm dumbfounded!" Jack said, completely stunned. "I know our time together was short-lived, but Russ told me a lot about you when we spent time on the run in France. I feel like we've been friends for years, and I didn't even know you were married, engaged, or seeing someone when we were over there."

"Oh, no, man, I meet Mela when I first got back to America. She's a Native American Indian from the Muwekma Ohlone tribe. They migrated west as we . . . Wait just a minute. When you guys, the white men, pushed them away from the east coast." Carver said it with a chuckle, and Carver continued, "She is the daughter of a man who is several generations removed from a chief."

"Do you mean Russ was at the hospital?" Jack asked. "He wasn't *in* the hospital was he?"

"Yeah, Russ was shot," Carver responded. "Didn't you know that?"

"No, I had no idea. I'm trying to find him. Where was he shot?"

Carver replied, "In the Battle of Vittorio Veneto on November third."

Jack laughed and said, "Yeah, okay, okay, jackass. Got ya. But I wanted to know where on his body he was shot."

Carver also started laughing. "Oh, so that's what you were asking? He was on another mission to free some prisoners and was rushing a farmhouse. He was running through a creek, and when he broke into the open, he took fire. He and his patrol got to the other side of the creek but were pinned down for about three-quarters of an hour.

Jack asked, "How big of a patrol was it?"

"It was twice the size of ours, six in all, but they were going into an active battle to take out Jewish prisoners in the hands of the Germans. The write-up by Jeffers said that he displayed rare courage and leadership. He led an advance that enabled his patrol to take their objective. He single-handedly took out two German pillboxes, which was reported by the patrol officer on the field, Second Lieutenant R. M. McKelvey."

Jack laughed again. "That's BS! Russ had a second lieutenant out there with him. Who do you think followed orders from whom?"

Carver said, "McKelvey said that when they got across the water and in the open, that's when all hell broke loose. There were several well-camouflaged machine guns on the ridge in front of them. They were pinned down by machine gun fire when five of them safely made the shoreline.

Jack asked, "Did they lose one or was he wounded?"

"He died," Carver continued, "but Russ went back in the creek to get him while under fire and made them carry him out. Under direct orders from McKelvey not to do it, Russ broke for some evergreens up the hill. He inadvertently exposed himself to some Germans with machine guns and took direct fire. He dove to the ground, crawled within thirty-five yards of them, and tossed a grenade into their laps, wounding one and killing two others."

"This sounds so much like the Russ we know and respect."

Carver said, "Oh, yes, but it gets better. Russ gagged the wounded German, got a length of Benji's leather strap out, and tied him to a tree facing in the direction that he was going so the guy could watch as his patrol was at the foot of the ridge. Russ once again exposed himself to open fire to locate another machine gun pit. He crawled within twenty-five yards of it and threw several grenades at them, killing two more and capturing two, this time at gunpoint. He made them walk down the hill to his patrol with his gun pointed right at their backs."

"Was he trying to get killed?" Jack asked.

"No, but it ain't over yet. He continued up the hill to a dirt road and spotted a sniper in a tree below his position on the road. Russ aimed down on him, and from his hip, he let loose with his machine gun. Russ continued to fire even as the German fell from the tree like a ruffled grouse during hunting season. Russ waved the patrol forward. As they advanced, they gathered their first prisoners. Russ had the objective in sight just up the road."

"This is great stuff for what I'm planning for our reunion."

"He started advancing on the house where the prisoners were, in the face of incoming fire from several windows," Carver continued. "Firing back at them, Russ got to a few vehicles just outside of the building, and his patrol started firing heavily on the house. The firing put on the house by his patrol allowed Russ to get the attention away from him long enough to get to the rear of the house and enter the building alone. Once inside, he killed two more German with Benji's pig sticker. When his patrol got into the building, it was obvious that Russ sliced the one's throat and then ran it straight through the other German's back and out the other side."

"This is the kind of stuff heroes are made of! But how did he get shot?"

"Well, it's not really known, but what Russ told me was that he freed seven Jewish prisoners. Once they were together, his patrol, the Jewish American soldiers, and the German prisoners were ready to move out. Russ took a minute to dump some water and a stone from the creek out of his boot. Turned out he had blood and a piece of his ankle bone in that boot."

Jack said, "This is an incredible story. It needs to be written up."

Carver nodded. "He was stabilized over there and sent home by Thanksgiving. My wife and I went to the hospital and had Thanksgiving dinner with him. I visited him a few times in December, and just before Christmas, he was sent to Walter Reed Hospital in Washington because he was transferring to DC to work in intelligence."

"Good God Almighty!" exclaimed Jack. "That's where I work now!" He began telling Carver what he was planning for Russ, Carver, and the memory of Benji. Jack was planning to put them in for at least the Army Distinguished Service Cross Medal. I'd even like to go for the Medal of Honor, but I guess I don't have the clout for that."

Carver said, "Well, Jack, thank you. Even though Benji died because of the mission, its success was all due to Russ. To award either of us for his actions would be unjust. Don't get me wrong. If I can come up with the money and the time, I'll be there for Russ, but I would have to decline sharing in that honor."

Jack said, "I assure you, you will be there, even if I have to pay for it myself."

Several days passed after Jack's conversation with Carver, and without Russ knowing a thing, Jack spoke with Russ's commanding officer in INSCOM (US Army Intelligence & Security Command). Because the department was so huge, it was likely that Russ had never spoken to this man. He was right; Russ's commanding officer had no idea who Russ was yet.

He agreed to look into Russ's record and work with Jack and the *Stars and Stripes* on a ceremony. He said he'd do that for anyone under his command. He asked Jack to send him the information on the two missions as he knew it; he would help in whatever way he could. He'd even write letters for the ribbons, but he agreed with Jack. He did not believe the actions were worthy of the Medal of Honor.

Jack went to work locating Russ's parents. He got Pop on the phone. Before Jack could explain who he was, Pop decided that Jack was a salesman of some sort, and he said, "I don't deal with this kinda crap. Do you want my old lady?"

Jack said, "Well, yes, sir. That would be fine."

Pop continued holding the phone close to his mouth and yelled at the top of his voice, "Mae, some jackass is on the phone selling something. Get rid of him."

Mae was coming across the room, saying, "Well, if you don't want to talk to him, why give me the phone, you old grouch?" She answered the phone. "Hello, we don't have the money to be buying anything."

Jack said, "Mrs. Kaye, I'm not a salesman. Your husband didn't give me a chance to tell him who I am. I'm a friend of Russ's. He saved my life in France."

Mae excitedly said, "Oh my goodness! Is this Jack? Little Russ's father and I loved the article you wrote! Many of our friends commented on the article as well."

"Yes, ma'am," Jack responded. "Thank you for the compliment, but I'm calling to talk to—"

Mae interrupted. "He has told us a lot about you, but he and Dani just left to introduce her to some of the relatives. He will be so happy you called. Dani will soon have the baby, you know."

Jack said, "But, ma'am, I had no idea he was at home, and I'm calling for you and his father. Russ cannot know about this call. We are planning a large surprise for him. Sort of like the surprise you just gave me."

"What surprise was that, Jack?"

"Dani . . . and a pregnant Dani at that! How, when, why did all this happen?"

"Oh, didn't you know about that?" Mae asked.

"No, Ma'am," Jack said. "The last time I saw or spoke to Russ was about two weeks after we met. I was with him when he met Dani, but we clearly left her behind."

Mae said, "Well, they must have done a little hanky-panky when you had your back turned. Russ left her with child and with our contact information."

Jack's mind was reeling. *They did a little* hanky-panky? *He gave her his mother's address? Are they married? What about her father and brother and the farm?*

Mae continued as if she could hear what he was thinking. "It seems as if someone told the Germans you guys were there and they came looking for you. She was in town when the Germans rushed the farm. They torched the farm, trying to burn you out. They executed her papa and brother before leaving. She was devastated when she returned from town. It just so happened that Russ was back her way for some late night mission a few weeks later, but he could not tell us what that mission was. Russ and Dani communicated the best they could, and he sent her home to us."

Jack snickered to himself about the secret late night mission. He decided that Russ's mom was blind in the mind if she didn't pick up on the implicit message being spoken there. He said nothing about that but instead asked, "Have they gotten married?"

Mae said, "Well, it just so happens they are getting married in two months, and I know he'd love to have you there. Could you and your wife come in for the wedding?"

"Well, ma'am, I'll soon be engaged but we're not married yet, and I don't know if we can come. I also need to get his surprise finished before his wedding or I can't come, because he can't know anything at all about my being in the area. If I could do all of this before his wedding, I'd be honored to come. However, I cannot speak for Winnie, my fiancée. But I will ask her the next time we talk and let you know."

Mae was clearly excited. "Tell me more about this surprise."

Jack, with a certain amount of pride in his voice, said, "I'm trying to get him either the Medal of Honor or the Army Distinguished Service Cross Medal for his bravery during the prison break-in. I recently heard about a second raid he led on a house where they were holding several Jewish prisoners."

Mae said, "Really? See, Pop and little Russ don't tell me these things for fear I'll worry. How many fellows were in the break-ins you speak of?"

"Well, during the one where he saved my life, there were three soldiers on Russ's team, and they saved thirteen prisoners. In the other one, where Russ was shot, there were six on his team and seven prisoners. Both times, he was the lead person calling all the shots. For the second mission, there was even an officer who was following Russ's lead."

"When is this ceremony? We might like to come to it."

"I'd love to have you there, but a date hasn't yet been chosen," Jack said. "Based on your news, I'm going to try to make it happen before the wedding. Any soldier wants a ribbon like that hanging on his dress uniform at his wedding. I now have your phone number. Let me give you my number so we can communicate over the next several weeks. I have no number at home, but at work, it's Washington, DC, number two-three-eight-eight. Frankie will always answer the phone. I'm often not there, as I'm anywhere from Massachusetts to South Carolina two or three days a week for work. However, I will get back to you as soon as I can."

Mae was enthusiastic. "This surprise party sounds exciting! Can I do anything for it? Little Russ loves my pepper cabbage. Would you like me to make some for the get-together?"

Jack chuckled. "No, ma'am, this event is not that kind of get-together. I'm sure we will be going out for a nice dinner afterward. However, the function will be a very dry military event with a lot of pomp and circumstance. The only excitement is going to be when his commander leads him to believe he has been chosen for another secret mission. The two or three others involved will play along that they are also chosen, and he'll be brought forward alone and presented the award by me. But until the award ceremony, he won't even know I'm there."

Mae said, "Well, if I can talk Pop into going down there, we'll be there."

"Hopefully you can," Jack said, "because I'd love to meet you and am really looking forward to seeing Dani again too. You know my job is helping children—not so much those of Dani's age but nonetheless children who lost their families due to the war. The program also provides financially for children fathered by our GIs or children crippled by the actions of the war."

"That sounds like a wonderful job," said Mae. "Let's keep in touch, and I'll start working on Pop. Though it really isn't the Christian thing to do, keeping a secret from little Russ . . ."

Jack pulled the phone away from his ear, and with a queer look on his face that wrinkled his eyebrows, he pursed his lips and twisted his nose. He looked at the phone, thinking it was like talking to his parents, and said, "Then we won't call it a secret. We'll call it a surprise."

She giggled like a schoolgirl and said, "Okay, Jack, it is a surprise, then. I'll call you in a few days to see how you're getting along with the planning of the surprise."

*   *   *

Days passed by, nearly two weeks in fact, with nothing after Jack's conversation with Mae Kaye, and then suddenly Russ's commander placed the call. Frankie took the call Jack was waiting for; however, Jack was away in Myrtle Beach, South Carolina. It was the commander of intel.

Frankie said, "Sir, Jack is on a southern tour of six cities and will not be back until late Friday. He asked me to get information from you. Then I can get hold of him so he can call you between meetings."

The commander said, "Let Jack know than Bernie called. We got the Army Distinguished Service Cross Medal, not the Medal of Honor. I've received the okay to use the officers' club from sixteen hundred hours until seventeen thirty on the Wednesday before his wedding because he already applied for leave for the wedding starting Thursday, May 8. His wedding is on Friday, and he has to be back on duty by Tuesday. He has my number; have him get back to me."

Frankie tracked Jack down at his hotel that evening, and Jack followed up with a call. Jack was getting in on Friday evening, and the commander invited him to dinner Saturday at the officers' club to show him what the facility offered and to start planning the scheme to get Russ to stay around later that evening. Of course, Jack needed to make all the plans to get Russ's family there. At this point, the commander knew nothing about getting Carver's and Benji's parents there, who they were, and why they were significant.

He made a call to Carver and asked him to come. Carver had the time, though limited, but saving enough money for transportation was a big stumbling block. Jack said he would look into a few possibilities to help Carver out, see if he could pull a rabbit out of his hat, and get back to Carver.

On his way home Friday afternoon, Jack was not going to sit in one of the ten-passenger seats any more than the man on the moon was made of green cheese. He crawled into the copilot seat as he generally did and carried on conversation with Donnie, the pilot of the F-1 seaplane; he was from Baltimore. Jack did this to get an education about flying a plane as much as anything, as someday he wanted to fly his own plane. This time was different, as Jack was on a fishing trip of sorts in the sky.

Jack asked, "Donnie, do you know how I can fly across the county twice in a week and not pay much money?"

Donnie laughed like a hyena, and his belly started jiggling like that of the traditional Santa Claus. He started passing gas like the popping of fireworks in unison with the high notes in his laughter as he said, "Who wants to know? Is it legal? What's in it for me? A dozen cases of beer since this Prohibition crap is in place may spark an interest to talk a bit further. Prohibition has taken my suds away. Help me out there or put fuel in my plane and you can get damn near anything from me. Why do you want to fly across the country to that God-forsaken place? It's going to fall off the face of the earth someday."

"No, no, it's not me needing to fly," Jack clarified. "I want to fly a friend in for an award ceremony for the man that I've told you about who saved my life. In fact, he's the other guy who broke into the prison to free us; he also lived to tell about it."

Donnie said, "He's a hero, and he'll be on my plane. I'll work out the details to get him here and back; you work on the beer. Get as much suds as you can get without getting my buddy Jackie in hot water and the fuel for the plane is on me. It's the least I can do for a hero. I'll let you know what I come up with. I just need the dates you want the package to travel."

"I'll need him here on Tuesday, the sixth of May, and he'll be going back the weekend of the ninth or tenth."

"I'll call you at the office when I get one of them there i-tin-er-knee thingy-dingies together listing travel times," Donnie said.

Jack chuckled at Donnie's attempt at pronouncing "itinerary." He said, "Aye-aye, Captain. I'll go to work on getting some good old Montoursville Hidden Mountain Logger for you. It's made in Loyalsock Creek's hidden stills. It may not be what your palate prefers, but it's much better than rotgut."

Donnie said, "So long as it's a step up from the skunk piss I'm drinking now from a Tennessee favor I called in, we'll be good."

A few days passed, and on Monday, Donnie called Frankie and said, "Is Jackie pooh about?"

Frankie all but spit her coffee across the room, as she could not see anyone ever having the nerve to call her boss Jackie pooh. She said, "Just a minute, please."

Jack came to the phone after a brief pause. Not wanting to discuss the delivery of illegal alcohol on a government phone, Jack quickly put a halt to a conversation that may have led to questions later. He said, "Donnie, thanks for calling me back so quickly, but I'm tied up right now. Is there any possibility we can meet later this evening? Tonight I'm going to dinner at my brother's, over near you. Maybe you could come by and talk with me there. It will be there, at Perry's, where your package will be shipped next month."

Although Donnie was not the brightest light in Maryland, even he could read between the lines, and he said, "Sure, Jackie pooh. Where does Perry live?"

Jack asked, "Do you know where the A&P Grocery store on Main Street in Columbia, Maryland, is?"

Donnie replied, "No, but it shouldn't be hard to find. It's not like there are a dozen grocery stores in any town around here."

"Meet me there at five thirty. That's where my brother works, and we'll go to his home from there."

Donnie said, "How did you make out with—"

Jack interrupted him, thinking that maybe the light bulb had burned out. "Donnie, I'm too busy to talk right now. Let's talk tonight."

Later, Jack was driving his 1911 Chevy series C Classic on the not-so-unusual ride from the base over toward Baltimore, the route he often took for work or to go to his brother's for dinner. He realized that this would be the first time his Baltimore contact was going to meet him halfway and be introduced to Perry. It wasn't long until he and Donnie were standing in the parking lot of the A&P about ten minutes before Perry was done with work.

Donnie said, "Not knowing your brother, I wasn't sure whether I needed to dress up, so I did."

Indeed he did, and he fanned his hands down over his pudgy—well, fat—body as if he were a model. He had on a powder-blue silk Jasper shirt with large puffy sleeves, wide royal-blue suspenders, and a formal Wyatt Earp-type bow tie that surely did not go with the rest of the outfit. This was covered up by a nice-looking light brown tweed vest. That was only problematic because it was worn unbuttoned by a large specimen of manhood who may have last buttoned it eighty pounds ago. Jack had to scratch his head and wonder if the baggy black bloomer-style pants or the summer straw dress cap with a burgundy ribbon was the most ridiculous mismatch to the rest of the outfit.

Jack could only smile at his friend and say, "You're a handsome Hector. I know Perry will be jealous of your outfit."

Moments later, Perry walked out of the store still wearing his butcher apron that hung almost to his shins. It was covered with blood from wiping his hands on it during the day. He came around the corner of the store and into the side parking lot. The brothers embraced and did this silly little head slap to one another, asking one another how their weeks were.

Jack introduced Donnie to Perry, and without missing a beat, Perry firmly shook hands with the total stranger. Coyly yet sincerely, Perry said, "Damn, don't know you from Adam or Eve, but I want your job if you can afford to dress in duds like that."

Donnie said, "Well, thank you! Your brother must really know you because he said you'd be jealous of my clothes. This is what being a pilot buys you."

"Trust me. Jack has not a clue what I'm really thinking," Perry assured him.

Jack said, "Oh, bro, I can almost guess what you're thinking, but I'm headed to your house to see your lovely wife and eat some of her famous meat loaf.

They went to Perry's house for dinner and enjoyed a tasty meal. Adele excused herself after dinner conversation to clean up the dishes, and the men went out to sit on the porch to talk. Perry said without much hesitation, "So my brother wants a favor from you, and your payment method could cost him his military career and reputation."

Intimidated by Perry's approach and the boldness in his tone, Donnie was not only taken back but also a bit scared as to the possibility of having walked into a trap. He said, "We could discuss other payment arrangements if we have to. I don't wish to cause problems."

"Ain't a problem with me," Perry said. "My other two brothers, Jeff and Max, will take care of all of the questionable things to be done up there, and I'll have it sitting in the old barn over yonder for you. You will pick it up while I'm at work by backing your vehicle into the barn. You will not carry it out into my yard. Adele must not know anything about it, so I'll let you know when she'll be out playing bridge with girlfriends. We'll just keep Jack out of the whole process. Can you live with that?"

Donnie said, "It all sounds great to me."

"We can only get you eight cases of quart bottles," Perry said. "Max said it's going to have to be four cases on one run and four more cases a few weeks later in order to meet the demand up home from others and get you taken care of too. He does not want to raise suspicion with authorities. Max thought to keep it fair, either he or Jeff would bring you the first half a week or so before the trip and then the other half when your job is done."

Donnie grinned and said, "That's fine with me."

"From this minute forward, there will be no further conversation on Jack's work phone—or mine, for that matter—about this," Perry said. "Jack is totally out of the payment arrangements except your discussion of fuel cost, and if you need to talk with me any further, you will call me and only me at my store and order a nice pot roast to feed five. I'll tell you when to pick it up, and you'll meet me at the store at that time. Is this all understood?"

Donnie said, "Well, I can't always afford pot roast that large. Could we make it for two? Other than that, it is crystal clear, sir."

Perry laughed and said, "You aren't really ordering a roast. You're asking for a meeting. When I tell you the time to pick it up, I'm telling you when we can have a meeting in the parking lot of the A&P."

Donnie said, "Oh, damn! You must think I'm dumb."

Nobody said a word at first. Then Jack said, "Okay, so how are we getting Carver here and back?"

"Well, it was tricky," Donnie said. "I had to rely on an old drinking buddy of mine. Major Reuben Fleet was in charge of army pilots in the war, like Walters and Boyle, who took the first US mail operation the other month. Seems these fellows are using surplus war planes like the de Havilland DH.4 biplanes to deliver mail across the country."

Jack said, "I wasn't aware that was completely up and running yet."

"It really isn't. Nevertheless, with Fleet's connections and it being for a ceremony for a war hero, he jumped in hand and foot. My only cousin, Derek, does what I do here, just on the west coast. He'll take the Los Angeles to Phoenix leg. Another fellow drops water in the event of a fire in the mountains of Colorado. He'll fly him from Phoenix, Arizona, to Denver, Colorado, for three dollars in fuel, so long as there's no fire burning in Colorado at the time. From there, Carver will catch a mail plane into Omaha, Nebraska. That's where the mail service ends right now, but Major Fleet asked another war pilot to take him to Chicago, Illinois. I have relatives out that way that I can visit and hang around for a few days if I need to, so I'll take the Chicago to Baltimore, Maryland, leg. You can pick him up by car there and get him to Washington, DC. Going back, I'll fly him from Baltimore to Chicago, and everything will be exactly in reverse from his trip east."

"Sounds hectic," said Jack. "Are people waiting if one or another leg is running late? Also, when will he leave and when will he get here and vice versa when returning?"

Donnie said, "The only leg we need to worry about is the airmail delivery from Chicago to Omaha, and Major Fleet tells me not to worry; we're all military, and we're there for one another. Carver would have to fly back Wednesday, right after the ceremony, or on Friday, which means he would have to miss the wedding. If he stays for the wedding, we'll fly him back on Monday. Both coming and going, he will need to leave by zero four thirty and will land at the final stop about zero eight thirty the next morning. The flying time will be about twenty-five and a half hours, at speeds of just over one hundred miles per hour."

Jack decided that Carver would decide how long he stayed. With that, the conversation switched gears totally, as Adele served her own desert concoction on the porch. Many people living in the Montoursville area are aware of the Amish folks' shoofly pie. Well, Adele made her own version of that, except in cake form. It was a molasses-type cake with a wet bottom and crumbs on top of the cake layer. It was to die for, and she made it because she knew Jack loved it.

When the get-together ended later that evening, Jack took Donnie with him to return him to his truck, which he'd left at the A&P. They had small talk about the French War Orphan Fund and flight plans, which he found somewhat funny. Jack laughed to himself as he thought that Perry must have scared the hell out of Donnie with his orders about not talking about his payment for getting Carver to Washington, DC, ever again.

Nothing of excitement happened for Jack over the next several weeks. He gave a few speeches in New Jersey about the children's fund and had a meeting with Henry Ross in New York. He also had several conversations with Carver to arrange for his flight. As for the plans for the bestowing of the Army Distinguished Service Cross Medal, he was made aware of event times and seating arrangements. Jack asked who was going to attend the program from Russ's family and friends, and Russ's commander was handling all the pomp and circumstance. Jack's only part in the program was a five-minute speech on how Russ saved his life and what it means to him.

It seemed like the dinner with Donnie, Adele, and Perry was just a few nights earlier when Jack found himself picking up Carver in Baltimore for the big event. They talked on the way back about how everything was going to unfold. Russ's family, Dani, Benji's parents, Carver, and a few other friends were going to be seated from a side door just as the program started. Jack hoped that Russ's attention would be on the speaker and that he would not turn around to see what the commotion was all about.

*   *   *

Russ believed that he was being considered for an important mission and that one of the five men he was sitting up front with would be chosen. The other four were in on the caper. They would be eliminating the men one at a time, explaining what qualities they had that put them in contention and what they lacked for the mission. Jack was to be hidden in the back to give a brief statement after Russ was on the stage staring at the press core, other officials from base, his bride-to-be, his family and friends, and fellow GIs from his squadron.

It seemed that almost as quickly as they discussed it in the car, the ceremony was unfolding in prime time. The ceremony fell together as perfectly as the conviction and the hanging of three Molly Maguires in Bloomsburg for the murder of Alexander Rea, the founder of Centralia, on October 17, 1868. Though the hanging happened more than ten years after the murder, planning this event took less than ten weeks. However, it felt like ten years to Jack. He anxiously waited to see Russ again. Just as Centralia was founded and built around an active coal mine back in 1866, this event was built around our own little Molly Maguire, who was a bit cocky and not afraid of anyone.

One by one, the five men were eliminated, and only Russ remained. The commander asked Russ to come forward. As he stood up, he gave an ever so quick glance to the others in the room. Russ noticed that many in the room were in civilian clothes, but he did not look hard enough to see any faces. He thought it strange that so many civilians worked on base. As he walked to the stage, he wondered what secret mission would have this many people involved. Russ immediately knew that something was up when he found himself standing on the stage staring at his mother. Mae Kaye was on the edge of her seat, looking as if she were going to wet herself any minute. With her sat Dani, Pop, and his little brother, Cal.

His commander came forward and simply said, "Sergeant Kaye, I guess you are seeing some familiar faces here. You probably realize that something special is happening but that there is no special mission. Someone would like to say a few words about what's going on, and then we will continue."

As the commander was speaking, Jack walked out from behind him, and the two men saw each other. The commander said, "We have a special guest speaker for today's gathering, a man who says he owes his life to Russell Kaye."

Russ looked dumbfounded at the commander, still wishing this were about a special mission, but at the same time, he was puzzled as to why his mother and father and even Cal and Dani were sitting in the audience. Right beside Dani and his family was a fellow that in the lighting looked like Carver, but he thought in the back of his mind that it couldn't be. He was in California, after all. They all looked alike anyway. There was a black couple with them, but he had no idea who they could be. It was not like Pop to sit willingly with black folks. After all, Pop was a real racist—not the hood-wearing, cross-burning kind, but bad enough that sometimes it even made Russ uncomfortable. He looked back at the black man and thought, *Holy hell, that is Carver!* Confusion was the best word for the moment.

As the commander continued to talk, Russ and Jack made eye contact, and then they hugged one another and greeted each other. The commander introduced Jack, and then he stepped forward and said, "You can continue your mutual admiration party later. Men in the military don't hug. Let's get through this first before the MPs arrest you both."

Being the more insightful of the two men, Jack suddenly felt a lump welling up in his throat. He knew that he would have to make a joke of some sort to settle everyone's nerves.

Jack turned to the audience and said, "My name is Jack Earl. This guy and Carver . . ." He pointed at Carver and said, "Stand up so others see who you are. Russ and Carver, along with another wonderful man, Benji, who couldn't join us, as he lost his life in the mission, saved my life. Benji's parents are also here today." He motioned to Benji's parents to stand which started the entire audience clapping to recognize Benji and Carver. Jack continued. "The three of them broke into a fully staffed prison and ruined a German guard's routine exercise class that I was involved in. A few Germans over in France were using me for their personal punching bag. One might say that they were the ones exercising; I was just getting beaten to a pulp. Once they were tied up and gagged, Russ allowed me to take out some of my frustration on them. By the way, Russ, thank you for that."

A few folks who knew the story chuckled, and the others were in awe, as if it were like a rookie ballplayer getting the walk-off grand slam in the bottom of the ninth to win the important game. Jack relaxed and was able to move forward.

"What you are about to witness has been a goal of mine since the day I got on a ship to leave France. Once I found out that Russ and I were stationed at the same base, thanks to Carver, I've wanted to look him up. I've resisted because I would have ended up telling him about this day. I even called his parents one day, and unbeknownst to me, he was on medical leave and staying with them. His mom told me I missed Russ and Dani by moments. We went to work that day. Mae and Russell Sr., thanks for your help."

He paused for a moment and looked around the room before speaking again with a slight hesitation. "See, three men—Russ, Carver, and Benji—risked life and limb to break into a castle that the Germans were using as a prison to free thirteen prisoners of war on a special operations mission. I was being beaten across the face with leather gloves because I would not give them answers to questions that I truly knew nothing about. The three of them, Russ, Carver, and Benji, with a little help from me, incapacitated the two guards and locked them in a room. With a bit more work and taking out four more guards, twelve prisoners got out safely, although one man was shot and killed by guards. Benji was the only one injured. One of the prisoners was assigned to help Benji get to a waiting barge that would take us to safety. He left Benji lying at the edge of the trail to save his own life, because Benji was slowing him down. Benji's leg was almost blown off, and it was bleeding badly."

He paused and looked right at Russ. A warm smile came to Jack's face, and he put his hand out in the direction of Russ. "This man risked his life again with me at his side. We went back looking for Benji, into an onslaught of dozens of Germans looking for us. Benji was shot, needing help and left behind somewhere. I found out later that Russ promised he would get all three of them back or they would rot together behind enemy lines. I went with Russ to rescue the fallen liberator because his leadership was infectious.

"We spent over a week never knowing from one moment to the next if we would get back to the base where Russ started. He made some incredible decisions to keep us safe during that week, a few that I disagreed with and called him out on, but they turned out to be the best for all three of us. Having no medical background, Russ and his wife-to-be right back there—Dani, please stand—performed emergency surgery on Benji, which gave him several more days of life he otherwise wouldn't have had. He died with Russ cuddling him in his arms like a child and praying over his soul in the chapel of a church."

Jack looked directly at Carver and said, "Carver will agree with me on this next statement. Russ was a man of his word when it would have been easier and safer to bury him in the church graveyard. Again, he promised the two men going on this mission that they would all come home or none of them would come home. Because of all of these actions, I initiated paperwork for him to receive the Army Distinguished Service Cross Medal. Carver declined being included because he believed Russ was the driving force." Jack then asked Carver to come forward with him, and they all shook hands. Jack and Carver stepped back and stood at ease to watch the ceremony.

The commander stepped up and first said, "Sergeant Kaye, I guess you have figured out this has nothing to do with a special mission. The gentlemen sitting there with you all agreed to play a role in this special event so it could unfold this way. It was all him, your friend Sergeant Earl, who did this. I am too damn conservative to do all that cock and bull. It may be good theater for the boys in the liberal media out there, but I'm a true Teddy Roosevelt Rough Rider. Part of me died when Teddy died back on that cold January day in 1919. I followed the orders of President Wilson, but he was a liberal and I am not. Teddy would not put on a show like this. Wilson would, so who am I to say what these events are to be like. Now Warren Harding is at the helm, and although he is a republican, he reminds me of a throwback of Wilson. There, I said it. It's out there for the benefit of the media. Now we will get on with the real program."

Jack was standing there thinking what an ass this guy was. Did he ever have any fun in his life? Jack glanced around the room, reading the faces of the people. A good 75 percent of them looked as if they agreed that this guy's underwear must be too tight around his waist.

The commander went through the pomp and circumstance of a formal program. Though it had its moments of splendor, Jack had to wonder how much the Russell Kaye he knew was enjoying this part of his program.

The commander started out by saying, "Russell Kaye, you were awarded this honor because you went above and beyond the call of duty, selflessly rescuing other soldiers by breaking into a fully staffed prison with only two men. Even with the German army searching for you, you went back to rescue one man who was left for dead. You risked personal injuries, imprisonment, or death. Wear it proudly, knowing that this medal represents the thanks of a grateful nation.

"The Distinguished Service Cross is awarded to a person who, while serving in any capacity with the army, serves with distinguished honor," he continued. "That's how Sergeant Kaye differentiated himself from others with his extraordinary heroism. While engaged in an action against an enemy of the United States in this military operation involving great conflict, he opposed the foreign force numerous times. The two acts of heroism noted here involved extreme risk of his life and were so extraordinary that they set his actions apart from those of his comrades."

He continued like this for several minutes. The more the commander said, the worse Jack felt for Carver and Benji as well as for Benji's parents because the praise was all heaped on Russ. Jack even felt a touch pissed. By the time the commander was done, Jack was having second thoughts about why he ever even wanted the commander involved with the ceremony.

The commander seemed to be showboating for his own personal military jacket because one of his people was receiving the second-highest award in the military. Jack should have known from the moment the commander started with his political pandering where this was headed, especially when he said, "I'm a dyed-in-the-wool Republican, and the fellow that planned some of this program must be one of those candy-ass liberals." This was as far from the truth as it could be. It was just that Jack was more relaxed and wasn't walking around every day of his life with a Rough Rider saddle glued to his ass.

It came time for Russ to speak after accepting the medal, and Jack couldn't make eye contact with Russ. All Jack was hoping was that Russ remembered to include Carver and Benji in order to help redeem the burning pit in his stomach caused by the commander.

Russ stepped to the microphone with a blank stare, as if gathering his thoughts, and said, "Mama, I'm sorry that I never told you how rough it was over there. I just didn't want you to fret. Pop, thanks for being so hard on me. You made me the man that I am. Your efforts helped me get where I am today. Cal, I thank God you were too young to be there and see what my eyes have seen."

With that, Cal eyes were getting glassy, and Dani reached out, put her hand on the back of Cal's neck, and started massaging it, for she knew all too well the pain of what Russ was referring to with the loss of her daddy, brother, and the farm. He continued by saying, "Other than the friendships forged there, the only good thing to come out of that war was my soon-to-be bride, Danielle Aimèe, meaning beloved one . . . and she is."

Russ continued, saying, "Getting the medal was a solemn moment to remember the loss of Benji, someone that through the short time we spent together I came to think of as a brother. His ultimate sacrifice to me is what defines the word 'hero,'" he said. "For that reason, I don't think I have done anything beyond my duty." He nodded toward Benji's parents. "Mr. and Mrs. Greene, it is your son who is the true hero here. I will never forget him, and I believe he is here with us and with me every day of my life. I swear that the day I was shot, I felt his presence ever so strongly."

Benji's father sat paralyzed and crying, but his mother stood up and said, "Russell, our son is no longer here to wear a ribbon on his chest. You are. Your acknowledgment of his contribution to the mission is the entire honor I'll ever need to have . . . and to hear from you and your lovely wife now and again. She has shared with us all what the two of you did to try to keep him alive and the loss she has incurred in doing so."

For the benefit of the press and his commander, Russ said, "Dani suffered great losses for trying to help us. Just days after we left, while she was in town getting groceries, Germans came to her family home looking for us. They executed her brother and father and burned their farm to the ground."

You could have heard a pin drop. Then there were the flashes of cameras taking pictures of Russ's family. To get the press back into what was happening on the stage instead of on the families, Jack said, "After the program, remind me that I have two things of Benji's that I would like to return to you." He paused and then said, "I thank everyone for your time today and will turn the program back over to my commander."

His commander was more relaxed when he came back, as he noticed that the others made informal presentations, taking the program in a very different direction. Within minutes, the program was dismissed after a short benediction.

Doing things in the quiet and unassuming way that Jack usually did, as soon as the awards ceremony was over, he had the families gather outside the officers' club. Then he introduced Winnie to all his friends. The group began getting to know one another. Finally Jack said, "Folks, folks, we have reservations for ten people for seven thirty, and it's a half-hour drive from here. If we left two minutes ago, we might get there on time, so chop—chop!"

They rode in three cars to the restaurant and were seated. Russ was worried about Pop breaking bread with Benji's folks and Carver. For Russ, Dani, Jack, and even Carver, it was a special time. Dani and Carver hardly knew one another, with the exception of sitting together during the awards ceremony. Cal may have felt like the odd man out, but he and Dani were pretty good buddies. When she and Russ married and settled in Langley, Cal was going to be lonely for the sister he never had.

One thing Dani knew from living in Harrisburg with the folks and Cal: no two brothers are exactly alike. Cal was soft-spoken, and he wouldn't think of swearing. He was short and chubby but not fat, and he was balding at nineteen years of age. Pop regularly accused Cal of shaving through the screen door. Even after years of ridicule from Pop, Cal was a sensitive young man, and he would tear up easily. In many ways, she saw her little brother in Cal.

Russ, on the other hand, had an opinion about everything and did not mind cursing to make his point. Nor did he hold back on cussing someone out to let him know he was not happy. He was tall and lanky, with wavy brown hair. He had just turned twenty-two years old and was clean-shaven. Just the opposite of Cal, Pop's ridicule turned him into a pompous ass from time to time. He would sooner pick a fight than walk away from one. He had steel-gray eyes that many women were attracted to, but his Dumbo ears probably could carry him away on a windy day.

Dani asked if she could say grace, and it was a lovely blessing:

Dear Heavenly Father, Thank you for our gathering here today as we break bread for many reasons. We come not only, O God, to You as a source of health and healing, with the loss of my family and our beloved friend Benji Greene, who gave his life for the cause of the French and the United States. With Your hand, we also ask that you guide us through Your Spirit to a place of calmness. Grant to us a consciousness of Your dwelling and surrounding presence as we live with them in our hearts, that we may permit You to give and us to accept Your health, strength, and peace, through Jesus Christ our Lord.

Thank You for bringing Carver safely here from California; they tell me it is far away. And thank You for allowing the Greenes, Mom, Pop, Cal, and Winnie to come together to celebrate Russ's award and our wedding Friday. Also, thank You for the food we are about to take, that it might nourish us and make us strong. I ask this all in the names of our Father, Son, and Holy Ghost, my Holy Trinity. Amen.

The meal went well, and Russ started to relax, for he realized that his father was on his best behavior and that he was not going to make any racist jokes or slurs. Russ wondered what drug Mae had given him. Then it happened. It wasn't about race at all, but Pop said, "Russ Jr., I guess once you are hitched, you'll become one of those God-fearing skirt clutchers who blindly follow the little woman to Sunday school, church, Bible study, and church choir. It'll do you some good and keep you out of bed so you don't have forty kids. I'd be chasing her all the time if I were you. You know what they say about French girls."

"Pop, don't be such an old letch," said Mae. "Behave yourself."

"Woman," he said, "just because there is snow on the roof don't mean there ain't fire in the furnace."

Mae said, "Well, there must have been a quick spring thaw. In case you haven't looked lately, there's not any snow on the roof any longer—or there's nothing in the way of insulation between the ears and the furnace melted the snow."

Everyone laughed at the old-timers' insult session with one another.

CHAPTER

A WEDDING, JOBS, A HOUSE, AND A BABY

The Benji's parents accepted Russ and Dani's request to drive up to Harrisburg for their wedding. They were getting married at the Fourth Street Church of Christ in Harrisburg, at Fourth and Delaware streets. It was a treat for many who had never been there, as it sports the only New England-style curved wooden pews in the city. They were less-than-comfortable seat for the long-drawn-out Christmas and Easter services. However, the wedding was short, sweet, and to the point; and the beauty of the church enhanced the photos taken that day.

Russ, of course, wore his drab olive green dress uniform and cover for outdoors. The jacket was adorned with five ribbons and his marksmanship pendent and infantry logo standing out more than the gold buttons on the jacket. His tie and pants both matched the drab olive green jacket. The only other colors in his outfit were the khaki shirt and black shoes.

On the other hand, Dani wore sandals and a beautiful yellow princess-style gown with intricate lace on the skirt and bodice. Mae was persistent that for something old, she would wear the pearl necklace that had been in the Rodgers family for years. Her beautiful raven hair was up in a bun, into which greens, white-and-yellow daisies, and bright yellow buttercups were interwoven to match the bouquet she was carrying.

Cal, Russ's best man, was dressed in his Sunday best, which was really a hand-me-down suit from Russ, with the seams let out since Cal was heavier than Russ was. Jennie Lee Rodgers, Mae's youngest sister, who was twelve years younger than Mae was, was the maid of honor, and she wore a dress that was a similar style as Dani's. The bodice of Jennie Lee's dress was a slightly paler yellow than Dani's was, and the skirt portion of her dress was a pale asparagus green.

Mae's oldest brother, Bill, the favorite of many—and said by all to be the only normal one of the boys—was always at the house for Sunday dinner, and he became very fond of Dani. Dani was also smitten with Bill and his family but absolutely fell in love with his youngest two children. Little Georgie and Sally Jane were the obvious choices for the ring bearer and flower girl. They both wore yellow tops and matching green-and-yellow handmade bottoms. Georgie had knickers on, and Sally wore a skirt.

The wedding was quite unconventional for a wedding of the time since Dani's *père* and *frère* were killed by the Germans in the raid and massacre. She wanted to have as normal of a wedding as possible, and being so far along with child, she needed something to ground her wedding.

She went on a search for someone to give her away but did not have to look far; she turned to her best friend in America. Cal would play a strange role in the wedding. Not only was he his brother's best man, but his first important role was to give his friend and intended sister-in-law away.

Cal's chest was nearly bursting with pride. For one of the first times in his life, he was feeling the joy of being important. On the other hand, there was Pop, wishing she had asked him since he was a father. He was not her father but a father nonetheless. It told him loud and clear, without words being spoken, that people did not appreciate his attitude—and that she cared more about his favorite punching bag, Cal, than he ever did.

The wedding ceremony was touching, and from time to time, it even brought tears to folks' eyes. Reverend Bentley from the Fourth Street Church of Christ preformed as beautiful a service as one could want. The tear-jerking part came when Father Philip from Sacred Heart Roman Catholic Church spoke.

He spoke openly about the joys of life and how grasping the Trinity, and how the belief in its power of the Father, Son, and Holy Ghost makes a difference in one's life. Among other things, he talked about Dani, who had lost everything material through the hell of war. She had grasped on to the Trinity she'd learned about in church, and it changed her life.

He spoke of the orphans like Dani, and even younger, who were created by the Great War, crippling hearts and creating wounds and discussed what others must do to help them. He encouraged people to reach into their hearts and their purses as they do at his church, giving graciously to the American Red Cross for the French War Orphans Fund.

Jack was stunned by what he was hearing. Winnie was holding his hand, and she tightened her grip, digging her nails into his hand. They all walked away from the wedding feeling the effects of the war and how strong people can move on.

The reception wasn't much in the way of a formal affair. Many of Mae's friends from the fire hall made their favorite dishes; it was a simple buffet of picnic-type foods. Some of Mae's brothers also made hamburgers.

Paxtang Fire Station, a brick two-story building at 336 South 2nd Street, was right behind the hospital and by the train bridge. It's where Mae's brothers ran fire calls. It was part of the volunteer fire company, which was deferred to by all other companies in the city because they were fearless on the lines in a fire. They were known to get in fistfights at fires in order to be the ones to walk into the orange crush first. However, this day, they were like little puppy dogs, trying their best to make Russ and Dani's day special.

It was a bittersweet parting for Russ when they left for their short honeymoon. He didn't want to leave Jack and Carver, but he quickly realized that with married life, certain things would change. He now had a wife who needed his attention too. They were spending two evenings at the New American Hotel in Mauch Chunk, where folks like General Ulysses S. Grant, President William H. Taft, Buffalo Bill, Thomas Edison, and John D. Rockefeller had spent time. Dani was a bit uneasy about the trip, as many people said the inn was haunted. Some folks said chairs were turned upside down while guests slept, items were moved around, and orbs and shadows appeared in photographs. There were stories about small children seeing ghosts. But they enjoyed themselves and saw many relaxing sites, and the mountains in the distance made it even more serene.

The problem was that, as with all good things, reality stepped in and it was back to work. The weekend was much too short, and it seemed the entire ceremony was for not. Dani went back to living with Mama and Pop, and Russ went back to the base. At least he could now go on the list for base housing because he was married. However, he knew it could be months until housing came through; he just had to wait.

Time passed slowly. Other than the few times he met Jack after work and his weekends at home with Dani, Russ was miserable. It was funny because he had never really cared about having a relationship with a woman before, except for male libido urges, but this woman had gotten to him.

As the beginning of June, Jack and Russ met for midnight chow at the chow hall on base, and Jack mentioned that things were not good for him at work.

Jack said, "Russ, a year ago, on February eighth, the paper started in the States. At the one-year anniversary, circulation was at a half million in the States. Ross took over in December, when I came on, and rumors floated about him and his inability to make the paper run successfully. As quickly as the rumors started, so did the troubles under Ross's management. If the *Stars and Stripes* paper goes away, what will become of my job?"

"Come on, Jack," Russ said. "You're worrying about stuff that may never happen. You're the sensible one of the two of us. Keep that positive attitude."

Jack spit his juice across the table. "Talk about keeping a positive attitude! You're so miserable that you could make an optimist cry."

Russ used a few colorful attitude words that always seemed to flow out of his mouth with the ease of milk from a fertile Guernsey after having a newborn calf. The two of them laughed at one another when they realized that two nurses were within earshot of them. The big difference was that Jack's face was also red from the embarrassing language.

As Russ bit into his egg sandwich, Jack said, "Do you eat with that mouth?"

Russ nodded his head, and after he swallowed, he said, "Yep. I even kiss my wife with that mouth."

A couple more weeks passed, and on June 18, it seemed they were still in the same place. They were both as miserable as a couple at a summer evening beach gathering that is infested with sand crabs, and to get away from them, they plunged into an ocean full of jellyfish.

Russ was still on his tirade about base housing . . . or lack thereof. He'd checked earlier in the week, and he was suddenly 112th on the list, when he had been down to 97th a month earlier. It seemed that several folks who outranked him had transferred in. He was disgusted and thinking he would never have Dani with him. What was he going to tell her over the weekend?

On the other hand, Jack went to a meeting only to find out that his biggest fear had come true. Under the leadership of Henry Ross, the *Stars and Stripes* was shutting down. His job in the military was over. What was he going to do? They were going to have several meetings over the next few days to find out what was going to happen with the staff.

Over the next several days, Jack was told that within weeks he would be parting the military unless his intent was to cross-train and reenlist. He would be having a complete medical evaluation, some dental work, exit interviews, and paperwork for an early discharge if he were to get out. He was angry with Ross for his lack of caring for the project, and he just threw his hands in the air.

Jack was at dinner that evening with Perry and Adele and told them he didn't know what he was going to do.

Perry said, "I don't know if you want to go home to nothingness in Montoursville or if you're planning to stay down here for a while. I believe I could help get you a job at *Frederick News Post* in Frederick, Maryland."

Jack thought about it for five seconds and said, "I'm not interested in going home. I'm already out on my own and don't want to take any steps backward."

Perry started laughing uncontrollably. "You're an ass, bro, and you know that ain't going to go over well. Winnie has more to say in what you do than you do."

Jack said, "No, she will do what I want her to do."

Chuckling, Adele said, "How about I give her a call and tell her you said that."

"No, no, you don't understand," Jack said. "She'll do what I want because she wants me to be happy. And Winnie wants to do whatever will get us together quicker."

Adele started laughing harder. "Let me see . . . You get out in a few weeks and go home versus getting out in a few weeks and going to work here and waiting for a May 20, 1920, wedding. How is that going to work under your plan?"

"Well, it . . . uh . . . um . . . We could get married earlier than May 20. Yeah, we could . . . get married in October or something like that."

Perry grinned. "Yeah, and I'll start a rumor that it's a shotgun wedding."

"Adele, is the meat loaf ready yet?" Jack asked.

*   *   *

Jack suffered through the ridicule and harassment of the evening, and in his mind, he made plans to head home for the weekend to discuss the situation with Winnie's parents. He decided that he'd call Winnie to discuss the idea before the weekend.

During his first conversation with Winnie's parents, Jack wanted to discuss the changes that were going on in his life and explore their thoughts about changing the wedding date.

Mr. Jadite was hesitant about the idea, saying, "I don't want my friends at church to sit around and wonder for months whether it was a shotgun wedding. Too many people are expecting a wedding in May of next year."

After extensive conversation, the wedding date change was accepted. The next obstacle was going to be planning the move to Maryland. This brought back all the suspicion about Winnie's nonexistent pregnancy. Aaron, her father, insisted that it would look as if they were running away to hide the shame on the family. Then he looked at both of them and said, "You two aren't trying to tell us something, are you? Winnie, you've been acting strange lately."

Jack didn't have to say a word, because Winnie became enraged that her father would even question that. "Poppy, you disgust me. How dare you accuse me of such a thing? The mere thought that something such as that would enter your mind about your baby girl is revolting. I'm ashamed of you. Don't you think I've listened in church?"

Jack was speechless, thinking *Dani goes to church regularly, but they are pregnant before they are married. Hmm, this would not be a good time to mention that.*

Eventually, the family meeting accomplished Jack's goals. The date of the wedding was changed to October 13, 1919. Winnie was going to go to Perry and Adele's house for a few weeks while Jack was still in the service. Jack had to make a promise to go home every weekend so the ladies—Sarah, Winnie, and others—could work on the wedding since the date had changed. This way, Jack and Winnie could start to look around for a home. The biggest problem with the rest of that evening was Mrs. Jadite and Jack having to walk around on chilly eggshells. They both tried to make light of things, but Winnie and her father said not one word to each other the rest of the night. One thing came very clear for Jack that night: do not make Winnie mad.

They made the call to Perry and Adele to arrange for Winnie's visit. To be on the safe side, Jack told Winnie what he was about to say to his brother because of the harassment they'd given him the other night. He wanted her to know because of what had happened earlier with her dad.

The phone rang several times, and then Adele answered. He couldn't resist saying, "I'm calling from Winnie's house. Like an obedient woman, she is doing what I told her she's doing. My question is, if I bring her down with me, can she stay with you so she can help me find a place to live?"

Adele said, "So in other words, Winnie told you this is what you're doing."

"Give me a break," Jack said. "Let me talk to Perry."

Adele purposely held the phone to her mouth and called out to Perry, "Your brother wants to make you think he's the boss, but Winnie has told him what he is going to do and what he can say."

He talked with his brother a bit and soon had made all the arrangements necessary to bring Winnie down to their house for a few weeks. He also told Perry that he wanted him to start making contact with those folks at *Frederick News Post* he had spoken of. Jack was ready to make the move because he was so frustrated and didn't want to sit around and stew about it.

On Sunday, June 22, the couple left Winnie's home. Father and daughter strained to say good-bye. Winnie's father said, "I would tell you to behave, but I'd get yelled at—so good-bye and have fun doing whatever you are doing."

Winnie's face started getting red again, contrasting with her light brown hair. She looked as if she'd just walked out of a day in the sun. "*Father*, you . . ."

Caroline interrupted. "Aaron Jadite, your behavior is as ridiculous as that of a two-year-old. You're going to push her out of your life and make them do exactly what you're blaming them of doing."

Aaron barked at his wife, "When I was a boy—"

Caroline interrupted again. "When you were a boy, blacks were slaves, your daddy was fighting in the Civil War, and you were a logger. You were chasing me all over because he wasn't at home to straighten you out, and you were almost half her age when you were trying to act like a jackrabbit." She paused for a second to read his face to see how much more she could get away with. "Compared to you, the two of them are angels, so let them alone now."

The couple left and headed south. After a bit of laughter over Winnie's mama taking her daddy on, the subject turned to the situation at hand. They discussed what they wanted in a home, the style of furniture they both liked, renting versus buying, and where in the DC area they should live. They talked about apartments, duplexes, and houses. This was as silly a conversation as they'd ever had. Both had little idea what they wanted, much less what their partner wanted.

They were so engrossed in the conversation that time passed quickly. As a little child would do, Winnie eventually asked, "How much longer before we get there?"

Jack chuckled and said, "Really, Winnie?" Then he realized that she had never been to Perry's house. "Oh my Lord! This is what you call a God moment," he said, turning into the one-fourth-mile dirt driveway to Perry and Adele's house. Perry, Adele, Jack, and even Winnie were soon standing in the parlor of the house and hugging each other.

Perry said, "Brother, I was busy last evening getting ready for your arrival."

"Well, I'll be spending some time here but will be driving back to the barracks each night," Jack said. "I'm not sleeping here. You didn't need to do anything fancy for me. This is between you guys and Winnie, not me."

Adele said, "You're right that you're not spending the night here, but that isn't what he's talking about, yuckle."

Winnie twisted her mouth to the left side as her nostril went upward also. She simply said, "Yuckle?"

Adele said, "It's my way of calling him the south end of a northbound horse without swearing."

Winnie said, "Oh, yes, yuckle. I've heard that term used on Jack once or twice before today."

"Hey, wait a minute . . . ," Jack protested.

"Remember the night you left for the trip to New York, just before Christmas?" Winnie reminded him. "Then there was the lack of attention you paid me the whole time you were at Bloomsburg. Need I go on?"

"Okay, okay," Perry said. "Before there's bloodshed in my house and you get a divorce before you get married, let me say something. Jack, you are to call Dora Biglow at the *Frederick News Post* tomorrow morning and tell her that Jim Reagan wants you in for an interview for the opening in the national news department. Your job would be to take news script off the AP wire and pick out stories to write for the local newspaper."

Jack said, "I'll do that tomorrow, but I have to report to the base first and see what I'm going to have to do to withdraw from the military over the next several weeks. I'll go in for an interview, but I cannot possibly commit to anything yet. Still, I will call." He looked at Perry and added, "Thanks, man. I didn't expect action that quickly."

Perry told Jack what Jim had said. "It ain't the greatest job doing rewrites of other people's work, but it is a foot in the door. He has also followed some of your work with the orphan thing you did."

Jack said, "No, no, getting in the door is the most important thing. The better jobs come when you prove yourself. Just in case someone asks, how do you know this Jim?"

"Do I have to tell you?" asked Perry.

Jack responded, "Well, I guess not if you don't want me to know, but I'll be embarrassed if someone says—"

Perry interrupted. "You know how I haven't been available for you to stop by on Wednesdays for the last six months? It's because I joined the church choir. Jim is the bass, and I'm a tenor. We stand beside one another, and we've gotten to know each other pretty well."

Jack said, "Oh my Lord, Perry. I'm sorry I asked you to help get that beer the other month."

"Well, I didn't enjoy it, and Adele liked it even less when she found out. I justified it in that I didn't touch it at all. The truth is, I wanted nothing to do with being involved in breaking the laws of Prohibition. But trust me when I say that I would love to pound down a beer or two."

The couples chipped in and got two pizzas for their dinner from the new pizzeria that just opened in town. They cost a total of twenty cents because Perry wanted a specialty pizza, one that amazed Jack and Winnie. Perry called it a Hawaiian pizza. It was topped with green pepper, onion, ham, and pineapple.

When the evening ended, Jack returned to the base, and Winnie settled into the room she would live in for several weeks. The next morning, Adele and Winnie drove around so Winnie could start getting the lay of the land. They picked up both area newspapers to look for available properties. They were seeing properties between $3,800 and $5,500, ones that had everything Jack and Winnie needed or wanted, which they had discussed on the ride down. The problem was they would need as much as 50 to 60 percent down, and the typical loan would need to be renegotiated every year because all mortgages were based on a variable rate of interest that changed from year to year. Furthermore, the mortgage had to be paid off within six years.

Meanwhile, Jack went to the base to start the process of getting ready to part the military. Jack also called Dora Biglow and made an appointment for an interview a few days out, on June 24.

When Jack got back to Perry's after the things he did at the base, he and Winnie discussed over dinner the things they'd learned during the day. Things such as his schedule over the next week, his upcoming interview, when they could start looking for houses, and what Winnie and Adele had found out about mortgages through banks.

The mortgage thing stumped Jack, and he wondered if they were right. Perry said, "Jack, this is exactly what we had to do. I honestly don't think you are going to find anything different out there."

Jack said, "If you're right, we're going to have to put twenty-one hundred dollars down on a thirty-five-hundred-dollar mortgage. Is that what you're telling me?"

Perry said, "Yes, and here's the kicker. Your mortgage would be about twenty-five dollars a month, but you can go rent the same house for about twenty dollars a month. If you can also save about thirty-five dollars a month for six years while you rent, you will have about twenty-five hundred dollars and can buy a starter home with that. You'll be in the same financial place in the same amount of time without killing yourself up front. I'm not saying that coming up with twenty dollars a month for rent plus saving thirty-five toward buying a house will be easy, but it may be easier than coming up with twenty-one hundred dollars now."

Winnie said, "You sound like you're speaking from experience."

Adele said, "That's exactly what we did here. Jack, your parents told us just what Perry told you."

They thought it over and began their search for available places to live. On Wednesday, they started looking for rental homes in towns between Bowie and Perry's home. They looked at a few ads and laid out a game plan, as Jack had a hunch he was going to end up at the *Baltimore Sun* or the *Baltimore City News*. He wasn't sure why he felt that way. Perhaps it was related to his frequent journeys to and from Baltimore with Donnie.

*　　*　　*

Jack really was going to the *Frederick News Post* interview, but just for interview practice. However, they also looked at a few ads for homes west of Perry's house, just in case something came of the *Frederick* interview. During his forty-five-minute drive on the morning of the interview, Jack went over what he wanted to say. When he arrived, Dora's secretary had him fill out an application; Jack was shocked by the amount of information they asked for. He wondered what the company expected of applicants.

He was asked into Dora's office, and as he entered, he was taken back. She was well endowed. However, she was also a very large woman to begin with, with salt-and-pepper hair. Jack figured that if he was 165 pounds, this woman was at least 275 pounds.

She introduced herself to Jack and was as emotionless as he had ever seen a woman. He knew in his heart that she was only going through the motions of an interview, as she probably did not like Jim Reagan, whoever he was, forcing her to do the interview.

The interview questions were blunt and direct, and her attitude was frigid and hardhearted, to say the least. Judging by her mode and motions, Jack was sure that ice was pumping through her veins. He was just about to say, "Let us be honest, ma'am. You don't want me here, so why don't I just leave?"

She asked, "You are still in the military, so why is it you're interviewing for a civilian position?"

"Ma'am, I'll be out of the military on July twenty-second. I don't want to wait until then to start putting my feelers out."

"Jim showed me several of the articles you wrote for the *Stairs and Stripes*."

Jack was a bit embarrassed and humbly said, "I realize that the job here is a completely different type of writing, but some of my early writings were considered more like action pieces than my work on the orphan fund."

Dora said, "Well, one article I have was the prison break you were involved in." She reluctantly added, "Nice piece."

Jack thanked her.

"If we agree to a venture, could you work fifteen to twenty hours a week between now and, I believe you said, the twenty-second of July?" Dora asked. "My problem is that the position needs to be filled immediately."

Jack said, "I can see myself working more hours than that most weeks, but I can guarantee that I could work that many hours at the very least."

Dora then asked him to wait in the outer office so she could make a call, saying she'd see what they could do. After he'd waited about twenty minutes, a gentleman came in the office, waved, and said, "Hi Cindy," to the secretary. He didn't wait for a response from her but merely walked right into Dora's office.

Another five minutes passed, and Cindy picked up her phone, glancing up at Jack. "Yes, ma'am," she said. Hanging up the phone, she simply pointed to the door and said to Jack, "They will see you now."

Jack walked back into the office and had what seemed like a half-hour conversation with Dora and the gentleman, whose name turned out to be Mr. Peterson. An offer was made. If Jack accepted the job at thirty-eight cents an hour part time, they would guarantee him forty-five cents once he went to work full time. For part time, Jack had to get in at least eighteen hours a week, but no more than thirty-two hours. When working full time, he would work forty-hour weeks, with sixty-eight cents an hour over forty, with a maximum of forty-five hours full time. He would have to leave early on Fridays if he hit forty-five hours. He would have five holidays, two sick days, and five days of vacation after six months, part time included.

Knowing that he was making about half that amount of money in the military, he accepted the position. He was to call them the next day to see what time he could start working on Monday, June 29.

He drove home knowing that he was going to be back out on the road in a few hours. The idea of finding a house in towns like Bowie, Laurel, Glen Burnie, Crofton, and Jessup was out of the question. As he remembered it, the problem was lack of properties for rent where he needed to live.

He wanted to get home and tell Winnie first so he headed to Perry and Adele's house. Once he told them the good news, it was as if he had two nagging wives who wanted to go house hunting. They went to West Friendship, Woodbine, Mount Airy, Brinkley Manor, and Monrovia, viewing eight homes in all. Winnie and Jack wanted to see the inside of only two of them, one in Woodbine and one in Mount Airy. The one in Woodbine reminded them of Perry and Adele's place and was just twenty-four miles west of Columbia.

They saw both homes and settled on the Woodbine house. It had three bedrooms, a large country kitchen, and a sitting room. It was off the beaten trail, in Howard County. Woodbine was named after the abundance of woodbine plants growing in the fields by the Patapsco River, at the juncture of the B&O Railroad, north of Lisbon, on Route 26. It was said that during the Civil War, Confederate cavalry crossed the Patapsco River at Woodbine on their way to the Battle of Gettysburg. Most of the people in town worked at the large canning factory on the Carroll County side of the river.

Though they got everything settled with the house, they had to wait until the first of the month to move in. Jack had made the call to the newspaper, letting them know when he would be in on Monday. Because he had nothing to do at the base the rest of the day or on Friday, they left for Pennsylvania Thursday evening. The idea was to get some things for their new house. They made a great run, getting cooking items and some furnishings. Because he was off work until Monday, Jack's brother Jeff agreed to run more things down to them when he was done working on Wednesday, July 2. With Jack's new job and setting up house, it was an exciting time for Winnie and Jack. Little did they realize how frustrating life was for Russ.

Russ was miserable. As the days passed and he heard about Jack and Winnie's good fortune, it felt even worse. Jack and Russ got together at least once a week to talk for a while. It was almost as if Jack were counselor to a man he once considered cocky and pushy but who was still the most well-adjusted man he knew. Jack had no good answers for him, but just being together seemed to help Russ.

Michael William (Mikey) Kaye was born on June 14, and along with Russ's family, Dani's newfound friend Cal was with her instead of her own husband because Russ had no time off and Mikey came on a Thursday. Russ had to wait until the next evening before he could head up the road. He didn't even get to talk with Dani; he only spoke with his mama. Her words rang in his ears for thirty-six hours: "Son, your little peanut is here; Mikey is eighteen and a half inches long and weighs five pounds, seven ounces. Both he and Dani are fine. Do you want me to tell her something in the morning when I run into the hospital before going to the Broad Street Market?"

All Russ could do that night was sit around feeling sorry for himself and wishing he were out of the service one minute and then the next minute wishing they had base housing. He then vacillated to wishing he had leave time or the family was closer. He even got angry because he had been shot and spent so much time at home recovering. Why in hell was Cal in there acting like the baby's father? Why wasn't he off spending time with Sally Ann Spookenheaver, his newfound love, instead of with Russ's wife? Russ kind of understood why Cal would rather spend time with Dani than with Sally Ann. She was usually so unpleasant to be around that most people used her initials (SAS) and made up her nickname of "Sassy." Then Russ even got mad about Prohibition because he felt the need to tie a good drunk on.

The next day, his anger continued to grow. To add insult to injury, Russ's immediate supervisor, Army First Class Hank Plank (they called him "Hank Plank the human tank" behind his back), did not cut him loose until fifteen minutes before the end of his shift. Anyone who has ever been in a government office knows that once lunch is over on a Friday, nothing happens. The human tank never had children because he . . . well, just because. Why didn't he just have Russ work some overtime during the week so he could take extra time off on Friday? What damn good would fifteen minutes be?

Russ got to the Polyclinic Hospital fifteen minutes before visiting hours were over. "In a ward, there are no exceptions to the visiting hour rules," said the charge nurse. Russ decided that she was the perfect match for the human tank. If she sat around a room, she sat *around* the room. This came from a six feet one man who would weigh in at 150 pounds if he was soaking wet. Two-hundred-pound people with attitudes always caught crap from Russ—at least in his mind.

He spent every waking minute of visiting hours with Dani and little Mikey for the next two days. When Sunday evening came, he had to head back down the road; Dani and Mikey had three more days in the hospital. He felt the anger coming back. Both Dani and Russ were upset about it, but they could do nothing just then to change things.

Jack was on his own on July 22, a single home renter with a full time job, and Winnie was back home planning their wedding. Russ was seeing more of Dani and Mikey, as Jack was letting them come down for four or five days at a time on a regular basis, so long as they provided some money toward food and cleaned up after themselves. Jack and Russ had long evening conversations during which they bared their souls to one another. They were becoming best friends, and it seemed as if the relationship would endure. It was as much about the bonding between the two of them as it was about Dani and Mikey visiting Russ.

CHAPTER

13

ANOTHER WEDDING AND AN UNFORGETTABLE HONEYMOON

W eeks and months passed, and then there was another wedding at hand. Jack and Winnie's wedding was to be at St. Mark's Lutheran Church in Sunbury, Pennsylvania, on October 13, 1919. This was an issue with Jack's father as he wanted to perform the marriage in his own church; however, Jack quickly diffused it by reminding him that it was Winnie's and his wedding, and it would be how Winnie wanted it. They also believed it should be all about family, and they wanted him to be there and enjoy the day.

The church was founded in 1852 on Market Street, just after crossing the Route 15 bridge that spans the Susquehanna River. Reverend Henry Douglas Spaeth, son of the nationally known Lutheran theologian and teacher of Lutheran pastors, became its pastor in 1911. Born in Selinsgrove, not only was he familiar with the area and families that lived there, but he was also an exceptionally skillful minister.

Russ and Dani, along with several other people who had never been in this church, sat in awe. The chapel was unusual, as the seating was laid out in the round, with four aisles in a rectangular room. It was great for being able to see the activities, but there was no main center aisle for a bridal party to get to the front of the chapel.

The vaulted ceiling was adorned by a chandelier. The pulpit and baptismal and sacrament table area was on a three-foot-high alter. This was perfect for ceremonies and large enough to accommodate the wedding party.

The back wall had two large sculpted pillars about twenty feet apart, topped off by the base of a gable that had several windows over the sacrament table. Russ noticed a large stained glass window that reminded him of the window Jack took out of the church in France for him. Russ again felt Benji sitting beside him, as if he were sandwiched tightly between Dani and Benji. Russ felt himself adjusting in his seat to a more relaxed position. Russ was now at peace in church, and it no longer felt like a difficult task to go into a church.

Winnie was wearing a simple white wedding dress with elbow-length puffy sleeves, a fitted bodice with a Victorian neckline, and a full lace shirt. As the wedding expression about something old, new, borrowed, and blue goes, the old was her mother's pearl necklace that came over from England with her great-grandmother. The borrowed was a lace shawl to ward off cool weather that Dani brought from France. It was actually the one that Dani was wearing when she returned from town the day her father and brother were killed. The blue was the flowing ribbons from her bouquet. Of course, the new was the beautiful dress she wore.

Jack had to go out and purchase a modest suit because his only suit was about twelve years old and a hand-me-down from his father. He got a chocolate-brown and light brown broad—striped double-breasted wide-lapel suit jacket with matching chocolate-brown pleated pants with cuffs. He had a cream-colored shirt with a tie that was made from the same material as the ribbons on Winnie's bouquet. The orange carnation in his lapel was the same as those in her bouquet.

Adele was Winnie's maid of honor, and Perry was Jack's best man. Adele wore a dress of a similar style to Winnie's but in gold; Perry's plain suit was medium brown and double-breasted. The children of Winnie's sister, Joy, were the ring bearer and flower girl. Their names were Darren Jr. and Mindy. They were both dressed in their Sunday best church clothes.

The ceremony was simple yet breathtaking in two ways. Reverend Spaeth was totally in his element and brought many of the women to tears. Several men were choked up from time to time. As people left the church, Jack's father complimented the young minister, saying he'd been angry with his own children for not allowing him to officiate at their weddings. After hearing Reverend Spaeth's wedding ceremony, Rubin was glad they hadn't, for what he'd just witnessed was a most inspiring wedding.

The other breathtaking thing that happened during the wedding was that when Reverend Speath said, "What God has joined together let no man tear asunder," lightning struck the ground not far from the north side of the church. The stained glass windows lit up as if a gazillion-watt lighting system flashed on and off behind them. The lights in the church flickered, and the explosive clap of thunder was deafening. Several Baptist friends in the church let out a loud, "Amen, Lord, Amen." Russ almost crushed Dani's hand, and Jack took a step back. Visible tears welled up in their eyes as memories of a different time danced through their heads.

Pelting rain changed the traditional events after the service, and they all rushed to the reception at the Williamsport volunteer fire department. It would have been easier to have the reception at the Sunbury fire hall, but they were paid fire fighters. The lower level of their building was for the steamer and horses. The upper level was the bunk room. They had no space for such a social event.

Winnie's parents would not hear of a picnic-style reception like Russ and Dani had, although that was very amenable to the kids. They liked the idea of the casual style so they were able to float about and see folks at their leisure. Aaron thought that with that reception style, you would surely miss someone. There would be seating with family-style serving, and the couple could go from table to table. Winnie agreed so long as seating was mixed between families so it wasn't the Jadites on one side and the Earls on the other. The meal was wedding soup, meat loaf, broccoli, and mashed potatoes, with a side salad prepared by the Women's Auxiliary of the firehouse. The cake was a typical white wedding cake.

The reception was nicely done. Afterward, many of the fifty-some guests stayed there socializing as the pouring rain continued.

Eventually, despite the weather, the couple left for their honeymoon. Their destination was a cabin in Loyalsock. The rain was not a concern to them, as they had waited a long time for this week and nothing was going to dampen their plans. They were going to enjoy themselves completely!

On the way, Winnie said, "We are so lucky to have family and friends that are so kind to give us a honeymoon. Perry and Adele gave us two picnic baskets with a week's worth of food. My brother-in-law, Darren, rented the cabin from Kenny Weaver and made sure it was ready for us. Russ fueled up the car. It's like a free honeymoon."

Jack cleared his throat and said, "You don't see the possibility of a few gags along the way, Winnie?"

She said, "No, it's our honeymoon."

Jack smiled. "Okay, dear, we'll see."

Winnie said, "Well, it cannot be as it was when we went camping the last time with your brothers and parents. The only thing that saved your poor mother and me was that it was summer, the windows were open, and we hung the blanket in the center of the room. We girls had not even had beans, but you guys did and were . . . hogs. The way you befouled the room that weekend, that's the only word I can think of. Grown men having a contest for the longest, the squeakiest, the stickiest, and worst of all . . . the one that sounded most like a horn was simply ridiculous. I don't know which of you won the award for the biggest foul one."

All Jack could do was laugh and say, "Good times."

Winnie looked at Jack in a scolding kind of way. "Your mother kept looking at me and saying, 'Trust me. I didn't raise them this way.' Jack Earl, you will not act like that this week. Do I make myself clear?"

He wasn't even married four hours and had already learned what to do and say. "Yes, dear."

To get to the cabin they had to use a dirt trail that was more or less two ruts in a grassy area. For the most part, the ruts were full of water from the storm. They chanced it, drove through the water, and did make it to the cabin. Joy's husband, Darren, had boarded the door shut, making them second-guess whether they were in the right place. The giveaway was a sign inside the cabin, visible through the window: Jack & Winnie, Just Married. Jack was forced to remove the boards from the door in the rain because Darren was a smart-ass. Once they got inside, they saw that wherever Darren could lay strands of wet cooked spaghetti, he did.

Jack looked at Winnie and said, "Let the gags begin." She was speechless. She went about cleaning up the spaghetti while Jack brought the things in from the car. He also brought in a little bit of soaking wet wood in the hopes that he could get a fire started.

Thankfully, whoever was in the cabin before had set up the makings for a fire in the fireplace, and it contained some kindling and newspapers. There were also two pieces of dry wood to get it hot before trying to burn wet wood. There was a chill in the cabin, so he decided to start the fire. He took a stick match and lit the papers. Within seconds, the fire was burning the newspapers, but the perfectly rolled and twisted paper that Jack lit on fire turned out to be another warped joke. Limburger cheese had been layered between the sheets of newspaper by some jokester. They had to decide whether to endure the smell or to go out in the rain. They both felt queasy because of the smell but opted to stay dry.

Jack smiled and tried to humor Winnie by saying, "Honey, it's our honeymoon. We are going to have fun, even in the rain and regardless of the smell."

After a while, Winnie said, "I need to head to the little house out back even though it's still raining." She took a lantern and headed out.

She was back seemingly within seconds, and now she was infuriated. "Darren is lucky he isn't here; he would be singing soprano in the choir next week."

Jack asked, "What now?"

She answered, "A damn bucket of corncobs was all that was there."

Jack started laughing this time, but Winnie found no humor in it. After looking in every cupboard in the cabin, he finally found the roll of bathroom tissue with a note on it that read, "Sis, are you having fun yet?" Jack thought it was better to remove the note before he handed the roll to her.

Prior to that moment, Jack had never heard Winnie swear, but now she said, "Damn it. Darren is dead meat, and they're in on it too." As she was unpacking the food from the baskets, they saw that every can label was gone. "You will be having 'guess what's for your dinner' every night, hopefully including some sort of meat and vegetables."

Jack said, "I'm getting a bit hungry . . . but not for a meal. But before we go to bed, I'll need a little something to recharge my batteries."

Winnie cut up an apple and a banana. She said, "Well, here goes. I'm opening a can of whatever you are having with your snack." She worked away with the hand can opener. "It's smoked oysters in a mustard sauce." She fought back tears and said, "The gags just keep on coming, even from Maryland."

They ate, laughed it off, and finished their late night snack. They were getting to the point of consummating their marriage. Winnie, being a lady, was putting on her mildly suggestive nightgown to charm her man. Jack, on the other hand, was a man's man and just stripped to his boxer shorts. He blurted out, "See this length of rope hanging on the headboard? Do you think it is to tie . . ." And with that, he pounced onto the bed with all his weight. Apparently, Darren had cut every rope on the rope bed within a shred of being cut in two, and as Jack bounced on the bed, he and the mattress continued to the floor, making a heck of a ruckus. He was lying on a mattress that was on the floor, looking up at his startled bride.

Winnie, only half-dressed, asked, "Are you all right?"

He said, "Now that I'm looking at you with so little on, I'm fine, but a second ago, I was ready to kill your brother-in-law." She lifted her leg over the frame of the bed, saying, "I wonder how many more gags we will encounter," and joined Jack on the mattress. Neither of them seemed to mind being closer than intended to the cold, damp floor for the rest of the night.

The next morning brought more rain, and every leaf was now off the trees. Snow flurries danced about in the wind. One of Adele's mysterious cans was clearly a can of corned beef. They decided that breakfast would be fried eggs over corned beef with some toast. Winnie got everything ready and opened what she thought was corned beef, only to find that it was actually smoked herring. They looked at one another, and she said, "That is one for the day."

Jack said, "What the hell. Fry it up, I'll eat it."

"I believe I'll just do eggs, thank you very much."

They spent the first day of their honeymoon playing cribbage and spades, in addition to re-roping the bed, rather than hiking, fishing, boating, or any of the other things they had planned if it wasn't such bad weather. However, the lousy weather also provided more time to cuddle and be affectionate with one another.

The mystery lunch was bacon and cheese sandwiches, collard greens with bacon buds, and canned prunes. By three thirty in the afternoon, they knew the intent of the mystery meals. All the food in the baskets was food that created a lot of gas.

Jack gathered wet logs to start a fire outside and started to split them into small pieces to make kindling. Then he cut bigger pieces too. The water was dripping out of the wood, so much so that the papers under the kindling became wet. Jack went to the shed to look for a flare, with no luck. He grabbed a gas can and drizzled gas on the wood in the ring.

Winnie said, "Jack, gasoline will explode."

Jack said, "Don't worry, it won't explode. I do this all the time." Jack threw a lit match into the fire ring and took three steps away. The explosion that followed echoed across the lake and back again several times over. Before he could pick himself up from the ground, wet leaves, mud, and twigs had covered Jack. Once Winnie realized that Jack was not injured, she couldn't stop laughing at how silly he looked. A piece of the firewood had soared past his head like an asteroid and shattered one of the windows in the cabin bedroom. They had to use Darren's board from the front window to board up the hole.

By the time they were getting ready for dinner, the two of them decided that with the rain having stopped for a while, they would start a fire outside and cook on the fire pit. They chose to cook outside because they were both having their share of gas problems, thanks to Adele and Perry. They decided to have hot dogs. The mystery cans just happened to be baked beans, sauerkraut, and peaches. As they laughed, Winnie said, "Well, it looks like this week is going to be just like the weekend with your brothers."

Jack said, "Yes, dear, although you are eating the same foods I am. So what does that mean for you?"

They had a relaxing evening in the wooded yard. There was a bit of a chill, but it was good for cuddling. With the cloud cover, there was no gazing at the stars. They both watched the fire and imagined the flames being dancers giving them a show. Even with the fire, it became too chilly for Winnie, so they decided to go in.

To avoid letting the hot fire go to waste, they put hot coals, ash, and char from the burning fire in a bucket and carried it in start a fire in the fireplace inside. While Jack was starting the fire, Winnie went to the outhouse. Jack was just getting a good fire started inside when he heard a gut-wrenching shrill scream coming from Winnie outside. He ran outside to meet her running toward him with her bloomers down around her knees, yelling at the top of her lungs and pointing at the outhouse. "Snake! Snake! Large black snake! I think it's a copperhead; I heard it rattle! It has to be at least two or three feet long!"

Jack didn't know what to expect at that point, as she was describing three different snakes. He walked into the outhouse and saw that the poor little ten-inch garter snake was just as scared of Winnie's reaction as Winnie was at seeing the snake.

Jack showed Winnie what he found, and she said sarcastically, "I bet Darren found some way to arrange for that snake, too."

Jack stood guard as she went back in and finished her business. When they returned to the cabin, the fire was crackling nicely. They were able to burn the damp wood that they had stacked the evening before.

Winnie asked Jack if he wanted a piece of wedding cake while they played cards. He said that would be great. Abruptly, from out of nowhere, Winnie said the words that every man wants to hear: "Do you just want to go to bed instead?"

Jack wanted to say, "I'm there!" However, being the coy soul that he was, he said, "That would be great, but I kind of had my mind set on cake now that you brought it up."

She said, "Well, you think of all the men in the German Army, multiply that times two, and that's how many ants are walking all over the wedding cake. How badly do you want cake?"

Jack said, "See ya in bed!"

By morning, the rain was back, and the couple spent the day playing cards and eating things like oat bran banana bread, smoked turkey, asparagus, brussel sprouts, cottage cheese, and Limburger cheese, taking several trips to the outhouse. They were not past the formality of being proper and were stewing in one another's gas, thanking Perry and Adele for it every time.

While they played cards, they decided that if the next day brought more of the same weather, they might as well wrap up the honeymoon and head home, visit the folks for a few hours, and then head down to Maryland. Jack would still take the rest of the week off, and they could get cleaned up, have some food that was not going to give them gas, and spend the rest of their honeymoon together there.

As the long day drew to an end, the couple got ready to head to bed. Jack went outside first because he wanted to stoke the fire and bring in more of the wood that they'd stacked out of the rain for the fire.

Jack dropped the logs on the floor of the cabin, making a ruckus, at about the same time Winnie was coming out of the outhouse. She shined her lantern up the trail toward the cabin. The same instant the logs bounced off the floor, the beam of light struck two skunks under the cabin, trying to get out of the rain. The skunks started spraying their "perfume" to their hearts' content. She ran for the cabin, but they must have sensed she was coming after them, so the skunks sprayed again. Anytime Winnie or Jack made much noise at all, the skunks let them know they were still there . . . all night long.

Winnie begged Jack to pack and leave in the middle of the night because the smell was ungodly as it permeated through the floorboards and into the cabin. He somehow convinced her to wait it out. The only humor they had through it all was deciding whether it was Darren's fault with the cabin tricks or Perry and Adele's fault with the gas tricks.

When Winnie woke up in the morning, Jack was already packing. Winnie said, "I guess this means it's still raining?"

He chuckled, "No, the sun is out, but the outhouse is completely surrounded by the Loyalsox Creek."

Winnie said, "If you ever ask me to go camping again, we will have serious issues. If I have anything to say about it, I'm never going camping again."

CHAPTER

CIVILIAN JOBS AND HOME SWEET HOME

T he next several weeks became very hectic for Russ. In Early November, he and four others were called into Commander Plank's office. They met with him and the civilian equivalent to Plank's position, Jim Cooper. Cooper was a good-looking well-dressed bigger fellow, about six-one and pushing 270 pounds. With his perfectly combed hair, classy wardrobe, and crystal-blue eyes, many men would think of him as a pretty boy. Russ was surprised when he shook hands with this man. Russ had large hands, but they felt like a child's hand in Cooper's grip.

They took Russ and the other four by total surprise; they didn't see it coming. The situation was that because of the drawdown of the military since the war was behind them, several military positions were being eliminated. The five of them were in line to be the first to go because they had less than six months of military service left. Three of them would be offered positions with the civilian forces of the INSCOM.

Army intelligence within the US boarders and overseas was being developed. Colonel Ralph VanDeman was the chief of military intelligence and of the War Department. VanDeman was concentrating on a new issue: the real threat of German spies in the homeland. Over the last few years, they created a secret division called Corps of Intelligence Police. Their job was to conduct undercover investigations of individuals and organizations. There was a growing concern about immigrants. Every guard unit and national army unit had members from this corp within it to secretly report on suspicious activities or behaviors of soldiers in their unit.

Now that the war was over, the United States started a Cipher Bureau in 1919 to break diplomatic codes, officially a department of the Military Intelligence Division. Suspicious groups would be investigated, and corpsmen were to keep their eyes open and ears to the ground. They were monitoring for spies by observing strange conduct of individuals and small groups as well as activities of immigrants.

Cooper said, "You will receive a letter in the next three to five days that will inform you as to whether you are or are not being offered a civilian job." Russ could not believe his luck and thought how great it would be if he was one of the lucky ones. He wanted to stay on and not have to go job hunting. He vacillated as to whether he was going to tell Dani before he received his letter, but he knew in the back of his mind that he shouldn't talk to her until he knew more about what was going on.

He didn't have to wait three to five days for the letter, as it was in the mail the following day. He had a job offer. All he had to do was sign the letter and send it back. The offer was basically the same job, just with a different supervisor. He would still be working with men in uniform as well. His separation date from the army would be December 23, and his first day of service as a civilian would be January 5, 1920.

The offer was for $1,050 a year and included a signing wartime veteran's bonus of $150. This would be based on a twice a month pay system, being paid on the first and fifteenth. His pay would be $39.04 minus taxes. The bonus would be paid within seven days of his signing of the acceptance letter. Russ felt like doing a summersault but knew he was not in good enough shape for that.

He read on to find out that this offer would include medical and life insurance on him and medical on Dani and Mikey. Per pay period, he would earn seven hours off for sick, holiday, and personal leave. It also included a buyout of leave time from the military of $1.50 a day. For Russ, that wouldn't be very much, because by the time of his separation, only four days would qualify. He did give Dani a call to get her input, but he knew it would be stupid not to accept it. Even if it wasn't the job he intended to keep as a career, it was a start and would get them closer to living together.

Dani was thrilled and was ready to come down the next day and start looking for a home. She got off the phone as he got ready for work. He returned his letter, thereby accepting the job. Like greased lightning, Dani was on the phone with Winnie.

"Winnie, it's Dani. I'm looking for a place to stay at the J&W Inn," which is what she jokingly called Jack and Winnie's because of all of the visits she had made there over the past several months.

There was no question or need to discuss it with Jack, Winnie said. "As always, honey, your room in the west wing is open to you. When will you be here so I can get extra food in?"

Dani said, "Winnie, I'll bring dinner for one night, and we can share the cost of food. Jack has always liked my pot-au-feu. That's French for my pot roast Jack went nuts over. I make it with low-cost cuts of beef that are cooked for a long time, with carrots, turnips, leeks, celery, cabbage, and onions. I season it with salt, black pepper, and a pinch of cloves. The stew is covered with a topping of Dijon mustard and coarsely chopped gherkins pickled in vinegar."

"Okay, but when are you going to get here?" Winnie asked.

"Russ will probably come up this weekend and I'll come down with him. We have exciting news."

"Are you going to have another baby?"

Dani "No, Russ is getting out of the service in about four weeks and was offered a job with the CIA as a civilian," Dani explained. "We have to find a home and move in the next few weeks."

Winnie said, "Wonderful! I think that also gives us a reason for an evening out for dinner."

Dani said, "We'll see. Russ is pretty much of a . . . I believe you call them a money miser."

"Where are you looking? Winnie asked. "Do you have any idea?"

Dani laughed and said, "Other than your house and the base, what do I know about where anything is down in that area?"

"Selfishly, I want you to live up this way so I can be around you and the baby. However, for Russ's sake, you should be down toward DC. If you're smart, you will live a half hour or so out; otherwise, you won't be able to afford it."

Dani asked, "What does that mean to us?"

"Well, the closest you could get to us and stay out of the city of Washington, DC, but still be near Fort Belvoir is where we should concentrate on finding a house. That would include Alexandria, Arlington, Falls Church, Bailey's Crossroads, and Annandale, which are all about an hour from us. A few of those might be too close to DC to find the property or rent costs you want."

"Could you do for us what you did for yourself?" Dani asked. "Russ will be at work this week, and I'm up here. I'm thinking of rentals in the same kind of neighborhood that you live in. I'd love to have Christmas there."

Winnie said, "I'll go to work on it this afternoon, honey."

Winnie did as she had promised and gathered the three major papers to explore the classified sections for properties. She realized that rents in Alexandria, Arlington, where much higher than she and Jack were paying, by almost seven to eight dollars per month, and she figured they were out of the question. The rents on properties in Falls Church, Bailey's Crossroads, and Annandale were within a dollar or two of what they were paying and would probably be more to their liking.

There were not as many properties to look at as when Jack and Winnie went looking, maybe because they were looking so much closer to Washington, DC.

She was certain that a place renting for $2.30 a week was not worth looking at for two reasons. The extraordinary cheap rent and week-to-week rent payments made Winnie think it was a seedy or dangerous area. The rentals that were in the mid-twenties a month were out of Dani's price range. She ultimately found only three properties that seemed worth going to see. One of the three seemed to have Dani written all over it.

The property was a gentleman's farm in Annandale. It was on twenty-seven acres, and twenty-two of the acres were being farmed by a small vegetable farmer, who also had use of the barn. The farmhouse and two acres were being rented for fifteen dollars a month; it included a half-acre garden and a pond for swimming and skating. There was a picnic area with a large fire pit for burning and cooking.

The town of Annandale was founded in 1685 by Colonel William H. Fitzhugh, who purchased over twenty-four thousand acres of land. It was untamed wilderness, but Fitzhugh converted the land into one of the largest tobacco plantations in Northern Virginia. After his death, his heirs started selling off small plots of land when they needed money. The community was named Annandale, after the Scottish village located at the mouth of the Annan River. Winnie thought that Dani would enjoy the mix of the population, and there was quite a bit of farmland surrounding it. The community depended on one another and provided for each other.

Winnie called Dani to tell her about it, and Dani said, "Get with Russ. If he's okay with it, rent it without my seeing it. I don't want something like that to get away. It sounds too much like home . . ." She paused for a moment. "Better yet, I'll call Russ tomorrow at work if he doesn't call me tonight. I'll tell him about it and tell him why we started looking without him, and then I'll tell him to call you so the three of you can go tomorrow evening if you all can."

The next evening, Russ, Jack, and Winnie went to see the farmhouse. Russ rented the farmhouse plus the two acres, and the family was able to move in the next weekend. It was a twenty-four square foot, two-story house, constructed of homemade river brick, with a white porch and a red metal roof. It only had windows on the north and south sides of the home. There were large chimneys of mountain stone on both ends where there were no windows. Inside were two large rooms on the first floor, and there was a makeshift bathroom on the second floor, just above the kitchen area. The plumbing from both rooms ran out to a septic system. The rest of the upstairs consisted of two rooms with no closet space.

There was a heat vent in the ceiling above each fireplace to heat the upstairs. The fireplaces themselves were the source of heat on the first floor. In more recent years, a coal-fired boiler was installed in the dirt basement. It created the hot water and the steam for the home's four cast-iron radiators, two on each floor. One had to be in the kitchen and another in the bath so the pipes would not freeze. The makeshift plumbing and all four radiators were on inside walls. The old house was not much to look at, but it certainly would work for a starter home.

Before they knew it, they were settled in their home and Russ was a few weeks away from his separation from the service. Between work, the service, changing jobs, visiting family, Christmas, and general life activities, both couples were sure they would have little time together. They decided to have dinner at Russ and Dani's house after church on December 14. Dani made her specialty, pot-au-feu, and crepes for desert.

While the gals were in the kitchen finishing cooking dinner, the guys sat in the front room shooting the bull.

Jack said, "How about the Athletics? Didn't they have a great season?"

Russ laughed. "Yeah, they ended the season with thirty-six wins and a hundred and four losses. Right. However, the Phillies weren't much better off with a forty-seven to ninety to one record."

"Yeah, I like the Phillies, but you know I follow the Athletics. For the life of me, I don't know why Connie got rid of Roy Grover for the likes of Harry Thompson. He did nothing for us. Good God, he had a six point seven five ERA with one damn strikeout all year.

"You must be a loyal fan," said Russ. "What is it now? Has it been five consecutive seasons they've been in the cellar? Connie should have never sold off all their star players."

Jack said, "Don't get me wrong. I favor the Phillies, but I like some of the players on the As. Talk about the cellar; the Chicago White Sox went to the World Series, but they tarnished their reputation and might as well be in the cellar, the dirt basement. The White Sox are a peevish lot. That club needs unity. They are just too divided—it's like there are two bands of players. Together they would probably be the best team that ever played the game."

"Baseball's reserve clause can prohibit players from playing baseball for anyone else. The White Sox owner paid his best two players, 'Shoeless' Joe and Buck Weaver, only six thousand a year. Then, to save money because he thought they were overpaid, he didn't wash the guys' uniforms that often."

"I didn't know that," Jack admitted.

Russ asked, "Why did you think the team was dubbed with the nickname Black Sox?"

"Well, what happened to the team this year?" asked Jack.

"Comiskey is a tyrant and cheap as hell," said Russ. "Because of his claims of having very little money, he pushed his players to sell their baseball ethics out for money. Speculators found players looking for extra cash, and the Black Sox just happened to be their golden prize this year. It could have been the Athletics."

"The only betting on Philly would have been on another loss or that we wouldn't hit another home run. They had only twenty-four home runs on the season and haven't scored well—their 2.03 run average per game was pathetic but consistent."

"Have you thought of this?" asked Russ. "The two worst teams in baseball are the Phillies and the A's, so here we sit talking about the Black Sox to make us feel better about our losers."

Dani called out, "Guys, it's time for dinner."

While they were eating, they fussed over six month-old Mikey and talked about how big he was getting, the foods he was eating, and all the things he was able to do. Then they talked and laughed about Winnie's and Jack's honeymoon.

Russ said, "With all this talk about a vacation, let's plan a family vacation together. It's not like we're not family."

"I know you are going to all get a laugh out of this after Jack just won his own personal Pulitzer Prize with the story of our honeymoon, but it's not as if any of us have a ton of money," said Winnie. "Let's think about a camping trip."

It certainly brought laughter.

Russ said, "Winnie, you're right. Even cheaper motels could cost us about ten fifty a couple per week. We'll have to do some brainstorming for an inexpensive vacation."

"I wonder how much a suite would cost," Winnie wondered aloud.

Dani polled the others. "Are you all more interested in the mountains or the shore? I believe that's the first thing we need to agree on."

"I'm a mountain man; look at where I'm from," Jack said. "Could I have more of that fancy-named pot roast? Russ, pass the coleslaw as well, please."

"You'll have to excuse my husband, Dani," Winnie said. "He'll think better with a full stomach."

Dani giggled and said, "Back home it's a compliment when a man eats your food. We're lucky. However, at home this dish is made with beef shanks, oxtail, beef short ribs, and the marrow out of the bone. You cannot get all those things here, so I just used pork ribs and boneless rump roast. It does lose some of the flavor I'm used to tasting. I take it that oxtail and bone marrow are hard to get around here." Jack had slowed the pace of shoveling his food and was staring at it. Dani just giggled a bit harder.

Everyone concluded that in the heat of the summer, the mountains held more appeal to them than the shoreline, though Winnie was still thinking a lot about the honeymoon from hell.

Jack informed them, "My parents were friends of Bruce Ricketts, who just died last year, and the family has a small park. We could go tent camping there, as he closed his inn a number of years ago."

Russ said, "What's its attraction?"

Jack said, "Ricketts Glen was once Native American land. The land has exquisite waterfalls. They're its main attraction. R. Bruce Ricketts had a hotel in operation for about thirty years, until 1903 or 1904, I think, and he built a walking trail along the waterfalls. He made a two-thousand-acre park that encompasses about two dozen waterfalls, the tallest about half again as tall as this house. At one point, you can walk behind the waterfall, and if you follow the trail, you can stand on top of it and look down over it."

"Where in today's economy did he get the money to build such a park?" asked Russ.

"Oh my Lord," Jack said, "the man owned eighty thousand acres that were mostly wooded. He and his friend Samuel Weaver built saw mills on the land, cleared seventy-eight thousand acres, and either sold or used the wood to build furniture. That's how he became so wealthy. As I said, Ricketts died last year. But his kids, his son in particular, are friends of my father's and would probably let us go camping there, I'm sure."

Winnie said, "I don't know about this. What about Mikey? Is he old enough to camp out in the woods? What if he needs a doctor? What if he gets bit by a large snake?"

Russ laughed. "What, Winnie, like a three-foot black copperhead with a rattle? If he gets bitten, we'll find a doctor. Mikey can't grow up in a glass house."

"Russ, you're a jackass," said Dani. "Quit picking on Winnie; she's my friend. I have a question for Jack. Other than hiking, is there anything else to do there?"

"We can camp out by Lake Jean and go fishing to catch our dinner," Jack responded. "They also have horses that I'm sure they would let us ride. We can go swimming and canoeing too."

Winnie said, "Dani, you and I can take Mikey into town shopping and stay in a motel if the weather stinks."

"I have a fascination with the Indians in Pennsylvania because of living in the Harrisburg area and hearing so much about the Carlisle Indian School," said Russ.

"Well, from what I have been told," said Jack, "the Iroquoian-speaking Susquehannock Indians from the Harrisburg area weren't at the Indian school. The Indians from the Ricketts Glen area that lived in stockade villages of large longhouses were primarily the ones in the school."

"And you are sure it was the Iroquois living there?" Russ asked. "Maybe we can research that one day of our vacation."

Jack replied, "History tells us that in seventeen sixty-eight, the Brits acquired land from the Iroquois in a treaty that included what is known today as the Ricketts Glen area. My folks told me about thirty years ago that an Indian pot in the style of the Indians of the Susquehanna region was discovered beneath a rock ledge by the Creek. So I guess any Indian could have lived there."

"So long as you promise that all this snow will be gone by then, I'm in for a trip like that. Come on, Winnie. Will you give it another shot?" Dani pleaded.

Winnie laughed and said, "Well, Russ, the women spoke, and now we know what we're doing for our summer vacation. My conditions are these: none of those big funny-looking snakes; no skunks; Dani and I choose all the food; there will be no fart food; and if it rains, we are in a motel. Got it, Jonathan William Earl?"

Russ looked at Jack and said, "Come on, it's not hard. Just say *Yes, dear*!"

Jack said, "Maybe I'll just leave you home, woman."

Russ shook his head. "Jack, listen to me: *Yes, dear.*"

"Russ, you used to be the manly man of the two of us," Jack ribbed Russ. "What happened?"

Russ strutted around the room and said, "It's called diplomatic reasoning. I learned it in Washington. You tell them what they want to hear, and then do what you want to do. Then blame it on the other party while silencing their right to free speech."

They all laughed at that one because they knew exactly what Russ was referring to. Woodrow Wilson was a master at that one. He made a case to go to war to Congress. Many Americans were against going to war. He then created the Sedition Act of 1918, which criminalized all criticism of the government. It was intended to stop the protesters and naysayers in the country from speaking out publicly. Under Woodrow Wilson, America was a nation under lockdown. However, he packaged it up with a pretty bow as if it were the will of the people.

As military men, Jack and Russ respected the office of president, but it was difficult to respect the man occupying the office when he approved such things as the Palmer Raids. Wilson once ordered the arrest of over ten thousand immigrants like Dani and endeavored to deport them illegally. In specific instances, he instructed the silencing of nonconformists.

When Christmas came, Russ and Dani were able to spend much of their time in Harrisburg, Pennsylvania, as Russ was off for one day short of two weeks between his discharge and the start-up of his new job. Dani felt it was important for her healing to have Christmas dinner in their farmhouse, just the three of them. She set a place at the table for her papa and brother. She knew that Russ would understand, but Pop would have had a ridiculing comment for her about that. She remembered early on that in response to a comment she made about missing them, he simply said, "They're dead. Now we're your family. Forget them." She never forgot the pain he caused her with those words.

Though it was Mikey's first Christmas, he didn't care as much about the gifts in the boxes as he did about the boxes the gifts came in. It was a toss-up as to whether each gift was a toy or something to teeth on. As far as his Christmas dinner, he was able to eat a little bit of mashed potatoes, gravy, and sweet potatoes.

On the other hand, Jack and Winnie were off for two four-day weekends. They made the journey to Montoursville, Pennsylvania, for Christmas, and the following week, they headed to Perry's for a New Year's Eve party. Perry managed to get two bricks from a grape grower in the Napa Valley. The following instructions were written on them: "After dissolving the brick in a gallon of water, do not place the liquid in a jug in the cupboard for twenty days, because it will turn into wine."

Five, four, three, two, one . . . Happy New Year! It's 1920!

RICKETTS GLEN
GETAWAY AND A RABBI

Russ walked out of the service and his old job and into a totally new job in the same building. His new office was a four-room suite down the hallway from his old office. He was surprised how different his job was going to become, yet in many ways it would be similar. With the formation of the intelligence section during WWI, the leader, VanDeman, organized a small staff to start the counterespionage and translation council.

Things were hopping from day one. Russ had heard a lot about the upcoming Palmer Raids while he was still in the military. They took place the day he went back to work. Throughout the United States, 4,025 suspected communists and anarchists were arrested and held without trial.

As many new endeavors launch, VanDeman started the new unit with a small staff of two civilian clerks in a makeshift office, led by Herbert O. Yardley. The job included breaking foreign codes. Yardley began to search for qualified personnel, bringing on board folks like Altus E. Prince, Franklin W. Allen, and John M. Manly, giving them key functions in the organization of the unit. Once organized, Yardley received two more tasks from Van Deman, which took them in another direction and necessitated reorganization.

By the summer of 1918, Yardley became aware through codes that Chile had close ties with Germany. Eventually, they had over eight hundred messages from Chili. Before November 1918, intel had solved Argentine, Mexican, and several other Latin or South American diplomatic codes. The main enemy of the United States was Germany. Our military thought that they had left Germany behind on the Western Front.

With British assistance, we exposed German conspiracies in Mexico. We learned of a German spy in the United States, Lothar Witzke. He was seized in Arizona. Based on items in his message, a military commission convicted Witzke as a spy and condemned him to death.

The staff now totaled more than 150 code-breakers, clerks, and translators, breaking almost eleven thousand messages. This effort provided a large and constant stream of information on the plans and attitudes of others toward the United States. Russ was going to surface here as a civilian.

Though he had little formal education, his specialty in the war was pulling men in trouble out of dangerous situations. In a role reversal, his new job was to go out in US communities and apprehend people like Witzke. Russ did a good deal of traveling all over the United States on the government's dime, but there was the downfall of being away from Dani and Mikey. He surely wasn't gone 24/7, as there weren't spies to pick up every week, thank God. However, he was kept busy in preparation for these journeys.

Jack, who was used to being in New York City one day and Charleston, South Carolina, the next was now sitting behind a desk writing script from the AP. The two commented on the total role reversal when the couples got together at Jack and Winnie's for dinner and cards in the middle of January 1920.

It was the couples' first dinner/pinochle night. They'd decided to get together to have dinner and play cards every three weeks as couples, alternating visiting each other's homes. The plan was to play multiple games each night, and the losing couple of each game would put half a cent into a pot for each point between the winning score and losing score. In the event that one couple had an off night, each couple could lose a maximum of one dollar a night. They would take the money in December and go out for dinner at Penn's Tavern in Sunbury for their Christmas get-together when they were home for the holiday.

They were sitting around chatting and wishing spring had arrived because they were ready for baseball. Russ said to Jack, "How about that BS with the Babe?"

Jack said, "Yeah, the 1919 Ships and Yards football along the Delaware River is over, and the story of the new football team in Philadelphia, the Frankford Yellow Jackets, is behind us. Now we're on to baseball season, and I'll say that the top sports story of baseball so far this year is that Babe Ruth was sold to the Yankees."

"Well, I don't give a damn what they say," said Russ. "The New York Yankees management announcing its purchase of the heavy-hitting outfielder 'Babe' Ruth from the Boston Red Sox for the sum of a hundred and twenty-five thousand dollars is crap. There is no man worth that kind of money."

Jack laughed. "You think that's bad? How about Shoeless Joe and Buck Weaver? Now that's ridiculous."

"I'd love to go to Baker Bowl to see a game," Russ said. "I checked the schedule, and the Phils are playing the Brooklyn Robins April twenty-second through the twenty-fourth. Want to go?"

Jack enthusiastically said, "Sure, are you buying?" They both laughed.

"Did you see in the paper that Matthias Enzberger was murdered on January twenty-sixth?"

Russ said, "Yeah, that came across the telegraph because he was important; the German minister of finance. The one that got me was John Francis Dodge, the automobile pioneer of Dodge Motors, who died on January fourteenth. He never even got to see the finished product of his invention."

Jack said, "I'm not a Dodge guy; I'm a Ford guy. I didn't pay any attention to it."

At dinner, Jack let Russ and Dani know that he had spoken to the Ricketts children. The camping trip was scheduled for June 26 through July 4. Since neither couple had ever engaged in a vacation such as this, they would need to purchase a fair amount of gear. They were all on notice to start getting ready. There was lots to do.

Winnie said it best when she indecently asked, "Jack, let me get this straight. Neither couple has a money tree, so your idea of spending less money is to go camping. Okay. Now you want us all to go buy camping equipment. Just how much money do you think we will save?"

Dani said, "*Ouch*. She just hammered you, my dear friend."

Russ started to laugh. "Are we back to square one about where we are going on vacation?"

Jack said, "No, I'm game for camping. Let's see what we can borrow from others and figure out if Winnie has a valid point or if she is just starting to backpedal."

Winnie retorted, "Backpedal? Me? I am not. Dani and I'll just go shopping in Wilkes Barre, and when she wants to do things in the woods with you two, I'll babysit Mikey."

The final thought on it was that they were going to start playing the plans out, and if either of the couples found they couldn't borrow equipment and it was going to cost them too much, they would make new plans.

The evening ended after an enjoyable night of three games of pinochle. Dani had never played the game before but caught on quickly after the first game. As it was, Jack and Winnie won the first two games, and Russ and Dani took the last game by a hair. The kitty ended up with ninety-two cents in it. The laughter came when Dani said, "Well, Russ, it looks like we will be taking them out to dinner. Thanks to me, eighty-six cents of the kitty was ours."

On January 25, a major snowstorm dumped five to ten inches of heavy, wet snow in the Washington area. Including Russ and

Dani, about 650,000 people in the area lost power because of the blizzard. Commutes across the Washington, DC, region were almost impossible. Many people were simply stranded for as many as four to eight hours on their way home. Some folks were stuck on the George Washington Memorial Parkway for up to fourteen hours. Many abandoned their vehicles on the roadway and walked home, making the problems worse.

They had their second big snowstorm in as many weeks from February 4 through February 6. It was a nor'easter, as the old timers call them, and it pounded the east side of Maryland with high winds and heavy rain. The storm dropped heavy snow in the western parts of Maryland, with tons of sleet over the area where Jack's and Russ's homes were, more in Jack's area.

High tides tore through the Atlantic Ocean's cities with heavy damage. Smaller buildings were ripped from their foundations and washed away. It slashed a channel between the coast and Sinepuxent Bay. High winds and light snow followed the storm on February 6.

Ice remained on the upper bay through the middle of March. The military was finally called in to bomb an ice pack that was blocking the mouth of the Susquehanna River where it enters the bay. The blockage created high waters way up to the north and west branches of the Susquehanna River. The ice buildup on the lower bay was also a problem until about four days after the storm passed.

Jack covered many stories, but one that deserved attention was when Congress passed the Railroad Transportation Act in February. It considerably increased the Interstate Commerce Commission (ICC) powers over the railroads. Jack thought things would become better for the railroads because as of the moment that the act went into effect, the government's hold on them would be gone. He believed that the less government was involved in business, the better off everybody would be.

The United States Railroad Administration (USRA) influence would end as of March 1. The ICC would then have the power to approve or reject possible railroad mergers and relinquishments of benefits. It would also have the authority to set rates. The government furthermore promised financial assistance to the railroads once the Railroad Transportation Act went into effect. This was to ensure the financial survival of railroads.

Jack had an interest in the big story in the nation on March 19. The United States Senate rejected for the second time the Treaty of Versailles, by a vote of forty-nine to thirty-five, falling seven votes short of the two-thirds majority needed for approval. Jack got permission to go into Washington on a lead story project to spread his wings.

The treaty was meant to be a formal peace treaty between the World War I Allies and Germany. The leaders of the "Big Four," Britain, France, Italy, and the United States, collectively met in Paris in the late spring of 1919. Their task while in France was to compose the treaty. President Wilson offered for inclusion his Fourteen Points for Peace, which intrigued Jack. It was a well-honed series of procedures proposed to ensure peace between all parties in the future.

The points included the creation of an international organization known as the League of Nations, which was a similar concept to something Russ and Jack had talked about while sitting around in Dani's barn one evening. They had not put a name to it, and they certainly hadn't thought it out to fourteen points, but they agreed that it was good for the four countries to come together as one in the face of Germany. Jack wrote an intellectual article that was picked up as an AP article going out of their office. His boss was truly thrilled to have that happen to a reporter who'd only been working for him for a few months.

Jack started writing a story off the AP, which began as follows:

On April 29, it's a shame that we pay homage to a Civil War veteran, William Henry Seward Jr., who is better known by what happened to his father. William Henry Seward was secretary of state under Abraham Lincoln. On the night of

April 14, 1865, Lewis Powell, a comrade and coconspirator with John Wilkes Booth, attempted to assassinate Seward.

Seward Jr., a Union brigadier general in the American Civil War, died today. He was appointed lieutenant colonel of New York's 138th Infantry Regiment, which became the 9th New York Heavy Artillery Regiment in December 1862. He had several promotions after many battles. Seward was slightly wounded in his arm. He also suffered a broken leg when his horse, which had been shot, fell on him at the Battle of Monocracy. He left the war as a brigadier general on September 13, 1864.

A few weeks later, Jack's lead story read as follows:

Today, May 16, the country lost Levi P. Morton. Morton was the vice president under Benjamin Harrison and was a representative to Congress from New York. He later served as the 31st governor of New York in the latter part of the 1800s. He was considered for the Republican nomination for the presidency in 1896, but the Republican Party chose William McKinley instead.

The next week, Jack did a small story on a fellow named Mohandas Gandhi, who started a nonviolent reform movement in India on May 24. Jack did not think it was going to be a major news article, although the AP was splashing it rather heavily that day. "Some think that this man will someday be the face of India's independence movement," he wrote. Jack ended his story with, "We will see."

On June 18, Russ was on a plane to Detroit, Michigan, with his overnight bag to another possible terrorist attack or possible German spy issue. Dani was on the phone with Jack to see what he could find out because Dannie was afraid when Russ went out to sites where explosions could happen.

Jack pulled the AP tapes on what was going on in Detroit and found there was a story he needed to highlight. Twelve employees at the county building were injured, two seriously, by a bomb in Detroit. It damaged the building down to its foundation. There were a significant number of panic-stricken employees, citizens on official business, and passersby in the street. Terrorism or spies from other countries were the first potential suspects. Therefore, Russ was called in.

Local police jumped to the conclusion that it was the "Purple Gang," a local mob-related group trying to terrorize officials. Nine members of their gang were on trial at that time.

The explanation by John T. Doyle, police inspector of the First Precinct, was that the bomb was planned for the Municipal Courts Building, where the Purple Gang's members were on trial. He concluded that possibly a stranger was appointed to place the bomb and, not knowing the area or the downtown buildings, mistook the bombed building for the courthouse. Because of the power of the bomb, he added that it was a miracle no one was killed.

The bomb squad from the Bureau of Investigation (BOI) gave a report to the local police as well as to Russ, Harvey Shankwel, and Eric Weedsman from INSCOM. They said it was determined that the bomb was powerful enough to bring down a building and able to kill hundreds of people.

If it had exploded in a confined space like a closet or a restroom instead of in the courtyard, it would have demolished the building and taken many lives. The bomb was left in a men's room with the intent of leveling the entire structure. The bomb blew up at about 2:50 p.m., and had it not been for Frank Stolpa, a constable, risking his life, the outcome would have been very different. Mr. Stolpa picked up the bomb, ran to a nearby courtyard, and tossed it as far as he could just seconds before it exploded. After a few days of investigation, Russ and the other investigators were satisfied that the Purple Gang were responsible for the bomb, and they turned it over to the local police before they returned to Washington.

He got home in time to pull together last-minute things before the five of them headed to Ricketts Glen. They borrowed things from folks at work, church, and their neighborhoods. Other than the items brought into work, they had to run around and pick things up. They had to pick up tents, chairs, and cooking gear from various friends. They had to pack clothes, food, and in Russ and Dani's case, they had to get things together for Mikey.

The plan was for Russ and Dani to spend the night at Jack and Winnie's and drive the other two hundred miles to Ricketts Glen the next morning. They would ride together in Jack's new canary-blue 1917 Willys Knight touring car. It was larger than Russ's 1916 Studebaker Series 17, and besides that, Russ's had a rumble seat for the passengers, and if the weather was bad, there would be a problem.

As for the camping gear, tents were at a premium for recreational uses. Only the heartiest people would go camping. Russ had friends in the supply squadron on base. Since he was on base every day, he called his contact and told him of his plight, and within days, he gave Russ two damaged tents. The strange thing was that both four-man tents were in their original packing materials. He told Russ that getting the poles out the front gate of the army base would be tricky, however, the tie-down pins were in the bag. He gave Russ a list of sizes of poles he needed to purchase. Now they both had tents for future camping trips. Winnie was very excited.

They also had cooking gear, lighting, and sleep gear. They purchased three six-foot, six-inch poles; eight three-foot poles; and a rough-cut seven-foot ridge board for each tent. The longer poles could all be strapped down to the roof of the car. However, the sixteen shorter poles had to go in with the luggage. In a nutshell, they found that they were going to need to take both cars.

They decided early on to stop at Mae and Pop's for lunch. Mae was excited because she had not seen the kids and Mikey for almost two months. The kids were one thing, but not seeing Mikey in a while was driving her nuts. Pop was less sentimental about his grandson.

His mind-set was that if offspring weren't around, they wouldn't spend the hard-earned money that he didn't have enough of anyway.

As if it were going to be their last meal for the entire week, Mae went all out making a lunch for them. She made Pennsylvania Dutch barbecued venison sandwiches, German potato sandwiches, pepper cabbage, and Russell's favorite: peanut butter cookies with Hershey's kisses in them. Adding the Hershey Kiss was just something nice she did for her boys on special occasions. Pop used to joke that if it's good enough for insane people, peanut butter is good enough for his kids.

No one was going anywhere until Mae brought out Mikey's first birthday cake and gift a few days early. For the first time in a long time, this brought a smile, be it forced or not, to Pop's face. "Hey there, big boy! Happy birthday, you little scallywag."

That's right. Pop's term of endearment for his grandchild was to call him a wicked or evil person who deliberately hurts others. The word "scallywag" was used popularly to describe post-Civil War white Southerners for their actions against blacks during the Reconstruction of the South. Pop either liked the sound of the word, didn't truly know what it meant, or had a stone for a heart when it came to his feelings and behaviors.

In 1895, with the use of peanuts, Dr. John Harvey Kellogg, started processing what he called nut meal. Kellogg distributed nut meal to his patients at his Battle Creek Sanitarium. It eventually became known as peanut butter. Joseph Lambert was employed by Dr. Kellogg. He began selling his own homemade brand from a hand-operated peanut butter grinder a year later. Pop was convinced that it was what made his kids like their mother and not like him.

Mae had planned this lunch to be sure there would be leftovers to send with the kids. That gave Pop another reason to be grumpy and complain. He said to her, "Mae, you are an enabler. These kids need to let go of your apron strings and make it on their own. Now on top of helping our kids, you're taking in a few damn coal crackers from Montoursville. Do I have a sign on my chest that says, 'Pop and Mae's Food Handout for the Needy'?"

They endured the awkwardness of the lunch and were then on their way. They made good time, getting there in about two hours, but the last part of the journey was thirty miles from Bloomsburg, on Route 487.

A one-way bridge was out about halfway up to the park. None of them knew another way to get there, and they had to turn not one but two cars around on the road. They backtracked to a filling station in Dushore that may see two cars a day other than those coming to and from the park. The most embarrassing thing was the sign they first saw when they got to the filling station: Bridge Out Ahead.

The station attendant gave Jack and Russ directions via Dutch Mountain Road, which they were supposed to comprehend without ever being in the area before. He told them that it was a bit of a rough road; for about three miles, it was only dirt. He certainly was right about being rough. It woke Mikey from a sound sleep, and he started crying. As she was trying to hush him, Dani suddenly started laughing.

"What in the Sam Hill is so funny?" Russ asked.

Dani said, "If you think Mikey is upset by these rough roads, what do you suppose poor Jack is going through with Winnie in his car?" They both started laughing.

Much of the road, or dirt trail, had to be traveled at less than 15 miles per hour. Once the detour got back out on Route 487, they were still down from the entrance to the park. It seemed to be about halfway up the side of a mountain and looked to be about a 2,500-foot climb at a steep thirty-degree angle, going up a total of 3.7 miles. That final section of the road was Red Rock, and it led out to Lake Jean. Most of that was dirt and rock, not much better than Dutch Mountain Road.

They found a lovely campsite where they could enjoy the sunset as it glistened off Lake Jean. There were also two Adirondacks cabins there. They had wooden floors, roofs, and three sides made of logs. The front of each had a knee wall of log and a screen door. The rest of the front was screened in from the ceiling to the knee wall and had canvas inside to roll down for privacy at night. There was a large fire ring and a pile of wood covered with a tarp. It would be great to stay in the Adirondacks and set up only one tent to keep supplies out of the weather.

When they got out of their cars, Jack asked Russ and Dani, "What do you think about using the Adirondacks?"

They both waited for a sign from Winnie as to what she thought. Finally Russ said, "It's a lot less work to set up camp, and the teardown is a lot easier when the week is over. What do you think, Winnie?"

She smiled and said, "I'll tell you when my liver and kidneys fall back in place." She then looked at Mikey, who still had red eyes and moisture in his eyes and on his cheeks, and said, "I see my baby boy didn't like the bumpy road either. Come here to Aunt Winnie." She held her arms out to him, but he just stuck his pointer finger and thumb into his mouth and buried his face into Dani's neck and chest. Rejected by the baby, Winnie said, "Let's use those cabin-like things, then."

They worked together to get the camp set up, and the guys started a fire. Russ sat whittling down four long straight twigs so they could cook hot dogs over the fire. As the first evening crept into the area and the sun started to set on Lake Jean, they were in awe at the sky's beauty.

Russ said, "Red skies at night . . ."

Everyone chimed in, saying, "A sailor's delight."

At one point, the orange, pinks and reds were so reflective and gorgeous that it was difficult to distinguish between the sky and lake. Winnie said, "Oh my God, I think I died and went to heaven. This is how I imagine heaven looking." She looked at the other three and said, "We made the right decision. This is going to be a great vacation."

They were all waiting for the *but* . . . and then it came. "But I am worried that it could rain and wash out these roads. Then how would we ever get out of here?"

They all lovingly picked on her a bit and continued to watch the sunset. Once it was dark, they sat around telling camping stories.

Dani finally asked, "So what's on the agenda for tomorrow?"

Jack said, "Well, we can always take a hike. There are twelve trails from a bit over three-fourths of a mile to almost thirteen miles long."

Russ asked, "Do you have any suggestions?"

"Based on the map I found in the outhouse, I would suggest we do the Ganoga View Trail in the morning," Jack said. "It's only two point eight miles, and we would see the park's highest waterfall."

Looking at the map, Dani said, "It looks like some trails cross over other trails."

Jack said, "Yes, from what I can see, we would walk up to the side of Ganoga Falls, which is also part of the Falls Trail. We don't want to do the entire Falls Trail on the first day because it's a difficult hike and is just over seven miles. I'd like to do that trail while we're here, but it might be a guy thing because of the distance."

"If it is the only way to see all the falls, it's a hike I want to take too," said Dani.

Jack said, "Back to the Ganoga Trail, there's one spot where we need to use caution, especially with Mikey. We will need to carry him. There are some zigzags and drop-offs near Ganoga. Then we can do lunch and figure out something cooler for the afternoon."

The week flew by. There were heavenly sunsets, but the sunrises were hidden most days by the density of the deep forest or fog. They took five different trails, for over fifteen combined miles of hiking, and then they took in the tallest of the falls, Ganoga, at ninety-four feet, and saw the other twenty-one waterfalls as well. Beautiful mountain laurel was in bloom, and they picked and ate blueberries and saw countless birds of different types. They saw, heard, or saw evidence of a good deal of wildlife, like deer, wild turkeys, grouse, a bear, a coyote, pheasants, squirrels, and common furbearers such as raccoons, mink, muskrats, beavers, and a bobcat. They also passed through a narrow passage among bulky slabs of sandstone sediments that were accumulated and dropped off by a glacier thousands of years ago. Overall, the four adults had many amazing pictures in their heads and memories to take with them the rest of their lives.

The greatest amount of exercise came from taking turns carrying Mikey around on all the trails. Unlike his mommy, who was five-six and 135 pounds soaking wet, Russ was six-one and a muscular 180 pounds. Mikey was already forty-one pounds and forty inches tall. He was pudgy but solid, much like Cal was when he was small. For fear they'd get cramps in their arms and drown, they all joked about not going swimming as soon as they got back from hiking the trails.

They did go swimming several times on warm afternoons, although it was a bit cool because it was mountain-fed water. They also went horseback riding on the thirteen-mile horse trail. They saw the steam trains along the side of Mountain Springs Lake, which was a source of ice in the winter, and the concrete dam used to hold back Lake Leigh. Several evenings they took leisurely rowboat rides. Winnie had few complaints and wished they'd had better weather on her honeymoon, which would have made it more fun.

Too soon, it was time to head back to reality and return to the grind. They were glad when they got back out to the main road and the ride became more comfortable. They traveled the whole way through on Mikey's first birthday. Both couples agreed that they wanted to be home for a day before the guys went back to work.

Before they left for the camping trip, Russ and Dani had decided that they would go home on July 3 so they could celebrate Mikey's birthday at home on Sunday, July 4. Besides that, Dani missed Mass the weekend they left, and she did not want to miss two weeks in a row. She was enjoying St. James Catholic Church in Falls Church, Virginia. Back in 1902, Father Tearney started to build the parish and got them strongly on their feet. Quickly they built a small stone church at the intersection of Park Avenue and Spring Street. By 1906, the elementary parochial school was erected, and she had hopes for

Mikey to start his education there. That would eventually be a point of discussion she would need to have with Russ.

*   *   *

The couples got together for their twelfth card night, this time at Dani and Russ's. Russ made his specialty, homemade pizza with ground beef, olives, cheese, and onions. The dough Russ made was a family secret, so he said. The rise in the dough within the pizza was minimal, but eating the outer crust was almost like eating a slice of sweet bread. When it was still warm and oleo was spread on the crust, it was a treat in itself.

Russ told them, "Honestly, this is so much better with beer. However, that's not happening because of the present situation in the country with Prohibition. The best we can offer you is ginger ale, cream soda, or cola."

While they ate, Jack brought up the big news story of the week. He said, "History was made the other day, on August 18, 1920. Women were given the right to vote." He jokingly added, "The country will go to hell now." With that, Winnie slapped him on the back of his head.

Jack continued, saying, "The Nineteenth Amendment to the United States Constitution prohibits any United States citizen from being denied the right to vote based on sex. How about that?"

Dani announced, "I want to get my citizenship by the time Mikey starts school. Then even I will be able to vote."

Jack wanted to change the subject, so he said, "With women voting, the country may just spin out of control. However, what about baseball? After last night, Lord only knows if the great American pastime will continue."

Russ said, "Yeah, the Indians are in first place going into New York. New York is only half a game behind Cleveland in the standings. Some say the Yanks would do anything to win, but do you think they would?"

"No," Jack said. "It was an accident; the baseball family is in shock. Ray is the only major league player in history to die from a pitched ball. This is true, but Chapman led off the fifth in his normal crouched batting stance, known for crowding the plate. Carl Mays, a submarine pitcher, was known for his spitball, which would often rise up toward the batter's head. Mays let one of his underhanded shots loose, and the ball hit Chapman on the left side of the head."

"I know, but something just doesn't add up," Russ said. "I'm not saying he hit him on purpose, but the man collapsed right then and there. The crack of the ball could be heard all over the stands, and spectators gasped as they turned their heads away."

"However," Jack said, "in Mays's defense, the ball bounced back to him. He thought it was a hit, and he fielded the ball and threw him out at first. It wasn't until he looked back at home to see why Chapman hadn't run that he realized he had knocked Chapman unconscious.

The evening ended with a total of almost twelve dollars toward the Christmas dinner. They had five more card nights remaining, which could leave them close to twenty dollars for their evening out.

*   *   *

A few weeks later, Russ was on the go again. At noon on September 16, a horse-drawn wagon passed by lunchtime crowds on Wall Street in New York City and stopped across the street from the headquarters of the J.P. Morgan bank at 23 Wall Street. Inside, it carried one hundred pounds of dynamite and five hundred pounds of heavy cast-iron sash weights. A detonation timer was set, and it exploded. The horse and wagon were blasted into small fragments, and sash weights passed through the air in every direction. The driver was believed to have left the vehicle before the explosion and escape undetected.

There were thirty-eight victims, most dying within moments of the blast. Many others were wounded, several of which suffered severe injuries. The bomb caused more than two million dollars in property damage, destroying most of the interior spaces of the Morgan building.

As Jack was writing the story from notes off the AP, he wondered if Russ was there. The AP wire reported that many agents from INSCOM were called in, along with the Department of Justice's Bureau of Investigation (BOI). It was not immediately concluded that the bomb was an act of terrorism; the number of innocent people killed and the lack of an apparent specific target had investigators puzzled. They wondered also if it was simply an attack on J.P. Morgan, suggesting in turn that it was planted by radical opponents of capitalism, such as Bolsheviks, anarchists, communists, or militant socialists. By three thirty that afternoon, members of the New York Stock Exchange had met and decided to open for business the next day. Crews cleaned up the area overnight, destroying much of the physical evidence and hampering police investigators from solving the crime. Investigators soon focused on radical groups opposed to US financial policies. The *Washington Post* called the bombing an "act of war". Agencies of the government eventually blamed anarchists and communists for the bombing.

The Sons of the American Revolution had previously scheduled a patriotic rally for the day after the explosion to celebrate Constitution Day at exactly the same intersection. On September 17, thousands of people attended the Constitution Day rally in defiance of the previous day's attack.

The bombing stimulated renewed efforts to track the activities and movements of foreign radicals. Public demands to track down the perpetrators led to a request for INSCOM to release the contents of flyers found in a post office box in the Wall Street area just before the explosion. Printed in red ink on white paper, they read, "Remember, we will not tolerate things this way any longer. Free the political prisoners or it will be sure death for all of you." At the bottom was printed american anarchist fighters. This quickly eliminated any thoughts of an accidental explosion. The flyers were similar to flyers found at the June 1919 anarchist bombings.

Russ was in New York for some time. The investigation stalled when none of the victims turned out to be the driver of the wagon. Though the horse was newly shod, their investigation could not locate the stable responsible for the work, and when the blacksmith of the shoes was located, he could offer little information as to who purchased them. Most of the investigation focused on anarchists and communists, including the Galleanist group, which it was believed was involved in the 1919 bombings. In particular, the Soviets and the Communist Party USA were closely investigated as the masterminds of the Wall Street bombing.

One of Jack's lead stories on December 10 was about Woodrow Wilson. Back in 1905, Teddy Roosevelt won the Nobel Peace Prize for helping to end the Russo-Japanese War. Woodrow Wilson was the only other sitting president to earn the honor of being awarded the Nobel Peace Prize. He received the honor for his tireless work in ending the First World War and forming the League of Nations. Wilson could not attend the ceremony in Norway, and therefore the US ambassador to Norway, Albert Schmedeman, delivered a telegram speech from Wilson to the Nobel Committee.

Early in the morning, before the alarm clock was set to go off, the phone was ringing in Russ and Dani's house. Russ got up to answer it. Dani said, "If they wake Mikey, I'll wring their necks. You can tell them that."

Russ whispered, "Honey, honey, if you do that, you will never become a citizen," he said as he patted her on the tush when he left the room.

Dani said, "You keep that up and you'll be required to return to bed before Mikey wakes up, big boy. Oh, that's right. Duty calls."

Several minutes later, he walked back into the room, grabbed his overnight bag out of the closet, and started to pack. Dani asked, "Where to this time, sugar?"

"This is BS," Russ said. "One of these days, this crap will be behind us and we will be able to lie in bed and cuddle until we want to get up."

Dani laughed and whispered in the sexy voice of a pregnant mother, "And what will we do with the kids in your male fantasy?" Then she said, "So where are you off to, sugar?"

Russ replied, "Harvey Shankwel and I are headed up to Ellis Island in New York. All we know is that we are to pick up a man coming to the United States by ship. A Turkish vessel is coming into New York with a rabbi from Israel aboard, or at least a man dressed as a rabbi, whom the German government arrested. The rabbi escaped while being transferred. We were told he is considered very dangerous. Can you believe that a rabbi could be dangerous?"

Dani said, "Well, I don't believe a rabbi could ever be as dangerous as Shankwel. I don't trust him any further than I could push his bony carcass. I just get a cold chill up and down my back when he is around me."

"Wow, what do you really think?" Russ asked.

Dani answered, "Don't ever bring him home. I don't want him to know where we live." Then she smiled. "You're still in the sexy boxers, buddy. Are you going to work like that?"

Russ laughed. "Maybe that's why I'm cold. I should jump back in bed for a few minutes." With that, he was under the sheets and cuddling up to his wife, who was in the early part of her second trimester.

Dani called his bluff. "You're such a sorry soul. It's the middle of the summer. You're not cold. What do you really want?"

Russ mumbled, "Je veux que vous mon pot préféré enceinte."

Dannie started belly laughing and said, "You want your favorite pregnant potty? You are such a romantic!"

They both jumped out of bed twenty minutes later and scrambled to get Russ out the door. When he kissed his wife good-bye at the door, he said, "I know I'm forgetting something."

She patted his fanny and said, "Yeah, you're leaving us behind."

In the briefing at the office, they were told that the German agents traced the rabbi to a Turkish vessel. They had radioed the captain that US customs officials and the INSCOM agents would pick him up as the ship unloaded to prevent passengers from being injured. The passenger in question was dressed as a rabbi.

Shankwel and Russ were told to arrest and detain the rabbi until German agents could get to the United States to pick him up.

CHAPTER

BASEBALL, HOT DOGS, APPLE PIE, AND MODEL T FORDS

Life continued in much the same way for the couples over the next eighteen months, and Russ was now a senior agent with the INSCOM. Jack had been promoted to an editor for the *Washington Times-Herald* in Washington, DC. It was the summer of 1922. Both couples had purchased homes. Russ and Dani lived in a newer, bigger home in Annandale, Virginia, and Jack and Winnie had moved to Bowie, Maryland. Russ and Dannie had another little one, Lois Anne. However, they call her Susie because Mikey, out of nowhere, started calling her his Susie doll. Jack and Winnie were the proud parents of their first little one, Brad.

Several two-cent stamps took letters between Bowie and Annandale, and there were a few phone calls back and forth during the past six weeks or so. Finally, the day the two friends had waited for arrived. Russ took the trolley into the train station, and Jack hopped onto the express train into DC. The guys met for a quick breakfast on August 2, 1922, which was a warm Sunday morning. After eating, they boarded the Philadelphia express and headed for the North Broad Street Station in Philadelphia.

The guys shot the bull on their 140-mile train ride. Russ made a few off-color comments about a blonde who was sitting not far from them. This led to some crude jokes from Russ about pregnant women, women voting or not, and keeping them in the kitchen and bedroom where they belong. Such talk was the norm for Russ and in part gave him his nickname "Foul One."

They went from there to recollections of their war days, Jack's church, and Russ's difficult search for a church. All Russ had decided was that he would not select the fish-eater church that Dani attended. They talked about their new homes, the repairs needing to be done to them, their wives, and their kids. They discussed the teams to follow during the baseball season and the terrible baseball being played by the Phillies.

As the two Pennsylvania boys got closer to the Baker Bowl in Philadelphia to see the Phillies game, Jack asked, "Who's this field named after?"

Russ told him, "William Baker, the Phillies owner. Have you ever been to this stadium?"

Jack said, "No, this is my first game ever, other than on the radio."

Russ started describing the stadium by saying, "There's a hump in the ground—the distance of the warning track from the right field wall going toward center field—and you can actually see it. It's where the tunnel for the train line runs into the North Broad Street Station."

As Jack had come to expect from Russ's mouth, he made an off-color joke about the hump and playing balls off it. This one even made Jack roll his eyes. Jack said, "And that is why we call you "Foul One."

Realizing they were in a tunnel underground, Jack said, "I wonder if we are under the hump right now." Then, out of nowhere, Foul One struck again. With a grin on only one side of his face, he spoke through his smile with his teeth gritted as if he were trying to whisper. He continued with the offensive comment about playing balls off the hump and the Cubbies.

Jack was stunned, even with the comment coming from Russ, and before Jack could even respond to the comment, the train quickly slowed to a stop at the North Broad Street Station, less than a block away from the park. Jack could only think, *Father, forgive this boy's transgressions.*

Walking toward the stadium, Russ said, "Is this the day the Phils will catch on fire?"

Jack laughed and said, "Let's hope it isn't like the fire back on August 6, 1894, when the stadium totally burned to the ground." They both laughed and continued to walk toward the stadium.

They entered the stadium nearest to Huntington and Broad Street in the right field corner and walked toward the home base side on the way to their seats. Russ started to laugh aloud, and Jack stopped dead in his tracks. He slowly turned around with that trademark smirk on his face and a gleam in his eye that made one realize that his mind was in deep thought. Slowly yet emphatically, Jack said, "What is going through your foul mind now, Foul One?"

With his wrist limply bent and his pointer finger pointed at his own chest, Russ said, "Who me?" Then he continued without Jack saying a word. "No, I was just thinking that if it doesn't burn to the ground like it did in 1894 while we're here, maybe the bleachers might collapse like they did in August 1903, killing twelve fans. Maybe coming to an August game wasn't such a good idea."

Jack grinned and said, "Good Lord, how did we ever become such good friends? You have such a sick, twisted mind. Thank God He loves your warts and wrinkles."

They got to their seats on the third base side of the field, between home base and third base. They were directly in line to look up at the right field line, where there was a huge sign that looked like a bar of Lifebuoy Soap on the outfield fence. The slogan on the sign simply read, "Health Soap Stops B.O."

Jack noticed a bunch of bare signs and said, "I guess they have lost a bunch of advertisers since the team stinks."

Russ said, "No. Their advertisements for liquor were covered up because of Prohibition."

The lineup cards were posted, and the coaches met with officials. The game was about to get under way. Jack shook his head as he scanned the stadium. He looked at Russ and said, "This team will not be here five years from now if people don't start supporting them."

"Yeah, it holds almost nineteen thousand people. I'll bet there aren't even fifteen hundred people here today watching this game."

"That's a shame," Jack said. "Even the A's pull more people than that to a game."

Russ agreed but said hopefully, "Well, maybe this will be the day for Cy Williams to open things up like he did two years ago against the Cubbies with the long ball."

Jack said, "I've wanted to see Lefty Weinert pitch since he's the only native Philadelphian starter in the lineup."

Russ said, "I came down with the hopes of seeing Russell Wrightstone play."

Jack chuckled. "That's not going to happen. The Phillies will have to play their A game, and he's at best a B ball player."

The floundering Phillies took the field on that warm Sunday afternoon, August 2, 1922. It was within a week of both the twenty-eighth anniversary of the fire that destroyed the first stadium and the nineteenth anniversary of the day the bleachers collapsed, killing twelve fans.

Something was strange with the Phillies lineup. As usual, Cliff Lee, Curt Walker, and Cy Williams were the outfield, from left field to right field. That is really where the usual lineup stopped. Lefty Weinert was on the mound, and Goldie Rapp was at shortstop. Jimmy Smith was at second, and making Russ Kaye's day, Russell Wrightstone was at third base. The only regulars in the infield were first baseman Roy Leslie and the catcher, Butch Henline. With six left-handed batters in the lineup, the Phillies had a stacked deck.

Russ was excited because he used to leave his Harrisburg home and stay with relatives in Mechanicsburg, where he worked picking strawberries for a penny and a half a quart. In the evenings, he played baseball for Mechanicsburg and had the opportunity on several occasions to play against Russell Wrightstone, who played for the Bowmansdale, Shiremanstown team.

As suddenly as lightning knocks out power to your house, it became evident to Russ what was going on. Vic Aldridge and Pete Alexander were scorching hot pitchers right now and played for the Cubs. Both could end up being a fifteen or so game winner before the end of the season, as the Cubs were still in the hunt.

Alexander was scheduled to start today, but he got ill earlier in the day. Therefore, Bill Killefer, the Cubbies manager, had a decision to make: move Aldridge up a day in the rotation or put someone else in and possibly give up a game. Therefore, Killefer made the decision to throw a rookie hurler, Vic Keen. He had been a Phillies prospect a year or so before, but that day, Vic would be facing the Phillies. He had family there watching because he was from Maryland, not far from Philadelphia.

Lefty was looking good early on. He had a one, two, three inning against Charlie Hollocher, Cubbies shortstop; third baseman Marty Krug in (his final season because he was going back to his mother country, Germany); and center fielder Hank Miller. It was a six-pitch inning.

The Phillies struck first blood off the rookie with a single by Cliff Lee, and a home run by Cy Williams. However, they left the bases loaded, sending the eighth batter to the plate. If there was anything the young pitcher from Bellaire could take away from the first inning, it was that he had three strikeouts. The Cubbies came right back at the floundering Phillies with a run in the top of the second while sending six hitters to the plate. The Phillies ran the young pitcher out of the game in the second and scored four more runs.

Tiny Osborne had to come in to get the final two outs of the inning, and the Phillies batted around for only the second time this season. There was little to cheer about for the next four innings, as no more scoring took place through the fourth. The Phillies seem to be in control, with a six to one lead after the sixth inning, but then the Cubbies made some noise in the top of the seventh. They scored four runs and had two runners in scoring position with no outs when they chased pitcher Lefty out of the game to the showers.

Of all people, Kaiser Wilhelm, the Phillies manager, brought in John Singleton. Singleton was having an atrocious season, and the Philly fans, in typical fashion, started booing before the right-hander even reached the mound. Singleton's first pitch to Ray Grimes, the Cubs home runs leader, was an early Christmas gift in the center of the plate. Grimes delivered the package airmail off the right center wall between Cliff Lee and Curt Walker as the two runs scored to give the Cubs a seven to six lead. Singleton's next great pitch was inside, and it hit the Cubs pitcher. That was enough for Wilhelm, as the 1,500 fans were sounding pretty much like a packed house.

Next up on the hill for the Phillies was the fireball pitcher, Petie Behan. Petie was the team-leading reliever, with only a 2.47 ERA. He was up against the wall as he faced the ninth batter of the inning; there were still no outs recorded, with runners on first and second. The Phillies were shading to the right side to try for a double play. A hit down the left field line would surely blow this thing wide open.

Petie stepped up onto the hill as cool as a cucumber. Bob O'Farrell came up to bat after the pitcher. With two strikes on him, Petie delivered a Christmas package to Farrell, who got hold of it and airmailed it out of the park. You could have heard a pin drop in the stadium. It was still climbing when it left the stadium toward the right field corner. The ball appeared to be headed out to the North Board Street Station. All eyes were on the home plate umpire, and he vigorously threw both arms toward the foul line. The whole stadium could once again breathe. The next pitch resulted in a pop fly down the right field foul line, and both Leslie at first and Williams in right gave chase, almost colliding but both missing the ball. The tenth pitch resulted in a crack of the bat that was as loud as a gun going off. The stadium once again went silent, and the only voice that was heard was that of the announcer as he muttered "Oh my God."

The ball was threading a needle along the third base line, about two feet off the ground. Russell Wrightstone sprinted thirty feet to his right, and in a desperate attempt, he dived face-first about twelve more feet toward the ball. He hit the ground with his face and chest leading, giving his total body to the play as he trapped the ball between the ground and himself, not allowing the ball to get out into the field. He was literally lying face-first on third base after sliding a few feet, which enabled him to make a force play.

He had the wherewithal to get his body into a sitting position in front of the bag, and from his butt, he threw a line drive perfect strike about three feet off the ground to Goldie Happ at second base for the second out. The announcer yelled his next words: "Holy Lord Jesus!"

Having a cannon for an arm because he was a third baseman, Happ rifled the ball from second base over to the outstretched mitt of first baseman Roy Leslie to complete a triple play.

"That's the fighting spirit," said the announcer. He continued in his excited rant. "I think that's the Phillies first natural Triune play this season."

Jack and Russ's heads snapped toward each other like two perfectly synchronized mimes. Furthermore, the facial expressions of these two mimes were almost identical, eyes wide open and mouths looking as if they were fishing for flies.

Russ asked, "What the hell did he say? He was supposed to say 'triple play.'" Not being an overly religious man, Russ had no idea what "Triune" meant. He had heard the word once or twice before, and while he was trying to remember where and when, he said, "Did he say '*Triune*'?"

"August baseball strikes again: a fire, collapsed bleachers, and now a Triune," Jack said. "What do you think about that?"

Russ said, "I don't know what to make of it. I've heard the term, but I can honestly say I have no idea what the hell Triune is."

Jack snickered at his buddy. "I need to get you to church a bit more often. When I tell you, you'll never use words 'hell' and 'Triune' in the same sentence again."

Russ gave him that what-are-you-talking-about look and asked, "Is it some religious thing?"

Jack said, "Think of what the announcer said during that play: Oh my God, Holy Lord Jesus, and then the Spirit. He actually referred to Them and then said the word 'Triune.'"

"Oh, the Father, Son, and Holy Spirit. We call it 'the Trinity.'"

"In Sunday school, I learned that the first recorded use of the word 'Trinity' came in Christian theology in about AD 180 by Theophilus of Antioch, if I recall my teachings," Jack said. "He used it, however, to refer to a 'triad' of three days, the first three days of creation, not the Father, Son, and Holy Ghost. He then likened it to 'God, His Word, and His Wisdom.' Tertullian, a Latin theologian who wrote in the early third century, is credited with using the words 'Trinity' and 'person' to explain that the Father, Son, and Holy Spirit were one in essence—not one in person."

Looking confused, Russ asked, "So 'Triune' is . . . ?"

"'Triune' is simply a group of three, such as the three puzzle pieces that together make one picture. Thus, it is simply an older Latin word for 'Trinity.' 'Tri' means three. 'Une,' or 'ūnus,' means one. A Triune consists of three parts that make a whole."

"I get it," Russ said, "and now I remember when I heard it. Remember about eighteen months ago when I went to New York for the Jewish rabbi? He keep screaming at me, 'Christian, help me, help me! The Triune is in jeopardy, and it is Israel's only hope.'"

"Russ, I believe that there is a hidden meaning for us, you and me, by the announcer saying what he did," Jack responded. "I don't know what it is yet. However, when I was at my Aunt Beebe's funeral a couple of days ago, one of my cousins pulled out a poem that Beebe wrote while she lived in Scotland, before she came to America. The poem was to honor her father, who was a Presbyterian minister. It told of his love of a Triune God and a key to Israel's future. Actually, I've carried a copy of it in my wallet since the funeral. Here, I'll show you." He pulled a folded paper from his wallet and gave it to Russ to read.

From the church on Canal and Castle St. in Paisley, Scotland, a message for all men from the graves of John Barbour and Margret Semple

Our family history is little known and hard to believe.
From Jerusalem to Bourduex to Paisley, our secret will leave.
The legacy of lives devoted to the Triune God is not complete.
Descendants from Scotland go to the new land to find a place
to rest their feet.
Their fated Triunes' future God patiently awaits.
The clarity of the call to return to the Promised Land will be
definitely fate.
The Son of God left his mark on earth; this we cannot deny.
The Holy Spirit moves in a way that to us just mystifies.
John's children will not be fishermen, as a general rule.
They will be too busy lumbering, tilling soil, and teaching school.
But when it comes to Sunday, they will tread the narrow route.
They are fishers of men, not of pike and trout.
There will be one descendant of John saved by rusty grace,
Who will find himself in the Triune race.
On this boy and friend, our fate will depend.
Godspeed and best wishes from John to the daring young man.

Peace of Christ be with you,
Emma Beebe

"I don't understand," Russ said. "Why us? Really, Jack, why me . . . of all people?"

Jack said, "To answer your question, believe it or not, God sometimes seeks out less-than-perfect people, even heathens, to spread His gospel."

Russ and Jack were stunned over both of them separately hearing of a Triune and now at a baseball game together. They quietly continued watching the game.

The Phillies charged off the field with heads held high; they were pumped. The first batter hit a single, and the next was hit by the pitch. The Cubbies then turned a double play when the runner on second tried to advance to third. Next up was Russell Wrightstone, who popped a Texas league single into right field. The score was now all tied up at seven. When the inning ended, Russ busted out in laughter to the point of holding his ribs.

"Russ, what in heaven's name are you laughing at?" asked Jack.

Throughout burst of laughter and moments of uncontrollable giggles, Russ said, "Don't you get it? I didn't have a damn clue what a Triune was, but this time I'm one up on you, Jackie pooh. You haven't even focused in on it."

"Focused in on what?"

"It's tied seven to seven in the seventh inning. Doesn't seven-seven-seven represent Satan in the Bible?"

"No," responded Jack, "number seven is the most familiar number in the Bible, and it represents spiritual perfection or completion. Literally, it means divine fullness, coming from a Hebrew word meaning 'to be full or satisfied.' Maybe we *are* the ones God is asking to do something special."

Jack smiled and continued. "If you want to look at it in another way, God's action number is three: the fire, the bleachers, and now the seven-seven-seven outcome. I just think it's peculiar that three times over several years during August baseball games, remarkable things have happened."

The strangest part of the seven-seven-seven idea that Russ joked about is that the game ended in a tie of seven to seven. Folks left the stadium with mixed feelings. Fans always came to see their team win; they never wanted to see them lose. However, losing was nothing new for the Philadelphia fans in recent years. They had not had a good season since 1915. The good thing was that Jack and Russ were leaving with neither a win nor a loss but a puzzle of faith to figure out. Were they reading something into a simple tie score in a baseball game? But then there was the fact that the announcer said the word

"Triune." They made their way back over to the train station and even had time for a quick sandwich and drink at a local diner before the train ride home.

They walked through the train station to the platform and did not have to wait long before they heard the words from conductor at the rear of the last car: "All aboard! Southbound train number seventy-one, Philadelphia Penn Station, Wilmington, Baltimore, Washington, DC, departing at five twenty-seven. All aboard!"

As they boarded the train back to DC, Jack and Russ were chatting about the game and the highlight of the scoring. Russ then said, "Okay, Jack, you'll have to tell me more about this Triune thing."

Jack said, "Yeah, when the announcer said that word and you looked at me, I thought we were in the same mind-set. In reality, you were just catching the fact that he did not say *triple play* at first. We'll have some talking to do later."

Once they were seated, Jack said, "So, Russ, tell me about that guy at Ellis Island."

"He came in on a Turkish vessel, and we were to pick him up," Russ explained. He was an escaped prisoner from German agents and thought to be impersonating a rabbi. He could have been armed and dangerous according to the reports we had received. In order not to draw suspicion to my position, I acquired some customs officer official clothing. I stood around acting as if I didn't have a care in the world. The rabbi stepped onto the dock on Ellis Island. I said, 'Good morning, Rabbi. How are you this morning?' The rabbi simply said, 'Shalom.'"

Russ continued. "I then told him that the Jewish customs office was in a hard-to-find location for some reason. I asked if I could show him to its location, and he agreed. We chatted casually as we walked, and he seemed to start relaxing, knowing he was off the ship and in the United States."

"Where did Triune come into play?" asked Jack.

"You're so inpatient," Russ chided. "While we were talking, I offered him Wrigley's Spearmint, and when he took it with his left hand, I assumed he was left-handed. I took him to a room. As we started through the doorway into the room, I slammed one side of my handcuffs on his left wrist. The guy went totally nuts. He tried to catch me with a right hook, and that's all I needed to kick his ass a bit. I managed to get the other cuff on, and I slammed him on the floor. When he tried to get up, I slammed him to the floor again, the whole time thinking, *I don't trust the Germans. What if I'm beating up a real rabbi?* However, the words coming out of his mouth made me know otherwise. I closed the door and locked both of us inside."

Jack asked, "What—if anything—did he say about the Triune?"

"He started screaming, 'Christian help me. Nazis are going to kill us. Triune is at jeopardy, Israel's only hope.' He said it several times while sitting on the floor, and then he screamed it in German . . . then Hebrew. I tried to calm him down, but after about ten minutes of his repeating the same words, I couldn't take it anymore. I grabbed him and punched him square in the face, shutting him up finally. Then he called me a simpleton jerk and spit his blood in my face."

"Oh Lord, that was the wrong thing to do," said Jack.

Russ smiled. "I threw him into the far corner of the room and dazed him. I started for the door. He came at me, screaming like an insane man. I just turned and lifted my knee right into the would-be rabbi's crotch.'

Jack just said, "Oh my God. With his hands handcuffed behind him, he couldn't even reach the pain to rub it. You are mean."

"I got out of the room and relocked it," Russ said. "I leaned against the door and tried to calm down before talking with my fellow agent. Then *boom!* The son of a bitch threw himself against the door. He scared the hell out of me. He kept ramming the door, screaming only in Hebrew this time, for another ten minutes. He must have knocked himself out, because it became quiet. I called for Harvey to guard the room and its occupant, and I went to get cleaned up.

"That night while I was sleeping, what the rabbi said kept playing over and over in my dreams. The next day, I went into work and started to see if I could find any information on what he was saying.

When we got home to DC, I found a special agent on Jewish Affairs and asked him about Triune and Israel. I didn't get much information, so I still don't think I totally understand what Triune is."

Jack said, "As I told you, you do know—just in different words. Why he said Triune in that situation, Lord only knows. At any rate, that makes me think of some things I've often wondered about."

"Well, help me out. Where did it take you?" asked Russ. "Tell me again how Triune and Trinity are the same thing."

Jack gave Russ that trademark grin. With a voice that was ever so slightly jiggling with the bumpy train ride, he said, "Like I told you before, my friend, you've heard of it many times, only by a different name. It's the same as the Trinity."

"Then why not say the Trinity?" Russ asked.

"Historically speaking, the word 'Trinity' does not appear in the scriptures at all. The idea of it is in the Bible hundreds of times from Genesis 1:26 on, where God said, 'Let us make man in Our image, and after Our likeness . . .' He continued, "And in Matthew 28:19, it is written, 'Go ye therefore, and make disciples of all the nations, baptizing them in the name of the Father, Son and Holy Spirit.' In 2nd Corinthians 13:14 aul ends his letter, 'The grace of the Lord Jesus Christ, and the love of God, and the communion of the Holy Ghost be with you all. Amen.' These are just a few examples."

"Okay, okay, I get it now," said Russ, "But where did someone come up with the word 'Trinity' to replace the word 'Triune' . . . and why?"

"Well," said Jack, continuing to teach Russ biblical history, "Trinity simply comes from the mind-set of a tri-unity or the Latin noun *Trinitas* meaning threeness, or three in one. The term Trinity came from the Church historian about the beginning of second century."

Russ, with a puzzled look said, "So are you saying that the Old Testament does not use the word 'Trinity,' but it is in the New Testament once Jesus was born?"

"No, as I said earlier, it came to be a term used in the church about 180 AD, if I remember my church teachings correctly. Theophilus of Antioch first used the term 'Triad'; however, it was not to refer to the Father, Son, and Holy Spirit but to the first three days of creation. Tertullian, the Latin theologian I mentioned, is the one who first used the term Trinity to describe the Father, Son, and Holy Spirit."

"That's right," Ross said. "You did say that. So is this when the term Trinity came to be a widely used term in the church?"

"Yes . . . but no."

Several people on the train had been at the game. They'd also questioned the use of the term "Triune" during the game. They turned in their seats as Jack continued.

"It wasn't until 325 AD, when the Council of Nicea established the doctrine of the Trinity and they adopted the Nicene Creed, that it kind of became universal."

Russ said, "Okay, I guess I get all of that, but what did he mean when he said it in that situation, and why did he say it in that situation?"

One of the passengers on the train who was listening said, "Maybe it was as simple as the guy just came from Bible study; maybe you're just making a mountain out of a molehill."

Jack said, "Yes, maybe so, but maybe there is a hidden meaning in it for all of us."

The passenger who had butted into the conversation said, "Oh yeah, Bible-thumper? Are you going to tell us next that the world is going to end on December 7, 1941, or something silly like that?"

Jack gave the guy a look and chose not to respond. Instead, he said to Russ, "That's what it means. However, I'm still perplexed as to why he said it at that very moment."

Soon they both drifted off into a light sleep. It seemed like moments later that they heard the conductor say, "Washington, DC." They got off the train and said their good-byes without mentioning the Triune again. They went their separate ways to get their rides home.

CHAPTER

DREAMS

On the evening of Wednesday, August 23, 1933, the National Weather Service was tracking a Chesapeake-Potomac hurricane. It had started out ten days earlier, on August 13, when a ship at sea first reported a tropical depression around the Cape Verde Islands, not far from Mauritania and Western Sahara. Because of where the storm was, early warnings extended from Cape Hatteras to Boston. Evacuations in North Carolina and the southern part of Virginia were advised.

A few days of watching brought a wide storm path, with winds at 60 miles per hour, pushing the growing storm toward America's East Coast. Smaller ships and fishing vessels headed for the shorelines. People from as far north as Gloucester, Virginia, the Chesapeake Bay, and as far south as Savannah, Georgia, were starting to batten down the hatches in preparation for the eighth storm and third hurricane of the very active 1933 Atlantic hurricane season.

Although not yet known, the most destructive hurricanes of the season would soon make landfall. The storm moved in a northwest direction and gained hurricane status on August 16. The hurricane continued to strengthen, and by August 22, the hurricane reached its height of strength, with unrelenting winds of 140 miles per hour. It was deemed a category 4 hurricane. On August 23, the hurricane made landfall on the Outer Banks of North Carolina and was downgraded to a category 1 hurricane as it weakened while moving inland.

The storm turned to the northeast, passing through Virginia, Maryland, and Pennsylvania before weakening to a tropical depression over New York. In the state of Maryland, the storm's effects resulted in severe crop damage, and many boats and piers were damaged or demolished due to high tides and storm swells. The hurricane produced heavy rainfall along its path, with a peak of over thirteen inches of rain as far off the coast as York, Pennsylvania, about a half hour south of Russ's parents.

The hurricane caused severe damage along the East Coast. Virginia was the hardest hit, for the storm's eye passed directly over Norfolk shipyards, where Jack landed when he flew home. Everywhere the hurricane went, it left death and destruction in its path; Maryland, Washington, DC, and Delaware were the worst hit.

In total, the hurricane caused $27.2 million in damage at a time when the average new home cost $5,750 and the unemployment rate was at its all-time high of 25.2 percent, in the worst year yet of the Depression, and there were thirty fatalities. Everywhere one turned, people by the thousands were questioning why God would let this happen. The Depression was bad enough. Why all the other things on top of it?

In Virginia, tides were reported to be up to nine feet above normal. The high tides and storm swell flooded a large percentage of downtown Norfolk and sank ten navy ships. Other reports along the coast were that the storm swell caused beach erosion and the James and York rivers overflowed their banks, causing even more damage.

Further inland, which affected both Russ's and Jack's families, strong winds knocked out power and phone lines while flooding destroyed roads and businesses. In Washington, DC, the storm pounded over six inches of rain, and winds of fifty miles per hour were experienced. In Maryland, the hurricane damaged crops and buildings, destroyed a railroad bridge into Ocean City, and created an inlet where there was never one before. On the coastline, the storm damaged or destroyed much in its path.

On Friday night, August 25, Russ, Jack, and their families went to bed without any power to light their homes or hot water in which to bathe. They couldn't even make phone calls. In the Kaye house, Mikey and Susie were afraid and camped out on the floor of their parents' room. They'd all experienced one of the most violent thunder and lightning storms they could remember. The storm rattled the windows, and lightning seemed dangerously close to their homes. Fire sirens rang out regularly to call in help to either cut up downed trees blocking streets or put out lightning fires. They had their share of rescues as well. Those who were foolishly adventurous drove around to see the flooding and ended up driving down washed-away streets.

As Russ lay there, his mind drifted away to the night sixteen years ago when he spent a few minutes in Château de Beynac with Benji and Carver. That was the same night that he met Jack and his team released so many prisoners from the castle. He thought of what he'd said in his prayer on top of the hill in the rocks. He remembered bits and pieces of it, including this: *I only come to you when I need you, and I need not tell you why I come to you on my knees tonight because you already know.* Now he was thinking, *Here I am. I rush though life and never slow down enough to thank You for all You have given me. I have a beautiful wife, two wonderful children, a decent if drafty house, a good job, great friends, and a good family. For all these blessings, I should do more for You, my Lord; however, I just am not a church-driven person. I do not like to sit in a room with a bunch of hypocrites who profess to be Christians. Then they walk out the church door, treat others poorly and complain about their lives. I'm not like them. Please know that I am yours to navigate in any way you see fit.*

Just then, a bolt of lightning lit up the room and the stained glass window that Jack had taken out of the church. Russ remembered staring at it after Benji died in his arms, and now it sat on his windowsill, leaning against the window. When the lightning lit it up, he saw colors in the glass that he never recalled seeing before.

Russ saw several shades of orange, which indicates comforter, teacher, and companion—combining the work of love in relation to the merits of the sacrifice as a healer, restorer, and teacher of righteousness. He lay still and stared at the glass, waiting for another bolt of lightning to light up the room. Russ began to wonder why this stained glass had him so intrigued tonight.

He recalled Shankwel once saying at work, "Why is it that they say they are religious when they talk to God, yet the doctors say they are insane if God talks to them?" Russ had had a guarded relationship with Shankwel ever since the rabbi trip to New York, when Dani said she did not like him.

The storm was still quite powerful, yet no lightning lit up the room as it had earlier. Russ was mesmerized and slowly drifted away into a deep sleep. In his dream, he saw a vision of a painting that was hanging in the room where Benji was shot inside the castle.

Russ had vivid memories, sometimes haunting memories, of Benji being shot and the struggle that ensued. However, he had never thought about that painting before it came to him in this dream. It was large, about eight feet wide by ten feet high, with a glittery high-gloss gold frame. The painting was of the crucifixion of Jesus Christ, with mother Mary on his right-hand side and Mary Magdalene on his left.

In his dream, he was in the large stone room in the castle, the one with the rounded ceiling, looking at Christ in the painting. The cross slowly faded away to just a shadow, and Jesus Christ, fully clothed in a bright orange robe, stood with the two Marys. He lifted his hands high above his head. Lightning flashes in the painting and a booming voice from the stone ceiling said, "Russ, I have chosen you. You were spared in the room that day by Me, your Father in heaven. I have a message for you. To find the Triune, you need to start with Plymouth. Jack will help you."

*   *   *

Meanwhile, in Bowie, Jack and Winnie where trying to wait out the storm playing cards by candlelight because Brad was scared and wanted to sleep on the couch. Brad said, "Hey, Mom and Dad, how many times is the word 'orange' in the Bible?"

Jack said, "I don't know, but I'd guess a great many. After all, orange dye was easily made for clothes; fire has orange in it; and it's the color that is thought to represent a comforter, teacher, and companion—one who is a healer, a restorer, and a teacher of righteousness. I'd guess a good bit. Do you know?"

Brad laughed. "Gotcha, Dad. We learned in Sunday school that the word 'orange' isn't in the Bible at all. Not even once."

"That seems impossible," Winnie said.

Brad said, "There may have been orange as we know it today, but the cheap dye you spoke of didn't have a name. The word 'orange' came from the fruit; they didn't name the fruit after the color. 'Red' is in the Bible but not 'orange.'"

Jack said, "Here's a little project for you. Find out if there was a Greek and Latin word for orange back then. If what you're saying is true, I bet there wasn't. Now you need to get to sleep."

Every few minutes Jack would sternly tell Brad to settle down and get to sleep. Brad wanted to sit up talking all night long, but Jack would have none of that. They got to bed about eleven that night, still without power. The storm continued to rage, with thunder and incredible lightning. The wind was strong on the city of DC, causing significant damage in the area. They were lucky to have only lost electric.

Winnie fell fast asleep as Jack was lying on his right side and saying his nightly prayers, once again offering a life of servitude to God. Because of the storm, he started to daydream about the abuse he'd taken at the hands of the German guards in Château de Beynac. In his mind, he was staring at the fire in the middle of the stables they used to keep themselves warm. He remembered staring at those fires and wondering if he would ever be freed.

Every time he heard the thunder, he thought of explosions off in the distance. The lights being out, he could see the lightning flashes through the bedroom window. They reminded him of camera flashes, which somehow reminded him of when Russ, Carver, and Benji came through the guard's door in the castle. The memory of how badly he was being beaten returned as if it were last week.

The fire he was staring at was, in reality, a result of an unlucky neighbor up the street whose house was struck by lightning. Jack was staring at the second floor, where a small fire had broken out in his neighbor's house. He was so mesmerized that he couldn't distinguish fancy from reality. The fire truck arrived as Jack drifted off to sleep.

Jack started to dream about that night and the guards who had so badly beaten him. He remembered Benji's actions at the foot of the steps, when he laid the guard out like a doormat with the pig sticker. He dreamed about the incident in the large room with the rounded ceiling, about poor Benji being shot, and then, when it couldn't get any worse, Russ telling—no, ordering—the escapees to crawl through the sewer.

He then dreamed about what he'd done before leaving the room. He looked back to see one last time the large painting with the shiny gold-painted frame. This painting was the one thing that kept him alive in that living hell. He would look at the painting and feel hope for a better day. He truly believed that that painting was the sole thing that made him into the Christian he was today.

In Jack's dream, he spent seconds that felt like hours looking one last time at the crucifixion of Jesus Christ, with Mother Mary and Mary Magdalene at the foot of the cross. He looked at Jesus Christ ascending off the cross and off the painting and moving to the rounded ceiling of the room. The cross began to fade away, and the women looked to the heavens in total awe. Christ was fully clothed in a bright orange robe. There were lightning flashes throughout the room, and a voice from the stone ceiling said, "Jack, I have chosen you. You were spared in that room that day by Me, your heavenly Father. To find the Triune, start with Bradford. Russ will help you."

He looked again at the painting, and it was as it had always been in his time of need.

Thunder exploded, lightning struck, and God's voice said, "Voilà. It is complete. It is done."

BOOK 2
BONDED WINGS
(EXCERPT)

CHAPTER

Dreams, August 26, 1933

Russ woke up to another gloomy morning with gray skies and drizzle that continued as the storm lingered on. He looked to his right, where Dani was still sound asleep. He loved looking at her when she slept because there was always such peacefulness in her face, even though she experienced such hell when she was younger. During the war, Dani went home from the market to find her family farm burned to ashes. Even worse, she found her father and brother with their hands and feet bound with ropes and shot in the backs of their heads.

Russ watched her for several minutes and finally rolled over and put his hand on her inner thigh and started kissing her ear. "Morning, my French beauty," he whispered in her ear passionately.

She whispered in a not-so-romantic voice, "Remember, lover boy, the kids are sleeping on the floor at the foot of the bed because of the storm."

Russ simply said, "Damn it! This is the price I end up paying for two good nights of romance."

He rolled over and sat on the edge of the bed, wiping the sleep out of his eyes with the palms of his hands. He cleared his throat and lit a cigarette, a habit he used to push that morning taste out of his mouth. It was a taste, as he would say, that felt like the entire German army had marched through his mouth during the night.

"Honey, I wish you wouldn't smoke in bed," Dani said.

"I never heard you complain about it before," Russ said, chuckling at the thought that he was turning into a lecherous old man.

Dani said, "Good Lord, I almost feel like I'm married to Pop."

He looked at his pack of Pall Mall non-filter cigarettes and thought how dumb it was to smoke. They were in the middle of the worst financial depression in the country's history, never knowing if he might lose his job yet still buying cigarettes. Russ decided that it was time to quit the damn things—tomorrow.

He walked across the room in his boxer shorts, looked out the window and up to the sky, and said aloud, "God, what was with that dream last night? What in heaven's name are You trying to get me to do?"

His cigarette burned down to the point that it singed the inside of his index and middle fingers. He gasped and said, "Other than you're going to burn my fingers if I don't stop smoking." He lifted the window just high enough to pitch what was left of the cigarette in the wet yard and walked out of the room. Out of habit, he started to set up to make coffee, only to remember that they still had no power. Still in his boxer shorts, he walked out onto the front porch and sat on a damp porch chair. Other than evening and dinner prayers, Russ's conversations with God were rare. Now he was looking for answers as to the meaning of his dream.

He said to the open air as if he were speaking to a spirit, "God, I feel differently today because of the vision and what was said in the dream. After last night, I feel You have chosen me for a special assignment. I know I should never say this, but why me, God? I don't go to church as often as I should. Pop feels I destroyed the family name for marrying a fish eater. So why me, Lord?"

Thinking to himself about the big rainstorm, he wished that God would give him a sign or a clue as to what He wanted Russ to do. He decided he was not going to talk about it with anyone. Then he said out load as he lit another cigarette, "Damn, damn, double damn, I need a cup of hot coffee."

Over in Bowie, because of the power outage, the god-awful portable windup alarm clock had to come out of mothballs, as the expression goes.

The little brass hammer speedily started slamming back and forth on the shiny black bells atop the five-inch round black clock on four little brass legs. *Dingily, dangly, dingily, dangly, ding.* Jack thought the shrill-sounding alarm could certainly wake the dead and kill the weak at heart. It rang over and over again until Jack lazily reached beside the bed and shut the dumb thing off, saying, "Why now, Lord? Give me just fifteen more minutes. That's all I ask. Why couldn't You give me fifteen more lousy minutes of sleep? After all, it was You that gave me the crummy night's sleep by putting me into the midst of that wacky dream last night. What was that all about?"

Winnie rolled over and said, "Mr. Earl, don't continue your conversation with God like he's sitting on the end of the bed. You'll wake young America. Remember that Brad is sleeping on the floor. Wake him and you'll be sleeping permanently, because I'll take you out. I'm not ready to get up yet."

Brad popped up from the end of the bed and said, "Mama, he didn't wake me. I've been awake most of the night listening to you two snoring in unison. Dad breathes in, you breathe out, Dad out, you in. Occasionally you both made strange noises. Some were like the one babies make when they blow bubbles. Sometimes you would swear at the end of it by saying 'poop,' and then you'd go through the same ritual again and again. The conversation he's having with God is no different from the one he had with Him for the last hour. I don't know how you two can sleep in this room either. I'm going out to the couch to try to get some real sleep, and I promise you I'll never sleep in here again. After all, I am twelve years old now. I'd rather sleep in the yard in the pouring down rain than in this room with you two snoring."

"Young man, you'd better watch your tone of voice," Winnie warned.

Brad retorted, "*Well*, I'm just saying that even the thunder couldn't outdo you two."

Jack finally chimed in, "Okay, okay, watch how you talk to your mother."

Staggering out of the room, Brad mumbled to himself, "Words aren't three-dimensional objects. How can I watch them?"

Jack asked, "What did you say, young man?"

Winnie had covered her head with the sheet, laughing to herself and thinking that all the crap Jack gave his daddy was coming back tenfold.

After Brad left the room, Jack said to Winnie, "I had the strangest dream last night."

Winnie asked, "What was it? You had twins like him?"

"No, I was back in the prison camp during the breakout." Jack started to describe the dream. "In one room was a large painting of Jesus Christ on the cross. Mary—his mother—and Mary Magdalene were at the base of the cross, looking up at him. In my dream, Jesus Christ was fully clothed in a bright orange robe. He ascended from the cross and came out of the painting. Then he went up to the ceiling, which was rounded like a dome in that room.

"The cross slowly faded away, and the women looked to the heavens in awe. Lightning flashes lit up the room, and a voice from the stone ceiling said, 'Jack, I have chosen you to follow me. You were spared in this room today by Me.' Then I looked at the painting one last time before my escape, and the painting was as it was in reality."

Winnie said, "Good Lord, the dream came all these years later. What a strange dream. Do you have an idea what brought that on?"

"All I can think," Jack started, "is that it had something to do with the storm. It was storming that day just before Russ, Carver, and Benji arrived at the castle . . . Oh my Lord, Winnie! Today's the sixteenth anniversary of the prisoner of war breakout from Château de Beynac. That must be why I had the dream. I still don't understand what it means, though."

Winnie looked at the maddening clock and said, "Well, you will have all the time in the world to think about it at the office today because no one else except you will even try to go in. If you are going, you'd better get moving or you'll be late. Let me go back to my beauty sleep. You know what I've always said: If Mama ain't happy, ain't anybody happy."

ABOUT THE AUTHORS

Michael Weaver is a lifelong resident of Pennsylvania, except for his years in the United States Air Force. Weaver was born in 1954, and he grew up in Camp Hill, a small town west of the capital city of Harrisburg, Pennsylvania. Dealing with dyslexia before much was known about it, he wasn't very interested in reading and writing. Ultimately, however, Weaver became consumed by local Civil War history.

Since then, he has been on the board of directors of a local Civil War historical society and was three-time chairman of local Civil War reenactments. He is currently the president of another historical society he founded in 2005. In his younger years, he participated in Civil War reenactments in six different states with an artillery unit; however, age has sidelined him from those events. Though a Christian, Weaver is not currently active in a church. For several years, he has been searching for a church where he feels comfortable.

After being self-employed for over twenty years in the home construction and remodeling business, Weaver found it necessary to change professions due to back and knee injuries. He then went to college and got an associate's degree in business. He accepted a sales position in the lumber industry but soon found that that was not a good fit. Therefore, he turned to his new found hobby—now his passion—history. He decided that he wanted to author a book, so he started researching and gathering historic information about the Civil War. Initially, Weaver used his spare time in the evenings and on weekends to write books. To date, he has written and published five books, with this being the sixth. The second book of this trilogy, *Bonded Wings*, is well on its way to completion.

Other writings by Michael Weaver

TITLE	ISBN	YEAR
Jenkins in Mechanicsburg— The Confederate Attempt on Pennsylvania's Capital	0-9716490-0-6	2000
Captain John Bigelow—More Than Just a Civil War Hero at Gettysburg	0-9716490-1-4 (paper back)	2002
Captain John Bigelow—More Than Just a Civil War Hero at Gettysburg	0-9716490-3-0 (paper back)	2002
Pennsylvania Civil War Snippets for Curious Minds	0-9716490-4-9 (out of print)	2003
Student Activity Workbook to accompany "Snippets"	0-9716490-5-7 (out of print)	2004
The Life and Times of Mahlon Haines— The York, Shoe House (Available for sale only in the gift shop of the Shoe House, Hellam, PA)	0-9716490-8-1	2007

W ill Scott is also a lifelong resident of Pennsylvania, growing up in New Cumberland, about twenty minutes southwest of Harrisburg. Born in 1961, he grew up in a very religious family and attended church regularly. Ultimately, Scott became extremely involved in church life. He has taught Sunday school and been on church Property and Search committees He is active in projects and volunteers hours to the needy by making repairs to their homes. Scott has also followed in God's walk as a missionary by going to Alaska to help build a church. Scott and his wife started a newspaper, *Good News Daily*, which is no longer in production. His journey in construction and his work on the newspaper, coupled with his rich religious connection with God, found Will feeling ongoing signs from God to put together a book based on a journey in the name of God. Scott needed help with this project, as he had never written a book. He feels that God directed him to Weaver.

Scott went to trade school and got an associate's degree in home construction. He has been successfully self-employed since 1981 in the home construction and remodeling business, having built several homes a year for many of those years.

Other writings by Will Scott:

Good News Daily; a Christian newspaper—2004-2008